ANARCHY

A SUPERVILLAIN ROMANCE

MISSING

ALPHA CASE

I0659350

Anarchy Missing – Alpha Case

Learn more about this series here:
www.SuperAlphaSeries.com
Copyright © 2017 by JA Huss
ISBN: 978-1-944475-20-8

Edited by RJ Locksley
Cover and Interior Drawings by Ambro Jordi
Cover Design by JA Huss

CHAPTER ONE

Something is *wrong* with me.

Heat consumes my body. Snow melts under my feet, pooling into a puddle of water until small tendrils of steam swirl their way up my bare legs, surrounding me in a mist that disappears somewhere around my torso.

The city is calling.

The blue-black clouds hanging low in the sky are crowning the mountains, proclaiming them kings and queens. And the new cathedrals peeking up from the tall buildings in the distance, which Thomas started building last spring, and which mark the four points of the compass on each side of the city, stretch up like they are reaching for those clouds.

A sharp pain shoots through my head and I have to close my eyes, shut the world out, and take a moment.

I take a lot of moments these days.

And still... there is the heat.

I am fire. I am burning up. I will combust, I know it. I will explode into nothing but fire and agony if I don't do it.

Don't do it.

But the knife is there. In my hand, poised above my skin. It carves the anarchy symbol into the hard, muscular flesh of my upper left arm with less precision than it did last time. It will produce jagged edges of skin, deep red cuts, and... relief.

1

Each time I get a little less careful. But it doesn't matter. Because each time the skin heals over and hides my moment of weakness.

The blood drips down my arm, hot. So hot it burns my skin red. Leaves a streak. But it too will be gone before anyone knows.

No one will know.

The heat escapes in the form of red light and steam. And now I'm wrapped up in the mist from head to toe.

A chill runs through my body and it feels *so* good.

The city is calling.

There is a voice in my head. Clear. Concise. Commanding.

The city is calling me.

And so I answer.

CHAPTER TWO

"Are you listening?"

I'm not, not really. Thomas and Linc are pacing as I stare out the window. Lincoln is pissed off about some hack job with the banks. Thomas is trying his best to be indifferent to Linc's anger—an angry Lincoln is a lot more dangerous than it used to be now that he's changed—and I'm trying my best to listen to the two conversations going on outside my head as well as the one going on inside.

The city is talking to me.

But it's like… it's like I don't understand the language. Not completely. It's like Spanish. Something I learned but forgot. I recognize some of it. Like when you can pick out the word for shoes, or pants, or the color blue because those are the only sounds you remember.

"Case," Thomas says sharply. He's standing right behind me. His heat bothers me and I want—very desperately—to turn around and push him back. Make him step away so the coolness I carved into my arm this morning will last a little longer.

"What?" I snap back instead.

"What the fuck are you doing?"

I turn to face him, letting my conversation with Cathedral City fall away into nothing but indistinguishable murmurs. "I'm thinking, dammit."

"Well, you better be coming up with an idea," Lincoln says. "Because shit just got real."

A heavy sigh escapes my mouth before I can stop it. I don't even know what they were talking about. I give the city one last glance over my shoulder and then leave it behind. Those conversations belong to the night. Or the early dawn, like this morning. Something to hide, for sure. "Tell me again what happened? I'm not following." I say it calmly. Almost indifferent.

Lincoln tilts his head at me. Almost confusion. Or like he's considering something. Wondering what my problem is, maybe.

Who cares?

The problem is, Lincoln, the city is talking to me and I can't understand what it's saying.

"The problem is that every bank in the city was hacked this morning, Case." Thomas isn't as curious about my behavior. It's hard to make him care about much these days.

I just stare at him, wondering how a bank hack fits into my life.

"My program," Lincoln says, raising his voice. "They hacked my fucking *program.*"

"Oh," I say, understanding now.

"Oh?" Linc snarls as he walks up to me. "Oh? That's all you have to say is, 'Oh?'"

"What do you want me to say?" I ask, pushing past him, making sure I bump his shoulder so he knows I don't want to be fucked with at the moment. And then I take a seat on the couch. I can still see the city from the couch. It's a gray day. Blue, almost. The clouds above the mountains that ring the city are threatening more snow, but the temperature is mild at the moment, so it will come down as rain instead.

"I want you to say your end is fine, Case," Lincoln growls. "You know, the same way Thomas just said his end is fine. That we're on track, this is a coincidence, and I shouldn't worry too much about the fact that someone just *hacked into my motherfucking program!*"

He yells that last part pretty loud. And when I look up at him, there are veins sticking out from his neck.

"Lincoln," Sheila says from off to my left. "Calm down before you explode." She's inside SkyEye systems right now. Came with Linc on the helicopter.

I'm the one who will explode if I don't figure out what the goddamned city is saying.

"Sheila," Linc says, "we need to know where this hack came from. We need to know the full consequences—"

"We know," Sheila says, cutting him off. "They stole seventy-five million dollars."

I glance over at Thomas. "Your money?" I ask him, suddenly a little more interested in the conversation.

Thomas laughs. "I don't keep my fucking money in the bank. But I bet you lost some, dumbass that you are."

I get out my phone and pull up my banking app, check the balances of all my accounts. "Nope," I say, shoving the phone back into my suit coat. "Mine's all still there."

"It is?" Sheila asks. "Are you sure?"

I look at her holographic body being projected from sixteen small black boxes mounted near the ceiling throughout the SkyEye office. She's so real here. Almost as real as when she's down in Lincoln's cave. "I'm sure."

She and Lincoln exchange a look, which makes Thomas squint his eyes at me. "Why didn't they take your money?" he asks.

I shrug. "How the fuck would I know? So what should we do about it?"

"Find the fucking hacker," Lincoln says, completely out of patience with me. "What else?"

"And how do you propose we do that?" I ask back, trying to ignore the whispers of the city.

"That's your job, Lincoln," Thomas says. "You're the goddamned distributor, Case. Figure out if we're still on track."

Lincoln doesn't care for Thomas's answer and he's had enough. Because he takes long, quick steps over to the door, throws it open, and then walks out, letting it bang against the wall.

Thomas stares at the little round hole in the sheetrock from the doorknob, then tracks Lincoln as he disappears down a hallway.

"I'll handle him," Sheila says, flickering out.

Thomas takes a deep breath, straightens his suit coat, and then turns back to me. "What the fuck is the matter with you?"

"What do you mean?"

"You're acting… weird. And it *is* kinda curious that you didn't lose anything in this little hack."

I laugh. "Are you accusing me of breaking into the banks and stealing that money?"

Thomas stares at me for a few seconds, like he's trying to figure it out. But he gives up with a sigh, because he knows I'm just not capable. Even if I am acting weird, I don't know how to hack anything, let alone a program written by Lincoln.

"I can put feelers out."

Thomas gives me a slow nod. "Yeah, you better. We're almost there, Case. We're so close. We cannot afford to fuck things up now."

"I don't know how long it will take," I say, standing up. The city has gone quiet and I'm beginning to feel better. "But I'll do my best."

I walk out the open door and make my way to the reception area of Thomas's top-floor office at SkyEye. The receptionist, Jill, is on the phone, but she smiles, pausing her conversation, as I give her a nod and walk past, heading for the elevator.

When I get down to my car I feel… almost normal again. The sun has no hope of breaking through the thick clouds today, but it's light out. It makes a difference. The city only talks at night and now that the day is getting started, it needs to rest.

ToyBox, my educational gaming company, is situated on the west side of Cathedral City. Right up against the mountains. You can see it from SkyEye, which is in the city center, across the town square from the main cathedral.

And even though I try my best to concentrate on my ultramodern silver chrome boxes, stacked into the foothills like… well, boxes… my eyes are drawn to the ruined spire of Blue Corp, up north.

We blew it up when we took out the Blue Boar last winter. It was a fantastic explosion of glass and steel. I saw it all from the helicopter as we made our escape, even though I was only semiconscious from the wounds I suffered.

That explosion is burned into my memory.

Thomas promised the city he'd rebuild it, restart it under new ownership—us—and things would go back to normal. But it was a lie. Thomas is a well-known liar. At least to me and Lincoln. The city… they see something else when they look at Thomas. A billionaire with all the answers.

Oh, he has all the answers, all right. But they are not the answers people are looking for. They are the answers we're looking for. The three remaining Alphas from Prodigy School still have big plans for this world.

Anyway, no one is rebuilding Blue Corp. It's been shut down and empty since we took it out. Thomas explained it away by pointing to the four compass-point towers he's building.

And people are so stupid, right? What do they think he's going to do with four compass-point towers on the edge of the city?

I mean, come on. The guy is a satellite phone mogul. They can't figure it out? Because to me, it's kinda simple.

He's gonna take over. He's gonna take over everything.

I shake my head as I navigate my car towards my giant silver boxes on the side of the mountain. Maybe people deserve to be ruled like subjects? Maybe they deserve the government they get? Maybe we are the good guys after all? Come to save them from their ignorance and complacency?

That makes me laugh.

We're no such thing. Not even close. We are here for ourselves. For revenge. For restitution. Reparations, if you will. We will take, and take, and take... until—

My phone rings in my suit coat. I pull it out, check the number, and then tab accept as I wait at a red light. "Yeah," I say.

"We got a lead," Thomas says.

"Already?" I ask. "Shit, that was quick."

"Sheila found a fingerprint in the code."

"What'd it say?"

"We'll talk tonight. Don't put any feelers out just yet. We should lie low until we can come up with a plan. Everything goes as planned, Case. Understand?"

"Fine with me."

"We need full distribution by spring."

"We're on track," I say, annoyed that he feels the need to school me. "I know what I'm doing."

"You're acting weird. Sheila wants to see you for a check-up. Today."

"I don't need a check-up."

"I think you do, brother." Normally Thomas is as detached as they come. Indifferent, and cold. Colder than the technology he makes. Colder than the space those satellites of his live in. But right now, he sounds... concerned. "Something's going on with you, I can tell. It would be a lot easier if you just told us what it was, but if you're gonna keep secrets, we'll drag it out of you."

He pauses. Waiting to see if I have a response.

But I don't. What would I say? The city is talking to me? My body is heating up like fire and it only dissipates if I cut myself and let the heat out with my own blood?

Nope. Not even close to being there yet.

"I'm fine," I finally say, filling the silence. Meaning it. I always feel fine during the day. It's the night that gets to me. "Really. And I'll go for the check-up. I don't mind."

They won't find anything. I get monthly exams from Linc and Sheila's army of robot minions down in the cave. Each time I go I wait for them to find something. Tell me what's happening. And each time they pronounce me clean. One hundred percent fine.

"But I have meetings today. A shitload of meetings that take priority. So I'll drop by later this afternoon."

Thomas is still in his pause. Then he sighs. "Look, Case..." he says. "If something's wrong—"

"Nothing's wrong," I say. "I'd tell you." Which is a lie. And I don't even know why I lie, because I feel the words to be true. I've always liked Thomas. Maybe even more than Lincoln, though Linc and I are more like brothers. Thomas and I are more like friends.

"OK," Thomas says. "OK. I'll let them know to expect you for dinner. And Case?" he says, pausing for a second. "I'll be there too."

He ends the call before I can say anything about that last comment.

It means he's worried about me. Which is kinda touching if I think about it. Thomas doesn't worry about people other than himself most of the time.

My light turns green and I drive the rest of the way to ToyBox thinking about everything that's happened since he came to town. How much things have changed. Lincoln and his new... enhancements. I guess that's the only way to describe what we did to him after the Blue Boar shot him in the chest.

We changed him. He was the one who directed the change. Years and years of planning and preparation went into what we did to him that night. But still, he's not really... human anymore, is he?

And then what they did to me the night we took Blue Corp down. A little injection of that jellyfish goop Lincoln created. That's all it was. Just a little injection to promote healing.

I heal, all right. I heal so well that every time I take the knife to my skin, make the cuts that give me relief from the burning heat inside my body, it closes up within seconds.

But there is something inside me. The red light, like the light that seeps out through the vents in Lincoln's hands. The red light of... what?

Heat? Pain? Damage? What is it? What's inside my body? Why does it hurt so bad? Why do I need to cut it out? Why is the city speaking to me in a language I don't understand?

What am I doing? Why am I doing it? Why can't I stop?

Something is *wrong* with me.

CHAPTER THREE

Something is wrong with this city.

I just can't put my finger on it.

I sip my coffee as I look out the window of my downtown loft and ponder my uneasiness. I might be overreacting. I did grow up here. I have lots of great memories of friends, and school, and… boys.

That makes me smile, at least.

My phone buzzes on the kitchen table, so I walk over, pick it up, and tab accept. "Louise speaking."

"Lulu," Cait, my new assistant at the DA's office, says, a little out of breath. "When are you getting here? We're having a crisis."

"What? What kind of crisis?"

"The banks. Jesus Christ. The banks have been robbed."

"What? Which ones?"

"All of them, Lulu. I'm telling you, things are going off the rails. The mayor is here throwing a fit. He's got all the assistant DAs lined up in Randy's office, barking out threats."

When she says Randy's name it comes off like he's a pariah. Which he kinda is. Randy is the head DA, my boss. I don't know what I have against him. It might be his thousand-dollar suits—who can afford that at the DA's office? Or the way his thick hair is always perfectly styled. Or the fact that he actually schedules his time at the gym.

Every night from seven to nine, he's there. It's on the department calendar for everyone to see.

It might be all of that. Or it might just be that he's a pretentious asshole.

"I don't have time to explain, but they're all asking for you."

"It's not even seven yet," I say, feeling defensive.

"I know. I'm sorry. But can you just come in early? They're making me nervous."

"Sure." I sigh.

"Great," Cait says. "See you soon." She ends the call.

Maybe this is why I feel something is wrong. The jerks who run this city are all… well, government jerks. And I know there was a major overhaul in city personnel last winter, but it's the same old shit. This is my second job as an assistant DA and I really thought the shakeup would've changed things. But I don't think it has. Cathedral City politics are just as bad as Wolf Valley politics. Probably worse, if that's even possible, because it's a much bigger place. More crime, more violence, more everything than semi-quiet Wolf Valley.

I had to get out of Wolf Valley before they fired me over my big mouth. Let's just say… it's not always a good thing when everyone knows your name in a town. I had a reputation for being ruthless. Which should be a good quality for an assistant DA. But when the bad guys are almost indistinguishable from the good guys… well. They just want a good little minion to do her job the way she's told.

I really hope Cathedral City doesn't end up being the same way.

Please don't let Cathedral City end up being the same way.

CHAPTER FOUR

I live super close to City Hall. I almost bought a house up north, in the upper-class suburban neighborhoods near the mountains. But it was so much money. And I had reservations about this city from the very start, so I wasn't sure I actually wanted to buy a place. And renting a house in the suburbs is a waste. They are too expensive. Especially for a single person. Who needs all that space when they're single?

So I rented a loft in downtown.

I feel a lot better about that decision. Renting is a great idea. I don't know if I'll like it here. I can't shake the feeling that there's something more to this place...

I sigh as I pull my car into the municipal parking garage and take the ramp up to the sixth level where I have a reserved spot. I don't want to feel this way. I want to fit in, and feel at home, and get a new life. Away from the one I had in Wolf Valley after college.

My parents talked me into that job. And I don't blame them. They just wanted me to come home after law school. I'd been away for almost seven years.

I only lasted six months before the city officials figured out I wasn't corruptible. Lady Liberty, they called me. In a sneering way. But I kinda liked the nickname. What's wrong with being Lady Liberty? You'd think that would be a compliment for a district attorney.

It is, Lulu, I tell myself. *Values, ethics, and a respect for law and order are good things.*

Since when are these bad qualities?

But everyone I met up in Wolf Valley saw government positions as nothing more than stepping stones. And not into the private sector, either. Like I might not be a prosecutor forever. I can see myself defending people. Some high-class trial lawyer who always wins and makes boatloads of money. I'd like that just as much as anyone.

But these people aren't looking for better jobs, they're just looking for better perks. And they want favors too. Special considerations. Park their cars anywhere they want and never fear they'll get a ticket. Get caught speeding and talk their way out of it by name-dropping. You know, the good old rules-don't-apply-to-me attitude.

Everyone wants a better paycheck. They want luxury cars, bigger houses, more benefits and financial security. I get it.

But anyone who gets that by abusing their power doesn't deserve it.

I said those exact words to my boss up in the valley.

He was not impressed. I was told to wise up and toe the line.

I quit instead.

The Cathedral City job was already on the table, so it's not like I took a big risk or anything. Still, I said those things and I meant them.

I still mean them now. So what a heart-crushing disappointment it will be if I have to do it again here. What will it mean for my future? Will I ever get another job? You can't have two new jobs in less than a year and expect people to take you seriously. Not when you're a lawyer.

No. I can't do that again. Not for a while. I need to make this job work. Stick it out. Confront what I don't like and try to change it from within. *Be* Lady Liberty, I decide. I will be that flame of truth in the dark.

I will not run. Not this time.

I get out of the car feeling small and, if I'm being honest, slightly depressed about my new life. Randy is only part of it. Mayor Salinas is always looming over us, wanting things to work out the way he plans. *Don't push this case too hard. Give this one a deal. Put this one away forever.*

Is that how it's supposed to work? Is the law malleable? Can you pound it into submission and shape it into anything you want like a piece of soft metal?

God, I hope not. If this is the way it works—if this is how it is everywhere—then I made the wrong choice when I became a lawyer.

I chose law and order because I'm an idealist. I think the rules apply to everyone, equally. That no matter who you are, you must follow them like everyone else.

Otherwise, why have laws? Why not just live in anarchy?

I shudder at the thought.

Our offices are on the sixth floor of the City Hall building, so as soon as I walk through the large glass doors, I'm confronted by dozens of people, all bustling around in a frenzy.

I guess everyone gets here early on panic days.

Note to self, start coming in at six am instead of eight.

"Lightly," Randy says, peeking his head out of his office door. "Finally."

I'm about to sneer at him when his face softens. He looks like shit. His hair is a mess and he's not wearing one of his thousand-dollar suits. He's in jeans and a white button-down shirt, sleeves rolled up, that isn't even tucked in.

"Finally," he repeats. With something that might be... relief.

"Jesus, Randy. What's going on? You look like you've been up all night."

"I have," he says, lowering his voice as I come closer. "I got a phone call from the mayor at two AM that the government systems were all down. So I came in to help sort things out with IT and that's when the banks were hit."

"Shit," I say, trying to see past his body. His office is filled with angry voices and upper-level officials. "You should've called me. I'd have come in to help."

"I know," he says, even softer. "But there was nothing you could do. I figured one of us deserved to get some sleep. Be fresh in the morning."

Oh. Well, that was nice of him. Maybe he's not an asshole. Maybe I've misjudged him. I don't do that often, so it would be a nice surprise—especially the way I'm feeling today—to be wrong about Randy. "I'm here now. What can I do?"

"Just…" He looks me in the eyes, almost pleading.

That's when the scent of cinnamon hits my nose. "Is that coffee I smell?"

"Oh, yeah," Randy says, absently. He lifts up a white paper cup with a crimson lid and holds it out. "I had Cait get coffee. You want one?"

"Oh, hell yes," I say, taking the cup. "I came in as soon as Cait called. Didn't get my second cup at home."

Randy slips out of his office and closes the door behind him. We are so close, we're practically pressed together, chest to chest. "If you really want to help me out, Lulu—"

Lulu. He never calls me Lulu. It's always Louise. Or Miss Lightly. Or, like a few seconds ago… just Lightly. Like we're old army buddies who've been through hell together and only use each other's last names.

"—just back me up in there, OK?" He nods his head to the closed office door.

"Whatever you need," I say. He turns to go back in, but I grab hold of his bare arm. My unexpected touch stops me and him at the same time, and I let go. "But what's happening?"

"Just follow my lead. We have huge problems, Lulu. Huge."

I enter his office right behind him. No one looks at us. No one pays any attention to us at all. They are all too busy talking in short, clipped sentences. Bouncing accusations and defenses off each other.

"This is an inside job," Mayor Salinas roars, his index finger stabbing a thick folder on his desk so hard, I cringe at the thought of how that feels. "If this gets out to the press, we're all fucked."

Jesus Christ. Something big *is* happening. I feel a little excited over it.

Then feel shame at my excitement.

But a big case is… sorta fun. Right? A challenge.

Salinas looks up at me. "Miss Lightly," he growls. "Nice of you to join us."

I'm about to get defensive when Randy interrupts. "I wanted Lulu to be fresh when she came in and took over. She's not late, Mayor. She's right on time."

Mayor Salinas calms down a little before he says, "Well, good. You're on for the duration, Miss Lightly. You can expect to eat at your desk or in your car. We're not going home tonight until we have a lead, do you understand?"

I don't. Not really. But I nod my head.

"Good," the mayor snarls. "I want Chuck and Juan to go over to the banks and start interviewing everyone. And I do. Mean. *Everyone.*" He punctuates each of those words with more finger stabs on the thick folder.

17

Chuck and Juan both nod. They've been special assistant DAs for many years now and have a lot more seniority than I do.

"Sally, Tim, and Tiffany will coordinate all the court cases today. If any of the judges give you any shit for shuffling lawyers around, you tell him to call me. Understand?"

Sally and Tim, both assistant DAs, nod quietly. Almost meekly. "Yes, sir," Tiffany says. "We'll handle it." Tiffany is the chief deputy, reporting directly to Randy.

There's silence for a few seconds, then Mayor Salinas bellows, "Well, what the fuck are you waiting for? Get your asses out of here and back to work."

Chairs scrape, bodies shuffle, and a few seconds later it's just me, the mayor, and Randy. I shift my feet as I take a long sip of cinnamon-flavored coffee, trying my best not to look nervous.

"Lightly," the mayor says, running a hand through his thick head of dark hair that does nothing to betray his middle age. "You and Randy have been appointed special investigators. We need something today, Randy. Do you understand? I'm not fucking around. I want heads rolling by tonight."

"Got it, sir." Randy actually looks nervous as the words come out. "Don't worry, Lulu and I will dig up something."

"You better. If you want to keep your job, you better figure this out." He storms out of the office, slamming the door behind him.

"What the hell?" I ask Randy, both of us staring at the door for a few seconds.

He turns to me and then sighs deeply, then walks around to slump into the seat behind his desk.

"Special investigators?" I ask, taking a long sip of the delicious cinnamon coffee. "What does that mean?"

"It means..." Randy rubs his hands up and down his unshaven jaw. God, he's almost... handsome like this. All messy and disheveled. The scruffy chin, loose dress shirt, and rolled-up sleeves have me seeing Randy in a different light. "It means," he continues, "we've got a mole in the CCPD and the mayor expects you and I to bring them in with enough evidence to prosecute."

"A mole?" Jesus. I feel like I'm in a Jax Justice spy movie all of a sudden.

Randy opens a folder and points to an eight-by-ten black-and-white photograph. "How well do you know this woman?"

I squint down at the photo. "I've seen her around court. Molly something, right?"

"*Detective* Molly Masters," Randy adds. "She's fairly new, some kind of military hotshot hired on by the last chief—"

"Shit," I say, seeing where this is going. "She's a leftover from his corrupt department?"

"Take a seat, Lulu. This is kinda complicated and I need to spell it out very carefully. You're not on this case by accident. And I think you're going to resist what I'm about to tell you, so let me take it from the top. Don't interrupt me, just listen and think about what I'm going to tell you. Think very carefully, Lulu. And don't draw any conclusions until I'm done. Can you do that for me?"

I might swoon a little at his masculine vulnerability right now. He needs me. For what, I'm not sure, since I'm the new girl here. But he needs me. It's... sorta hot.

"Sure," I say, taking my seat. "Sure. I'm a good listener."

Randy smiles at me. He's so much cuter like this than he is all buttoned up in that suit. "Good. Now look. Molly

Masters came to town last winter as a new hire." He pulls out a bunch of papers and starts pointing again. "Her hire paperwork says she was recommended by Alastair Montgomery."

"The guy from Blue Corp? The one who died in that explosion?"

"What did I tell you about interrupting?" Randy says, but not meanly.

"Sorry. Go on."

"She was recommended by Mr. Montgomery and hired by Chief O'Neil. And yes, Montgomery was killed in that explosion several months back. But that's only the tip of the iceberg. She's been connected to this guy." He pulls out another eight-by-ten photograph, this time of a man, about Randy's age, looking like some kind of biker gang thug. "Lincoln Wade. Have you ever heard of him?"

"Lincoln Wade." I toss the name around in my head, sure I've heard it before. "I think so. But I've been away—"

"I know," Randy interrupts. "But you do know *this* guy?" Another photo appears.

"Thomas Brooks. Yes, he's the CEO of SkyEye. Oh, Jesus Christ, Randy. You're not telling me he's the one behind this?"

"We don't know yet."

"Shit," I mutter.

"Shit is right. If we call this guy out, do you know what will happen?"

"A swarm of lawyers will descend upon us with threats and lawsuits?"

"Ding, ding, ding," Randy says slowly. "But again, that isn't the reason you're here."

"Why *am* I here?" I try to take another sip of coffee, but my cup is empty, so I just stare at it instead.

Randy presses a button on his phone and barks, "Lisa, bring Miss Lightly another cup of that coffee, will you?" Then he scrubs his hot unshaven jaw a few more times.

"What?" I ask. "What is it, Randy? Tell me what's going on."

He takes one last photo out of the folder and pushes it towards me. "You're here because of *him*."

I almost stop breathing.

Case Reider.

The one boy I desperately didn't want to leave behind when my father moved us out to Wolf Valley seven years ago.

"Yes," I whisper. "I know him."

"I know you know him," Randy says softly. He places a hand on mine just as Lisa appears with another cup of coffee.

I take it from her, muttering some thanks, and then take a long, long sip before coming up for air and letting it out in a sigh.

"He was your escort for the Debutante Ball."

"How do you know that?" I ask.

"I was there that night." He smiles sheepishly. "Someone else's date, obviously. I saw you with him."

"I haven't seen him in forever."

Randy waves a hand in the air. "Doesn't matter. We're not after him."

I feel so relieved.

"Not yet."

My relief disappears.

"We know for a fact that Lincoln Wade is a black-hat hacker, Lulu. And Detective Molly Masters has been dating him since she came to town. But the real problem is... Lincoln Wade and Case Reider have been best friends since childhood. Do you remember those two boys who went missing twenty years ago, without a trace, then reappeared several years later with no explanation?"

"Oh, Jesus."

"Yup," Randy says. "Those two boys were Case and Lincoln. We think Brooks was involved somehow, but we're not sure where they intersect. They are close now, at any rate. Lulu," Randy says, leaning across his desk to take both my hands in his. "We need Case Reider to get to Lincoln Wade and Molly Masters, and we need you to get him for us."

CHAPTER FIVE

I head out of work a couple hours early so I can get up to Lincoln's house in the mountains at a decent hour. As it is, I'll probably be there most of the evening, depending on what kind of tests Sheila wants to run on me.

I'm conflicted about how much I want her to know.

Do I want her to figure out what's wrong with me and make adjustments? Sure. I'd love it if she shot me up with something Lincoln's been cooking up in that cave of his and all this shit disappeared.

Do I want her to know just how deep these abnormalities run? Just how bad it's gotten that carving up my skin with a knife is the only way I can find relief?

No. A very big emphatic no.

But there's almost no chance of her finding out. I've been up here so many times for tests. And each time I feel the same way. Hoping she won't, but wishing she will.

The drive up the pass to Lincoln's massive six-hundred-plus-acre property starts out wet and ends up icy.

The snow held off all day until the exact moment I need to navigate twisted mountain roads.

My luck is amazing. I can't get any more blessed than this.

I startle myself with a loud laugh, then shoot a look into the rear-view mirror. My eyes are bloodshot from the nightly activities and there's a dark shadow forming underneath them.

My palm slaps the spot on my upper left arm where I always carve the same thing, over and over. There's no pain leftover from my self-inflicted damage. No tenderness. And if I wasn't wearing a coat and could look at it right now, there'd be no trace of redness, swelling, or scarring.

How many times can I cut myself in the same place and have it leave no mark?

Forever? Does that mean I'm... immortal? How much trauma would it take to kill me? Am I invincible?

I wish I could ask Sheila these questions. But I'm afraid Lincoln would tell Thomas. And after that... well, I'd be out of the plan. They'd send me somewhere. Or maybe just keep me prisoner up here in Lincoln Country.

"Don't be stupid, Case." I look at my reflection in the mirror again. "They'd send you straight to the asylum. But hey, at least I'd go to the new building."

Atticus blew up the old one when he kidnapped his mother. Who is also Molly's mother. Adopted one, at least. Who knows who her real mother is. Maybe she and Thomas are straight siblings? We'll never know. All those genetic records were lost when we blew up the Prodigy School back when we were kids.

We might have an unhealthy obsession for explosives.

"No," I say. It would be a very bad idea to tell Sheila about anything. Let her find it herself... if she can. I'll deal with that if it happens. But until then, I need to keep my head, keep my own confidence, and try my best to figure this shit out. Maybe when I'm there tonight I can search through Lincoln's lab notes? They always do the tests in his cave. And I know they have notes on everything they've done on the computer in that room. Back when Lincoln was experimenting on himself Sheila would record everything. Adding it to his lengthy health history. Maybe I could get my hands on that? Figure out what this jellyfish stuff really does, and maybe why it's working so differently on me?

Lincoln's new driveway is more like a five-mile road. But at least it's no longer dirt. When he started rebuilding the mansion that's the first thing he upgraded so the construction crews could have access to the lot where he wanted to build the new house.

The mansion isn't fully complete yet on the inside, but from the outside you'd never know. It's a massive ten-thousand-square-foot monstrosity with four levels including the attic and basement, and a guest house in the back that Molly jokingly calls the mother-in-law apartment.

Sheila doesn't stay there, of course. They did set up her light projectors, but she refuses on principle to be sequestered away from "the family". Sheila stays in the cave and has limited access to the kitchen, the laundry room, and most of the first floor.

Apparently she's been cramping Lincoln's style and the upstairs is verboten.

Didn't stop her from drafting new plans for a nursery connected to the master bedroom during construction.

I think I might smile for the first time all day just picturing Lincoln and Molly's face when they walked into their new house for the first time and found a completely outfitted baby's room.

You gotta appreciate Sheila's tenacity.

Molly isn't ready for a baby yet. She's just settling into her detective job for the CCPD. And Linc? Well, I don't know if Lincoln will ever be fit to parent a child.

Their house comes into view and I take a moment to appreciate the dark gray, stone manor.

It's snowing pretty good by the time I get out of the car and I find myself wishing I had just gone home.

Gone is the hope of finding anything out. I just know something is wrong and it's got nothing to do with what Sheila and Linc did to me.

But I just tuck my coat collar up around my neck and head to the door. It opens before I even get there, holographic Sheila ready to greet me.

"Case," she says, waving me in and ordering the door to close behind via some unseen mechanism. "You look like shit."

"Thanks," I say, slipping my winter coat off and stomping my shoes on the mat before I enter the massive great room. "Where's Linc?"

"Waiting for you downstairs."

"Molly?" I ask.

"Still at work. I told her to take it easy. She shouldn't be overdoing things in her condition."

"She's—"

"Not yet." Sheila smirks as we walk towards the hidden panel built into the wall on the north side of the main living area fireplace. "But she will be shortly. Mark my words."

I drop the subject of Molly's nonexistent pregnancy and just walk down the spiral stone steps that lead to the lab.

The wave pattern of the huge jellyfish tanks reflects along the walls, getting brighter and brighter until the steps sweep around one final corner and it all comes into view.

This is the new entrance. Linc has been super-paranoid about anyone using the tunnel to access the cave since we took down Blue Corp. We can't risk anyone following one of us and compromising it. In fact, the tunnel got a new foot-thick steel door to replace that broken-down old grate that used to prevent access.

"Hey," Lincoln says, lying down on a rolling creeper, his feet pushing off on a giant red tool box and sliding across the floor. He slips smoothly underneath one of his muscle cars, wrench in hand, and resumes whatever he's been doing down here all day.

Sometimes I envy Lincoln. No job, no responsibilities. Doesn't even have to leave his damn house if he doesn't want to. Just walks down to his dungeon and gets right to work doing… well, whatever the fuck it is he does down here. Lab shit. Computer shit. Who knows? Maybe mad scientist shit.

"Sheila says you're gonna get another workup," Linc says, still tinkering.

"Yup," I say, sighing.

"You got problems I should know about?" This time he slides out from under the car just enough to make eye contact.

"Nope," I say. "Where's Thomas? He said he was coming for dinner."

Lincoln eyes me for a few seconds before scooting back under the car to continue working. "He'll be here soon, I think. He's picking Molly up so she doesn't have to drive in the snow."

"Well, I could've done that. You should've told me."

"No big deal," Lincoln says. "Besides, Sheila wanted you here early so she could get started."

"I have the room all ready for you," Sheila says. "It's all comfy and clean." Big smile on her face like I'm some child she needs to convince to be good for a shot.

I roll my eyes and walk away from Linc, down the hallway to the operating room. "What's the plan then?" I ask. "Nothing's wrong as far as I can tell."

"Well, Case," Sheila says, appearing in the room before I even get there, "I'm not sure you'd even know what to look for. Which is why you're lucky to have me as your doctor."

The machines and computers all flick on and I let my eyes linger on the computer screen for a moment, just to check if they've got it locked down. They do, but Sheila opens it up and data starts scrolling from her internal commands.

I'm sure there's a screen lock, but I'm also pretty sure that it's on a timer that lasts at least fifteen minutes. Sheila and Lincoln used to work in here alone before she took over the bots and he was changed. When you have no extra hands, you can't be stopping to unlock your computer every few minutes.

I watch it as robot minions start crawling up my legs with monitoring wires.

"Take off your shirt, Case. They need skin."

I nod to Sheila, but keep track of the screen out of the corner of my eye as I take off my suit coat and tie, then pull my shirt out of my pants and start unbuttoning it. The minion bots wait patiently on the operating table until I'm done, and then get to work hooking me up to... well, whatever it is Sheila hooks me up to when we do this shit.

I'm used to the minions by now. At first it was creepy as fuck to have those spider-bots crawling all over my body, but really, they are just Sheila using another body. Not semi-intelligent autonomous machines.

One of them crawls onto my hand and pricks my finger, then holds a small glass tube against the flow of blood. Before I can even complain about the lack of warning, it scurries down my pant leg, drops to the floor and climbs up the lab bench where the biggest piece of equipment in here—Hammer, Linc's robotic arm—takes it and proceeds to smear it on a slide and place it under a microscope.

Another prick draws my attention back to the minions. This time they have a needle in my arm and blood is streaming through a tube.

I glare at Sheila.

"You're always such a baby when it comes to blood. Best to just get it over with."

"How long is this gonna take?" I ask. I'm hungry. "And what's for dinner? Better be steak."

"Patience, please. We can't rush the tests. I feel like I've been missing something. So I'm going to do more this time. Look for everything." She stops to stare at me in that motherly way she always uses on Lincoln. "You'd tell me if something was off, wouldn't you, Case?"

"Sure," I say. "Why wouldn't I?"

"Well… some people are more afraid of results than they are procedures. You might be one of them."

"When have I ever given you shit for all this… well, all this shit you do to me? And let me remind you, I never asked for the jellyfish goop. I was just fine before you guys stuck me and filled me with healing genes."

I must've said something wrong because Sheila is giving me a very strange look for that outburst. "What do you mean… healing genes? We didn't *vector* you, Case. We gave you some enzymes, that's it. Which break down in the bloodstream after forty-eight hours. Do you know something I'm not aware of?"

"No," I say, defensively. "I don't even know what 'vector you' means. I just repeat shit I hear."

She stares at me longer than I think is necessary, but I don't look away. She'll know I'm hiding something for sure if I do that. "Well, I'm gonna figure out why you look like shit."

"Maybe I'm just tired and overworked? You ever think of that? Thomas and his grand plan has me running all over the place these days. Not to mention all the shit that went down this morning."

"Maybe…" Sheila says. But I can tell she's not convinced.

"And stop saying I look like shit, OK? I take it personally. I'm sensitive like that."

She laughs and looks away. "Sure you are."

"I'm probably not eating right. I need more vitamins or something."

"We'll see," she says, turning away from the computer, screen-lock not engaged. "It's gonna take a little while for the tests to run. Do you want to sleep for a little bit? Rest up before dinner?"

And even though this is just the lucky break I needed and I don't need to be so enthusiastic, I say, "Yeah, sure," and mean it. I really could use some fucking sleep. I'm sure as hell not getting any at home.

"OK," she says, coming over to pat my leg. Being touched by Sheila is weird. It's not pressure, but a combination of heat and light.

Kinda like that shit leaking out of my body when I cut myself.

"You rest up in here and I'll help Lincoln finish up whatever he's doing to that car." And then she flicks the light off and disappears.

"Thank you," I mutter, lying back on the cold table. It feels so good on my bare skin, I almost moan. I kinda wish I had a Sheila. I like her hovering mother-in-law act. It would be nice, actually, to have someone caring for you all the time. Someone invested in your well-being. Someone to love you…

I almost drift off, that's how exhausted I am, when I suddenly sit up, remembering why I needed her to leave me in here to begin with.

The lock screen still hasn't engaged, so I slip off the table, fish my key chain out of my suit coat pocket, and then slide the flash drive I keep on it into the hard drive of the medical computer and go searching for what I need.

Ten minutes later I've got it all downloaded and this time when I lie back on the cold, steel table, I close my eyes and let the world drift away for real.

CHAPTER SIX

"Where did you learn how to do all this?" I ask Randy. We're up in the mountains about two miles from the western edge of Lincoln Wade's massive estate, looking down at a drone in the back of Randy's department SUV.

"Air Force," he replies absently. He's messing with a tablet. Presumably programming the drone to fly over the estate so we can get surveillance images.

We spent the entire morning coming up with a plan. I did my best to talk him out of us—meaning he and I—doing all this spy stuff ourselves, but he insisted that the CCPD has been compromised and we can't enlist them for help. The drone was his idea. I barely know what a drone does, let alone how to fly one.

"I was a surveillance expert. Joined the military when I was eighteen, got accepted into a special tech ops unit, and this was all I did for three years."

"When did you have time for law school?" I ask, backing up as Randy takes the machine out and places it on a tripod so he can launch.

"What?" he asks, not looking at me.

"Law school?" I repeat.

"Oh, I only enlisted so I could pay for college." He stops to wink at me. "I realize I'm kind of a catch, but I'm older than I look."

I take a sip of cinnamon-flavored coffee and consider that. He is kind of a catch. Still unshaven, still half-put together. Still hotter today than he was yesterday.

"Anyway, I got this, Lulu. Just hold on to the tablet and step back for a minute."

I set my coffee down on the tailgate of the car, take the tablet, and do as he says. He picks up a two-handed controller with lots of little dials and joysticks on it, and starts working.

The drone is bigger than I thought it would be when he first mentioned it back at the office. When you see them on TV they look small. Like toys. But this thing has a wingspan of four feet. It barely fit in the car, even with all the seats down.

The propellers whirl, Randy gets a child-like look of glee on his face, and then it takes off. Straight up, like a helicopter.

"OK," Randy says. "I've got Wade's house marked in red. Come over here so I can see the screen as I fly."

I scoot closer to him, using him as a windbreak. It's not snowing, at least. Not yet. Which is why Randy dragged me up here after lunch. But it's damn cold and the wind, though slight, is biting at my face.

"There it is," Randy says, looking down at my tablet where the drone's-eye view is on screen. "I'm gonna land on the roof."

"What? No, we can't land on the roof. That's private property. I'm not even sure being over his house is legal. Who owns the air space?" I might need to look this up. I feel like we're skirting the edge of the law here.

"The government owns the air space, Lulu. Besides, I got a warrant this morning. We're fine. I wouldn't risk getting this evidence thrown out in court."

"When did you have time to get a warrant?"

"Lulu," he says, losing his patience a little. "I'm the fucking DA. I have a hundred people working under me. I don't need to get warrants myself. I send someone in, they talk to the judge, and bam. It's done. Now, look at the roof. Do you see the chimney on the far east side of the house?"

"Yes," I say, looking down at my tablet.

"I'm gonna land it there, the robotic arm is going to mount a camera, and then I'll bring it home and we can get out of here. Sound good?"

"Yes." I sigh. "It's cold up here." And this feels like spying. I'm not a spy. I'm not a detective. I'm a lawyer. I don't think my job description includes covert drone surveillance.

He does all that as I watch. I desperately want more coffee. I want to wrap my hands around the warm cup and take long sips. So I stay quiet as he works everything out.

Thirty minutes later I'm an icicle, the drone is back in the car, and we're on our way home.

"What are you doing for dinner?" Randy asks as we make our way back into Cathedral City.

"Dinner?" I'm so tired right now. "I think I'll just go home and make a frozen meal."

"What?" Randy says, making his way to the right side of the freeway so we can exit at D Street. "No. Come on. I'll take you somewhere nice. My treat." He looks over at me and smiles. "To make up for the unusual day."

"Unusual doesn't even cover it," I say. I don't want to go to dinner with him, even though I've been thinking all day about how much better-looking he is today than he was yesterday. "I think I'll—"

"I insist," Randy says, stopping for a red light a few blocks from City Hall. "We can go to my place, order takeout, and then watch the video feed of Wade's house. I didn't see his friends' cars in the driveway while we were there, but I'm almost positive Reider and Brooks will show up tonight. At the very least, Detective Masters will for sure, because she lives there with him now."

Shit. Case. I have not seen him in a very long time. Not since that night he was my date for the Debutante Ball. Is one aerial glimpse of him worth spending more time with Randy?

"Well, OK," I say, giving in. "But I can't stay too late. I just feel… wiped out, to be honest."

"Work like this does that when you first start. But it's kinda exciting too, right? I mean, spying is a little exhilarating. Besides, I only live a few blocks down from you. Any time you're ready to leave it's a five-minute walk."

My stomach rumbles. "What did you have in mind for food?" I ask, a little more interested.

"Whatever you want, Lulu." We pull in to the parking garage, wind our way up to level six, and then he stops in front of my car. "You go home, freshen up, and meet me in your lobby in thirty minutes. I've got another idea for how we can get Case Reider to notice you're back in town. We can discuss that tonight."

Get Case to notice me. Just the thought of Case noticing me again sends a shudder down my whole body.

"OK," I say, opening my door. "I'll see you in thirty, then."

He drives off, heading back down the garage ramp, presumably to check the drone back in with the guy he got it from.

I get in my car and lean my head back. I feel so tired for some reason. Maybe Randy is right? Maybe this was just a very exciting day and it's worn me out. I just hope I don't get stuck at his place for too long. Because what I really want to do is go home, look Case up on the internet, and think about him and his life for six or seven hours.

I start my car and head down the ramp, wondering how Case Reider, that perfect gentleman who went to Debutante rehearsals for months and months just to make me happy back when I was graduating high school, could possibly be mixed up in robbing all the Cathedral City banks.

What happened to him? I have to wonder. Because the Case Reider I knew was a good, good man. He was sweet, and attentive, and… open. That's one word I'd definitely use to describe him. Open. Honest. It's what attracted me to him in the first place. He expressed his feelings openly, no matter what they were. Joy, anger, happiness, frustration. He always had it written on his face.

If his friends really are the ones who robbed the banks this morning, and he really is involved, then I need to know what changed. How did he get here?

I ponder that as I make my way to the garage of my loft, and when I get upstairs and change out of my work clothes and into a casual pair of jeans and sweater, I'm still thinking about it.

I check my watch, realize I still have ten minutes, and grab my laptop. I sit at the kitchen bar, open it up, and do a search for Case Reider, Cathedral City.

ToyBox Inc. pops up first, along with a picture of him.

Damn. I forgot how handsome he is. It's not how I remember him, because he's in a nice suit, clean-shaven, and hair neatly styled. But I like the new version.

"Case Reider is the CEO and founder of ToyBox Inc., a gaming company that he started in his parents' garage when he was seventeen." That was many years before I met him. So… he's been building this for a while.

I glance down to the second headline. "'ToyBox Inc. Partners with SkyEye in an effort to make a virtual game out of Cathedral City.'" That was just dated two months ago. Hmmm. "What kind of virtual game?" I wonder out loud.

My phone buzzes. I take it out of my pocket and check the screen.

Randy: *I'm downstairs. You ready?*

Lulu: *Be right there.*

I close my laptop and grab a coat as I head out.

I need a lot more time alone with Mr. Reider, I decide. A lot more time. He can't be involved with this robbery. Never. I don't believe it for a second. And even though I have a feeling Randy will be trying his best to make Case look as guilty as possible, I can't imagine I'd ever believe that the man I knew could be responsible for robbing all the Cathedral City banks.

If he is—I need caution, because it's clear his friends Wade and Brooks are probably not as up-and-up as he is— but if he is, I know there's a reason behind it. I know there is more to this story.

I might even be able to offer him a deal if he helps us.

Yes, I decide. A deal to save himself if he gives up his friends. It could work.

So maybe dinner tonight with Randy won't be a waste of time? Maybe whatever plan he cooked up to get Case's attention will be a good one?

I nod, just as I get out of the elevator and see Randy talking to my doorman.

Yes. I'm going to be going along with this plan.

I'm going to get Case Reider's attention again, no matter what.

And I'm going to get justice for the bankers and the city along the way.

CHAPTER SEVEN

"Hmmm," Sheila says. She woke me up about fifteen minutes ago. Thomas and Molly are here now and we're all sitting in the main lab squinting at the wall-sized screen as my results flash by.

"What?" I ask. "Did you find something?" I decide I really do want her to find something. God, I had the worst nightmare while I was sleeping too. I dreamt the Blue Boar came back to life. Like all the blood tissue and bone splinters of his head went in rewind and put his skull back together. And he turned Molly against me and she killed me with that lariat chain thing he made into a weapon. Maybe she did kill me? Maybe I'm some kind of ghost left over?

"That's the weird part," Sheila says. "I cannot find a single thing out of order. Your bloodwork is textbook, your heart rate, your brain waves. You're better than ever, Case."

Yeah. I sigh to myself. That's kinda how I feel about it too. Better than ever. I'm just not Case anymore.

Molly comes up to squeeze my shoulder. "That's great, Case. You know I feel so bad about what I did—"

"You didn't do anything," Lincoln interrupts. "Stop apologizing to him. It wasn't you who did that, it was the Blue Boar."

Molly looks sadder than ever and I catch Lincoln scowling at me from across the room. "He's right, Molls,"

I say, taking Linc's hint to make her feel better. "It wasn't you. It was him. He turned you into something else."

Maybe he turned me into something else as well?

"Can we fucking eat already?" Lincoln says, standing up. "I'm done with work tonight."

"We're not done," Thomas says.

I sigh.

Sheila says, "Let's go upstairs, Molly. Let these boys have their team time."

We wait in silence as they disappear into the staircase and then we hear the deep clink of the thick panel door closing us back up.

"Make it quick," Lincoln says to Thomas. "I really am just hungry. You know I need to eat a lot these days to keep my body chemistry normal."

"We have time to be hungry later," Thomas says. "There was a note."

"What note?" Linc and I ask at the same time.

"Molly heard something while she was at work. She told me in the car on the way here. She thinks whoever robbed that bank left a note."

"What's it say?" I ask.

"They're hiding shit at the department, she said. Keeping things from her. Like they don't want her on the case."

"Why would they do that?" Lincoln asks.

"Molly thinks they figure you're involved, Lincoln," Thomas replies.

"Hey." Linc laughs, holding up his hands. "I've got nothing to do with this one, Thomas. I swear. Was *not* me."

"I know it wasn't you," Thomas says. "I monitor your computers now."

"You dick," Linc says. But he says it halfheartedly, like he doesn't give two shits what Thomas does. Even if

Thomas found out Lincoln was doing something nefarious down here, there's no way to stop him. Neither Thomas nor I have the computer skills Linc does. We're kinda at his mercy in that department.

"It didn't come from here. Or my house." But Thomas looks at me. "I don't monitor you, but maybe I should?"

I shrug. "I don't know how to do that hacking shit. I make toys, asshole."

"You're acting strange," Thomas says.

"Strange how?" I ask, really interested. Because I know I'm acting strange and I'd like another opinion on it. "Sheila says I'm clean."

"I know. But I think she's just not looking hard enough. We've talked about it actually."

"Talked about what?" I ask.

Lincoln clears his throat. "Look, Case," he starts. "We think the jellyfish enzymes might've fucked with something."

"Fucked with what?" My heart is beating fast all of a sudden. Because even though I *know* something is wrong, I don't want things to be wrong. I just want it all to go away.

"It doesn't matter. What matters," Thomas says, "is that we get a handle on it as soon as possible."

"So how do we do that?" I ask. "Sheila says—"

"Sheila says her instruments aren't sensitive enough," Linc interrupts. "She wants to inject you with nanites."

"Nanites? What the fuck are they?"

"Microscopic computers," Linc answers. "Injected in your blood. They travel through your whole body and a few hours later they start sending signals back."

"You assholes want to inject me with computers? No fucking way. I'm not getting turned into some crazy cyborg like you."

"They degrade after three weeks," Thomas offers. "Disappear, like they were never there."

I open my mouth to say no, but Lincoln beats me to it. "Look, Case. We need to know everything. What's happening with you? You look like total shit. You've been acting weird for months, and to be honest, I'm starting to get really worried about you, man. We need to figure this out."

I start pacing back and forth in front of the jellyfish tank. This is the huge one. The big blobs light up through bioluminescence. "What kind of jellyfish are these?" I ask.

"Just comb jellies," Linc says, walking up beside me. "Why?"

"What do you use them for?"

"They have special cells."

"Special how?" I ask.

"Who cares?" Thomas interrupts. "We're not taking no for an answer, Case. You're getting the nanites."

"Special how?" I repeat, this time only looking at Lincoln.

"They can transform," Lincoln says. I stare blankly at him. "Into other kinds of cells. That's how I made all these changes." He pans a hand down his body. You can't see Lincoln's changes with his clothes on. But they are clearly visible when he's undressed. He has ports in his arms and legs that can power specially-made weapons. And he's got that light inside him. And heat too. He's wearing gloves right now, as he usually does. And this hides the vents in his palms where the heat and light escape.

I look at my own palms. They don't glow, but they are hot. Even now, they are very hot.

Lincoln notices and takes my hand in his, pressing our palms together. "Shit," he says. "You're burning up, Case."

"Sheila says I'm not."

We just stare at each other.

"What's going on?" Thomas asks.

"Maybe you just need some vents?" Linc says. "Like me?"

"Why would I need vents, Lincoln? If all you did was boost my healing capacity?"

"What the fuck are you two talking about?" Thomas is getting pissed.

I don't know much about what Lincoln has been doing down here all these years, but I definitely know more than Thomas. He was missing for most of that.

"Maybe you had… a bad reaction?" Lincoln asks me.

"Would one of you assholes please fill me in?" Thomas snaps.

"The jellies," Lincoln says. "They're special because they heal in a weird way. And this particular kind," he says, motioning to the giant blobs in the tank, "they have special cells that can turn into other cells. Maybe…" He runs his fingers through his hair like he's thinking. "Maybe what they did to us at Prodigy School changed our biology. And maybe all those things I thought I was doing to myself to accept the changes were just a natural progression, or evolution, if you will, that came from mixing the jelly cells with mine."

"And maybe when you gave me that injection," I say, picking up his train of thought, "it changed me too."

Thomas just looks at us. Blinks. "So I've got two freaks now? We're about to enact the greatest political and social takeover in the history of the world and both my partners are a couple of super-freaks?"

"We need those nanites inside you," Lincoln says.

"Now we're making sense," Thomas says. "We'll just inject them into your blood and let Sheila figure the rest out. Problem solved."

I don't say anything. Just head towards the stairs.

"Where are you going?" Thomas asks.

Lincoln follows me and by the time we get to the main level and walk out into the living room, Thomas is there too. "Wait, Case," he says. "Let's just do it now. We need to get back on track."

I ignore him and walk towards the door.

"Where are you going?" Lincoln calls. "We're having dinner."

"I'm not hungry," I mumble, throwing the door open and walking out.

"What the fuck, Case?" Thomas calls. "You're gonna ruin everything."

"We still have shit to talk about," Lincoln yells. "The note!"

I just keep walking until I get to my car. I don't care, I realize. I don't care about any of this.

I drive back to the city in silence. Don't even bother turning on the radio. My head is filled with luminescent jellyfish, and nanites, and… death.

But I'm not dying. I know this like I know my own name. I'm not dying… I'm changing.

Into what though?

I take the corner around the mountains too fast, my sports car slipping on the ice more than once. But I can't help wondering how far I could push my body before it breaks. I could drive this car off a cliff and see what happens.

I aim for the side of the mountain, for a guard rail up ahead, shift gears, press my foot to the accelerator, ready to give it a try.

But then I see… I see… the Blue Boar, standing on the side of the road—laughing and dancing. The way he was that night. Gleeful and insane.

I swerve, the whole car sliding on the slick roads. Skipping across the snow in the breakdown lane.

And because the car is nothing if not responsive, the moment my hands try to correct, it responds.

I drive the rest of the way home like it never happened.

There is something wrong with me.

Heat consumes my body. Snow melts under my feet, pooling into a puddle of water until small tendrils of steam swirl their way up my bare legs, surrounding me in a mist that disappears somewhere around my torso.

The city is calling.

It's whispering in the predawn darkness as I stand here on the roof of my house.

Case, it says.

"What?" I ask it back. "What do you want?"

But it doesn't answer.

So I get the knife and carve the anarchy symbol into my upper left arm. I watch the blood pour out with the heat and the red light.

And feel relief.

The deep cuts give me relief.

CHAPTER EIGHT

We order Chinese as soon as we get to Randy's apartment. He was right, it's a very short walk between us. Only two blocks. But I have to say, he's much more interested in the tablet, which is broadcasting a live feed from atop Lincoln Wade's house, than he is in me at this point.

He's not as hot as I thought, either. That disheveled look he was totally pulling off this morning is getting old and looking a little more like… unkempt.

I yawn.

"Oh," Randy says, noticing. "Sorry. You wanna get a look at him?"

"Who?" I ask. Bored.

"Case Reider."

"He's on there? Already? Jesus."

"Look," Randy says, turning the tablet towards me. "That's him."

I study the feed. It's pretty clear for a camera mounted up on top of a mansion. But a fog must be slowly rolling in, because there's a mist coming off the asphalt driveway. It kinda curls up his legs as he walks, making him look a little… mystical.

He's not looking up, so I don't get a good look at his face. But I'd recognize him anywhere. Just his gait is enough for me to know it's him. The long strides and the way his broad shoulders sway a little with each step.

I have a sudden longing to see him again. Just a coffee. A conversation. Catch up on what we've both been doing all these years. Well, maybe not that. I don't know if I'm ready to talk about that yet. But just an apology for leaving him behind so suddenly might go a long way towards getting him reinterested in me.

God, I'm stupid. Case Reider was doing my father a favor when he agreed to be my date for the Debutante Ball. The whole thing was arranged by our fathers.

No, he has not been pining for me, that's for sure. I bet he's got a ton of girlfriends. He's a big important CEO now. Friends with some of the most powerful people in the city…

Criminals, I remind myself. He's friends with the subjects of our investigation.

"So about my plan," Randy says.

"What plan?" I'm kinda annoyed with Randy again. I really just want to go home and not even wait for the food. I don't know what I was thinking this morning. It's gonna be a long investigation if I have to spend every day with him. And this is it, as far as the nights go. I'm not coming back here again.

"To reintroduce you to Case Reider. God, Louise, focus. If you're too tired to keep working, just let me know and I'll have a driver drop you off at home."

"Oh," I say. But I'm really thinking… *Hell, yeah.* I forgot about that little plan. I gather myself. Ravel all the frayed edges together and pull down on my sweater, adjusting it with my attitude. "Not that I want to get anywhere near that criminal, but what did you have in mind?"

"Just…" Randy starts, hesitant. "Keep an open mind, OK?"

"Go on." I'm suspicious. But if this is going where I think it is… then…

"I think you should go on TV tomorrow. Do an interview with Channel Nine. Mayor Salinas and the police chief both did interviews today already. And they'll do more tomorrow. But we could use your pretty face to let Mr. Reider know you're back in town. He'll see you on the TV, tell his buddies, and then they will make contact, Louise."

Why is he calling me Louise again? All day it's Lulu this and Lulu that. Now it's Louise.

"Define contact," I say, trying to keep myself focused on business.

"Maybe… a phone call? To start. And then meet him somewhere. A casual date. Then, if we get lucky, he'll ask you to dinner. We'll plant a wire on you and then—"

"Wire?" I ask, surprised. "I'm not a detective. Or an informant, Randy. This is not something I do. It's like… entrapment."

It's not *like* entrapment. It *is* entrapment.

"We don't have to do the wire," Randy says, backing down. "But Lulu"—now it's Lulu again—"I know he'd like to see you again."

"You don't know that." But I'm hoping Case does want to see me again. I just don't want it to be my job to set him up for a fall. Or twenty to life in prison.

"And it's not entrapment. The crime has already been committed. We just want info on who did it. And it was his friend, Lulu. It is Lincoln Wade. This job has his name all over it."

"How do you know him so well?"

"Who?" Randy blinks at me.

"Lincoln Wade," I snap. I feel so bitchy right now. Like I haven't had my morning coffee, but it's dinner time. Maybe I'm just really hungry?

"I knew him once. Back when were in high school."

"Oh. So why don't you just go interview him? See what he says?"

"Because he's going to lie, Lulu."

"If I do this, I'm not wearing a wire." I say it firmly, like this is non-negotiable.

"Fine," Randy concedes.

"And I don't want to be followed."

"Unacceptable," Randy says. "That's standard protocol."

"No," I say, standing my ground. "If I'm being promoted to informant then I work this case alone. That's what informants do. At least while they're gathering evidence. If I find anything out, then you guys follow me and we bust them. That's my condition or I'm not doing it. I don't want people following me. And I don't want him being suspicious. If his friends are as dangerous as you say, then I don't want to risk my own safety."

It's a whole lot of bullshit. I just want to get some time alone with Case and not be wondering if anyone is critiquing my reactions.

Randy agrees to that, the food arrives, and once I am eagerly chowing down my chicken fried rice, I'm feeling better again. Randy isn't even getting on my nerves as we work through dinner and make a plan for tomorrow.

The next morning Cait is there when I walk in to the sixth-floor offices, handing me some more of that delicious cinnamon coffee. "I admit," I tell her with a smile, "I dreamed about this coffee last night."

"Oh, you like it?" she asks. "It's from that new coffeehouse down on C Street. City Coffee, it's called. I'm going back to grab some to take home. I love it too. Do you want me to pick you up some?"

"Yeah," I say, stopping to take a long sip. "I'd love to wake up to this every morning."

"Consider it done," Cait says, skipping off to deliver cups to other people in the office.

Randy and I spend the rest of the morning planning out every detail of the interview tonight. I'm sitting down with Marla Bast from Channel Nine at four o'clock, and it's going to air during the six o'clock news.

Randy is back together today. Predictable dark blue thousand-dollar suit, red power tie, and perfectly coiffed hair.

But somehow, he's sexy again. God, I don't know why I'm so hot and cold with this guy, He's never been mean to me. In fact, all day today, he's been nothing but sweet. He even bought me lunch at the new pub across from City Hall. And we didn't even eat at our desks.

"Are you nervous?" Randy asks. The TV people are here, micing me up and doing my hair and makeup.

"A little," I admit. But not about the interview. I'm nervous because I know Case is going to know I'm back in town tonight. He might even try to call me. Maybe I should stay late tonight? Just in case he calls the office?

"Lulu?" Randy asks. "Did you hear me?"

"No, what? Sorry. I was thinking about the interview. I'm so nervous."

"Just be yourself," he says in a low voice. I know that's so the TV people don't catch anything unusual in our conversation. "You'll do great."

CHAPTER NINE

I tab accept on my ringing phone and say, "Yeah."

"Are you watching the news?" It's Thomas.

I'm not. I'm sitting in my house, holding the knife in my hand, wondering if it's a sign things are getting worse because I want to cut myself right now, and I'm hours early.

So far, the naked trips to the roof have only happened in the middle of the night. But all day long I've had a building urge to cut. Deep, deep cuts. Let the heat out. I'm fucking burning up. Maybe I do need vents in my hands like Lincoln has? Maybe that would fix all my problems?

"No," I tell Thomas. "I'm eating dinner."

"Well, turn it on. Channel Nine. Quick."

I reach over for the remote on the end table and flick it on. I press nine on the keypad, and then a reporter's face is on screen. "We've heard rumors of a note, Miss Lightly. Can you confirm that whomever stole seventy-five million dollars from the Cathedral City banks yesterday morning left a note?"

Her face is suddenly on my wall. A face I have not seen since that last time we danced at the ball.

"I'm afraid I haven't seen the note, Ms. Bast."

"But there is one?"

"I'm sorry," Lulu says. "I can't confirm or deny that. I just have no information about it."

"What can you tell us?"

"Do you see her?" Thomas asks, still on the other side of the phone.

"I see her," I whisper. "Did you know she was back?"

"No," Thomas deadpans. "And I'm kinda pissed off about that. I had an arrangement with her father. And before *you* get all pissed off, I did it for your own good. And hers. It's dangerous for her to be here, Case. You have to know this."

"I do," I say, still softly.

"She needs to go."

I sigh. "So get rid of her." I can't stop Thomas. Whatever he's gonna do, he's gonna do. That's just how he is.

"We can't. She's a fucking assistant district attorney and apparently, she's on this new bank robbery case."

"So what should we do about it?"

"I think you should meet up with her. Bump in to her somewhere. Casually, you know. Nothing formal. Feel out the situation. See where she's heading. They're trying to pin this on us, Case. I hope you know that. And this is clearly a ploy to drag you into something."

"Yup," I say. He's probably right.

"Don't fall for it," Thomas cautions.

"I'm not an idiot," I snap. "Besides, I'm totally over her."

"Mmm-hmm."

"I am. I'm happy to get rid of her. I know you're the reason she left town, but you never told her to just cut contact with me, did you?"

"Nope. Never did."

"And she couldn't pick up the phone?"

"Right, brother. That's the right attitude. We're very close, man. So fucking close to putting all this shit in motion. Don't let a girl take that win away from you."

"I know that too. And believe me, that goal is still the only thing that matters. I want it just as bad as you." I'm not sure that's really true. Thomas is possessed with what we're doing to this city. But I'm definitely committed. "I'll take care of it."

"How? No," he amends. "Don't tell me. Better if I don't know." I'm just about to hang up when he says, "Have you thought about the nanites?"

"No, I have not," I say, anger building at the mere mention of that stupid plan. I plugged that flash drive into my computer when I woke up this morning from my little trip out to the roof. But none of it makes sense to me. I really have no clue what Lincoln does up there in his cave. Most of it was code, anyway. Shit I have no hope of ever understanding. And the rest… just more big biological terms that read as gibberish to me. "But I did give you assholes an answer. And it's still no. I don't want that shit inside of me."

"Well, Sheila came up with another idea. Just a little interface on the back of your neck. It's not even sub-dermal. Just a sticker, really. With electrodes on it. On the back of your neck. It can monitor all kinds of things through your skin and maybe we can figure out…" He pauses. "Get a handle on what kind of things are happening to you. Then maybe you'll see it's no big deal and we can do the nanites. The interface will tell us a lot more if we combine the two—"

"You got an address for her?" I interrupt, looking at the knife in my hand. I don't really want to think about what's happening to me.

"Sure," Thomas says. "I'll text it."

"Cool. I'll take care of shit tomorrow."

"Case?" Thomas asks before I can end the call.

"What?"

"You'd tell me if something was wrong, right? We're still close enough to tell each other shit like that, right?"

I'm still staring at the knife in my hand. Is it so bad, really? That I need to cut myself for relief? People do that shit all the time.

Psycho people, the inner me replies back.

"Yeah," I tell Thomas. "Yeah, sure. We've always been close."

Thomas waits to see if I'll say anything else. But I don't. So he says, "Good." Then, "Good. Whatever you need, man, I'm still here. Just remember that."

"Got it," I say, ending the call and throwing the phone onto the cushions next to me. It buzzes a text—Lulu's address, I presume—but I'm already standing, pulling my shirt out from my pants and unbuttoning it.

Two minutes later I'm on the roof, naked. Knife in hand, poised above the fleshy muscle of my left arm, ready to carve.

The city whispers to me. Only this time, it sounds like the Blue Boar.

I cut deep. Let the blood flow with the light.

And the pain disappears.

"Do you see her?" Thomas asks,

"I see her," I whisper. "Did you know she was back?"

"No. And I'm kinda pissed off about that. It's dangerous for her to be here, Case. You have to know this."

"I do," I say, still softly.

"She needs to go."

CHAPTER TEN

"What am I looking at?" I came in early this morning after spending an entire night foolishly imagining all the many ways in which Case Reider would make contact with me again—one of which included a romantic party that looked suspiciously like our night at the Debutante Ball—only to find a two-inch-thick file waiting on my desk, and Randy sitting in my chair, drinking that delicious-smelling coffee and talking on the phone. "This is... what?" I ask, looking up at Randy, who kindly vacated my chair and is now hovering over me. Jesus Christ, I need... "Cait!" I yell. "Can you please bring me a coffee!"

"It's code," Randy says.

I want to slap him, but I take a deep breath instead. "I can see that. *Randy.*" I hold the scowl in. Where is my coffee? "But what does it say? This isn't a note. When you said note I pictured cut-out ransom letters. Or boxy Capricorn-killer print. What *is* it?"

"Are you OK?" Randy asks, squinting his eyes at me. "Did I do something wrong? Are you mad at me?"

"Oh, for fuck's sake," I mumble.

"Why are you so bitchy?" he asks.

"Sorry," Cait says, appearing with my coffee.

"Thank God," I say, taking it from her and slurping some down real fast. I give Randy an almost apologetic look and then point to the caffeine. "I just needed my coffee."

"Got it," Randy says, his words clipped. "Cait," he says, and before Cait can escape the tension, she turns and smiles. "Make sure our princess here has her coffee waiting from now on."

"Sure thing, Randy." She gives me a wink and a smile, then leaves, closing the door behind her.

Randy pans his hands at me and says, "Take your time, Lulu. Drink up. You let me know when you're ready to work, OK?"

I feel stupid all of a sudden. I *was* kinda bitchy. It's really not like me. "I'm sorry," I say, meaning it. "I just had a long night and didn't get any sleep. And Case did not try to contact me. Our plan didn't work."

"Well... come on, Lulu. He's probably being directed by those thug friends of his. Give it more than one night before you give up. And before you ask me again, let me show you the message we found in the code."

He leans over my shoulder, so close to me I can smell his cologne. It's not strong, not at all. But he's very close.

"Hackers sometimes place messages inside their code. See this?" He points to a jumble of words and characters in the middle of the print out. "That's it."

"It doesn't say anything."

"It's *code*, Lulu." He says that like I'm a slow-learning five-year-old. "Which means you have to decipher it. And we did. The Feds had it since it came in yesterday and they sent it back with an analysis." He lifts the printout up and yup, sure enough there is a detailed analysis from the Feds.

If I had just waited five seconds, I'm sure Randy would've told me about that little detail. But instead I flew off the handle and blamed coffee. "I'm sorry."

"Don't worry about it," Randy says. "I'm sure all this is kind of overwhelming to you. Back in town after all these years. Then this big case, not to mention your ex-boyfriend might be involved. I get it. Just relax."

I almost wish that little pep talk came with a sleazy offer of a shoulder massage and some inappropriate sexual innuendo, because at least then I could pretend he's partly to blame for my behavior.

But it doesn't. He's being sincere.

"Look," he says, pulling the analysis out for me to read. "They think this hacker is calling himself Bike Boy. And he's talking to a guy named Red Robber."

"These are... handles? Or something? Nicknames?"

"Yeah," Randy says. "Online aliases. Red Robber seems to be the guy who actually carried it out, but it's not clear yet. We think Bike Boy is Lincoln Wade."

"Why?" I ask. "Why do you think that?"

"We went through Detective Masters' emails and she refers to him that way when they are... flirting."

"Bike Boy," I say out loud. "Sounds kinda stupid. Who's Red Robber?"

"We don't know. If we didn't already know that Bike Boy was Wade, then we'd have assumed he was the Red Robber. Because from what they could gather from this message, it appears this hack was all coming from Red Robber's instructions."

"Hmm," I say, taking another sip of coffee. I'm feeling better. Maybe it's really the missing caffeine that made me irritable this morning? "What else does it say?"

"That's about all we got from that bit of code. But the Feds are combing through the whole thing and they'll let us know if they find anything else."

"So what do we do with this?" I ask, flicking the page in my hand.

"Well," Randy says, walking around to the front of my desk to take a seat in one of the chairs. "Not much. We need more info. Hopefully we can get that from your boyfriend."

"He's not my boyfriend. He was never my boyfriend. He took me to the ball, that's all. And then I left town a few days later and never saw him again."

"Well, maybe…" Randy says, looking intently at me. "Maybe you could… try to get him interested in picking up where you left off?"

"Date him? You want me to date him? What if he's a real criminal? I'm not dating a criminal. It goes against everything I believe in."

"Which is why I trust you to keep it all straight. Not get caught up in him again, Lulu. We just need an in, you know?"

"He's not going to trust me." I laugh. "I work for you!"

"But…"

"But what?"

"Maybe you… get fired?"

"What?"

"Just listen a minute, Lulu. I know this isn't in your job description but we're in a tight spot, OK? He's going to make contact, we know this. And what if you two go out to just… catch up on old times, then you get fired for inappropriate behavior?" I'm about to open my mouth to protest, but he continues. "Fake fired, Lulu. Not for real. Just a ploy to lure him into trusting you again. We have a feeling that this is just the beginning of their plan for Cathedral City. We think that Brooks guy—Thomas Brooks—we think he's about to do something nefarious. You know he bought Blue Corp after that explosion and the whole corruption thing went down last winter."

"Yeah. So?"

"Well, we have new evidence that he—and his friends, including your Case—were the whole reason Blue Corp blew up."

"What evidence? I haven't heard this."

"It's super-secret at the moment. We're holding that very close as we build a case. But it's all in the file." Randy points to the folder in front of me. "On that flash drive. We have footage of that night, Lulu. Someone was recording from a high-rise while the whole thing went down."

"Holy shit. Can I see it?"

Randy drags his chair around to my side of the desk, grabs the flash drive, and plugs it into my computer. Some footage begins to play that shows the tall spires of Blue Corp off in the distance. "Look," he says.

At the same time, someone on the film says, "Is that a helicopter? Zoom in on that, dude." Whoever is filming complies and zooms. The quality gets bad, blurs, then focuses. But it's still kinda grainy.

Then something falls out of the helicopter. "What was that?" I ask.

"We think it's a guy with a parachute. But just wait," Randy says. "That's not even the interesting part."

When the 'copter gets right over top of the tallest spire, something else comes shooting out. A few seconds later it crashes into the top of the glass spire.

"What the hell?" I ask. "Was that a… a motorcycle?" It can't be. Who the hell drives a motorcycle out of a helicopter?

"Keep watching," Randy says.

There's not much else to see as the seconds tick off. But it must've been a lot more impressive in person, because the cameraman keeps saying, "Holy shit. Did you see that? Holy fuck, I think that was a grenade!"

The helicopter hovers the entire time, then some kind of grappling line flies down, along with another man, and that's when things really go crazy with flashes of what I can assume is gunfire. That grappling hook thing starts bringing people back up. I count four, total. And then the spire explodes as they fly away.

"Wow," I say.

"That's not all," Randy says. "Keep watching."

The camera follows the helicopter until the tiny lights disappear. Then the footage goes black, but then it flicks to life again. "What was that?" the guy who is not the cameraman says.

"The Asylum just exploded!" the cameraman yells. "Holy fuck, holy fuck—"

Randy turns it off. "That's what really happened, Lulu. That night Blue Corp exploded. And then Thomas Brooks made an announcement telling the whole world he was taking over Blue Corp. Did you know that Blue Corp owns the power company? And the water treatment plant? When Brooks took over Blue Corp, he essentially took over this entire city."

I lean back in my chair, feeling exhausted after watching all that. "Wow. Was that really a motorcycle? That came out of that helicopter?"

Randy nods. "Bike Boy," he says, like this explains everything.

And it… kinda does.

Lincoln Wade is Bike Boy. He did that. He crashed a motorcycle into the Blue Corp spire and then blew it up.

And he's Case Reider's best friend.

"They're bad guys," Randy says. "Really, *really* bad guys, Lulu. And we need to stop them before they fuck this city up even more than they already have. That's why when Case Reider makes contact—and he will, Lulu—you're gon a get close to him. I'm gonna fire you because of it, and then we're gonna take these assholes *down*."

CHAPTER ELEVEN

Lulu Lightly started out as a family responsibility and ended up a missed opportunity.

My parents weren't bad people. They just did bad things.

That's how I ended up in the Prodigy School. I was payment on a debt that was long overdue. But they helped us Alphas when we decided to end the program and leave, so giving into my father's request to take Lulu Lightly to the Debutante Ball seemed a simple enough thing at the time.

Of course, they didn't tell me about the months of dance lessons I'd need. Or the rehearsals. But it turned out to be a lot of fun. I was a terrible dancer but it made Lulu smile. And after about a month of that, I realized I actually made her happy. Even if she showed up for the dance lessons tired and not in the mood, just a few minutes with me could turn her whole day around.

I stare at her from under an awning as she makes her way towards me. Carefully trying to avoid puddles of slushy ice as her boss chats with her excitedly.

I've decided he's a dick.

Neither of them look at me as they make their way into the pub for lunch and I won't be following them in. But was nice to see her in person again. To know she's OK, at least. Since she did leave town and not contact me again.

Of course, that was Thomas's doing.

Whatever.

I stick my hands in my coat pocket and the heat pouring out of them warms my whole body up as I tuck my head into the wind and make my way down the block to catch a cab back to my car, which is parked at SkyEye.

When I get there, the doorman says, "Mr. Reider?"

"Yeah?" I answer.

"Mr. Brooks would like to see you before you go home."

"Sure," I say, letting out a long breath. I feel... I'm not sure. Not exactly sad, but... melancholy, I guess. That's the word. An old-fashioned way of saying depressed.

Thomas rehabbed this cathedral to house his corporate office last winter and the main cathedral has been turned into a huge lobby with glass meeting rooms, a large reception desk, and elevators that lead up to the glass bridge on the third floor, where you can cross over to the auxiliary buildings.

That's where his office is.

On my way across the bridge I can see the main cathedral out of the corner of my eye, but I don't look at it. It reminds me of Lulu and our perfect night, and that— I sigh heavily—is not what I need right now.

When it comes to office arrangements Thomas isn't as pretentious as he appears. He has an unassuming corner space that faces east, of all things. East. The direction of nothing, really. Unless you count the asylum in the north. It's just mountains with no interesting buildings.

I take that back when I peer inside his office. Because I can see the new East Boundary Tower he's building. One of four directional towers we're going to use, in conjunction with the smaller corresponding towers that flank each side of City Square, when the time is right.

But it's not pretty and it's not interesting. It's just a tower made of steel and most of what I can see at the moment is the giant crane being used to build it.

"You wanted to see me?" I ask him, walking in and slouching down in the chair in front of his desk.

He's looking at his computer. Doesn't acknowledge me at all, but speaks to someone on the phone with him. "I need that completed in six weeks, Jim. Make sure we're on track."

"Yes, sir," Jim says from the speaker.

Thomas ends the call by punching a button and then turns to me. "So what have you decided to do?"

I shrug.

"That's not an answer, Case. This is a problem and you're the only one who can fix it."

"What do you *want* me to do?" I ask, uninterested.

"Take care of her," Thomas says, annoyed. "What the hell do you think I want? We can't have a single interruption in our plans, Case. Not one. I'm doing my part with the construction. Linc is doing his part with the program, and we need you to do your part with the distribution or it's all for nothing."

"I'm ahead of schedule, Thomas. I've got 1.1 prototypes up in every bus stop shelter and subway station in the city. Plus, the 1.2 version software is already in place in the new jail. Version 2.0 will be ready on time, no problem. None of my plans are affected by any of this."

"She's trying to set us up." Thomas glares at me.

"She won't get far," I say. "They don't know what we did. They might think they know, but they don't know."

"They're not who we should be worried about and you know that. Whoever pulled off that heist is the person we need to take care of."

"But that's not her."

"It's got something to *do* with her." He's looking at me like he can't believe I'm not worried about this.

My hands are sweating profusely inside my gloves. I decided this morning I need to start wearing them regularly. Just in case. I want to take them off but it scares me. Every time they do this I think they'll be glowing red. Like Lincoln's. And even though every time I look at them to check, they aren't, there's always a first time and I don't want that time to be now.

"You're going to make contact with her." He waits for my objection, but I've already decided to hear him out, just to appear like I'm thinking it over like normal. So I don't object. "You're going to press her for information, see what they have, and we'll take it from there. Do that by tomorrow night, then meet us out at Linc's house and we'll discuss."

"No," I say.

"Which part of that is a no?" Thomas asks calmly.

"The part where I make contact. I don't want to make contact. It's not a good idea."

"I don't care what you want, brother. I only care about the plan. And if we can't see this thing through to the end, then what the fuck have we been doing for the past fifteen years?"

"We don't need her. We can just get Lincoln to hack into the offices and take what they have."

"She's involved somehow," Thomas says.

"Peripherally," I counter. "She's nothing. She's not that kind of girl, Thomas. I guarantee that if she's involved, she doesn't realize it."

"Which is why you need to explain it to her, get her on our side, and then we can take it from there."

I glare at him. "Then you do it."

"I don't know her."

"Neither do I."

Thomas sighs. "Case, this is not negotiable. Nothing is negotiable. You signed up, we're all committed, and now you need to do your part—"

"I don't want to fucking see her again," I growl. "What part of that don't you get?"

He folds his hands in his lap and leans back in his chair. A signal that says, *I'm listening. Talk.*

And even though Thomas Brooks is the last guy I want to talk with about my feelings, he's all I've got. So I say, "I loved her, OK? I loved her, she walked away from me, and I never quite got over that. I can't see her again, Thomas. Not like this."

He squints his eyes at me. "Not like what?"

I envision myself telling him everything in the silence that ensues. About the heat, and the pain, and the knife, and the blood.

And the blackouts.

But then I envision his reaction and stop myself.

"Not in the middle of the job," I say instead.

Thomas sighs again. It's long and heavy. Filled with stress and exhaustion. "I could help you with that," he finally says.

I know what he's talking about, but I have to shake my head and blink at him to make sure I heard him right.

"It's just temporary," he continues. "But enough to get you through a few meetings with her. It'll wear off in a couple days. A week, maybe."

"I don't think so," I say. But inside I consider what it would be like to be Thomas. Wholly unemotional. Unattached, unaffected, unbound by anything but the loyalty the three of us have to each other.

Lincoln was pissed off after that Blue Boar bullshit. It was pretty apparent that the inhibitor we used to keep us from killing each other never worked on Thomas. But that's not all that's different about him compared to Linc and me.

He's got no emotions. And he made himself that way on purpose using a drug he stole from Prodigy School back when we were kids.

"How do you have any left?" I ask. I've wondered about this for a while now, but never cared enough to ask.

"I reverse-engineered it. Bought a pharmaceutical company. Had them make it for me. It's a much better version than I had back then. It's fast-acting, long-lasting now. But I have the old version too, Case. I could give you the old version. The more temporary one. Just to get you through."

In other words, he could drug the love right out of me. Turn me into an emotionless machine, just like him.

"I've got a meeting," Thomas says, standing up from his desk, a signal that tells me it's time to leave. "But think about it. I'll come by your house tonight—"

"No," I say quickly. I can't have him at my house at night. He can't see the way I have to fight with the pain and the heat once the sun goes down. "I'll think about it," I say before he can ask any more questions. "And stop by here in the morning before work."

He smiles, satisfied. "OK," he says. "OK. I'll get some ready for you in case you decide to take me up on my offer."

He says that because he thinks he's won the argument and he's gonna get his way. But I'm not taking that pill. Not now, not ever.

"Don't get your hopes up," I say, rising to leave. "You'll be disappointed."

I walk out, not bothering to take the bridge back to the main cathedral because the garage is on this side of campus, and make my way down to my car.

I have a couple hours before the shit gets bad, so I drive by the main cathedral and before I know it, I'm parking in a space just half a block down.

I get out and start walking, the memories pulling at me. Guiding me back to the last night we had together. To the one and only moment in my life that I truly felt... happy.

She's there. Standing under the enormous gothic arch of the cathedral. Looking up at the heavy wooden double doors, like she very badly wants to enter, but requires an invitation.

I knew she'd be here. It wasn't the cathedral calling me back. It was her.

"Lulu," I say in a low voice, once I'm almost right behind her.

She doesn't whirl around in surprise.

She turns. Slowly. Cautiously.

And when her eyes meet mine, I realize something.

I still love her.

CHAPTER TWELVE

I don't want the night to be over. The last dance is a slow one, giving us permission to hold each other close, and take advantage of what's left of our first perfect night. All this... is done. My obligation to her and her family is over.

"Did you have a good time?" I whisper into her hair. She's got her head on my chest. It's resting there like she's exhausted. I have one arm wrapped tightly around her small waist, holding on to her hip. And the other is pressing her palm against my collar bone as we slowly shuffle our feet. Just one slow couple in a sea of black and white. The dancing is over. Every couple here is regretful that this is the sad end of a very happy night.

"The best night of my life," Lulu whispers. "I don't want it to end." Her words echo my thoughts. She pushes back suddenly, taking me by surprise. "Come with me."

My hand is squeezed as she leads me through the other couples, practically dragging me towards the front of the cathedral. Past groups of proud parents, all holding drinks. Past photographers taking pictures for the society page that will run in tomorrow's Sunday edition of The City Times. *We move past everyone until we are outside in the cool night. The street is lined with black limousines, ready to take everyone home in an orderly fashion. Some couples are already on their way out.*

But Lulu tugs on my hand, urging me to follow her into the dark shadows of the thick stone columns of the archway standing guard over the entrance.

We turn a corner and there is a small vestibule with an icon set back into a niche.

"What are we doing?" I ask.

"Shhh," Lulu says. "Just sit down."

I realize she's pointing to a small stone bench, opposite the iconic figure set into the wall. I give her a crooked smile. "Lulu…" I say, hesitant.

But she pushes me. Both hands firmly on my chest, making me take a step back. I bump into the bench and sit.

I am transfixed as she lifts up her elaborate white skirts of her dress and straddles my thighs, positioning herself over my cock, which is jumping to attention as what she's asking for becomes clear.

"Here?" I ask, my voice a low whisper. "Not here, Lulu."

"Yes," she says, easing her mouth down into my neck. Her lips are warm as they press against my skin. Her hands are gripping my shoulders. "I want my first time to be with you, and I want it to be right now."

CHAPTER THIRTEEN

He stares at me. I barely recognize him. He's so much older, broader, more intent. One gloved hand flies to my throat, the other covers my mouth as he pushes me back into the shadows of the thick stone columns that hold the arch over our heads. We round the corner, backing me into the secret spot I found for us so many years ago at the end of that one perfect night.

I'm frightened for a moment. Caught up in the accusations against him. In the law, and my duty, and my job.

But the heat of his hands and the urgency in his push are enough to keep me calm. Make me want him. Render me powerless to refuse him.

Did I ever doubt that I'd give in?

"Where did you go?" he asks, once we're hidden from view, the only prying eyes those of the iconic statue set into the stone wall.

"Away," I say simply.

"You're back now?" he asks. Eyes almost pleading.

"I'm back now."

He sits on the stone bench and it's like… it's like we're kids again. At the end of that one night at the ball. But this time we are deliberate. Older. More experienced, but also more cynical.

My eyes never leave his as I hike up my dress, straddle his thighs, and nestle myself into his lap.

He hugs me then. Wraps his arms completely around my waist, pulling me in so close, I almost gasp for air.

One gloved hand flies to my throat, the other covers my mouth as he pushes me back into the shadows of the thick stone columns that hold the arch over our heads. We round the corner, backing me into the secret spot I found for us so many years ago at the end of that one perfect night.

CHAPTER FOURTEEN

"Right here," she says. "Right now."

I cannot stop looking at her. We are dressed up like bride and groom. Playing the game of adulthood for parents, and photographers, and all the other couples around us.

"Please," she says, taking her lips to my mouth.

I kiss her softly. This was not how I imagined it. I have wanted to fuck her for weeks now. Every rehearsal was torture as I weighed that desire against who I am, what I'm doing, and how she might— or might not—fit into my long-term plan.

But I'm powerless. She's so in control of this moment, and I only want to make her happy, so I help her as she wrestles with the skirts of her dress and guides my hand between her legs.

The pulsing throb in my cock takes over and my fingers slip past her lacy panties, pulling them aside so I can find her soft wetness.

She closes her eyes and bites her lip, but I never stop watching her face as I ease my fingers in and out, gently stretching her open.

"Are you sure?" I ask. "I can think of so many different ways to make this better, Lulu."

She opens her eyes. I know what I'm doing with my fingers is painful because I can read her so well. I know her so well. If I fuck her here, she will have to be silent. She will have to bite back the soft screams that will come from her mouth when I fill her up.

"It doesn't get any better than this, Case. I swear, there will never be a better time than right now."

Her hand rests on top of mine as I continue to stimulate her. She closes her eyes again, whimpering for me to do more. To keep going and take the gift she's offering.

CHAPTER FIFTEEN

His kiss is crushingly hard. He bites my lip as his fingers press between my legs, seeking me out in a way I've only dreamed about for all these long years I've been away.

He unbuttons my coat, his fingers deft and experienced.

I lift up my hips, reaching for his belt. Unbuckling it and tugging on the button to his pants. I'm dragging the zipper down and pulling him out, his long, thick, hard cock in the palm of my hand.

When I look down at him, he's hungry. He looks like he's starving for me.

"I'm not letting you get away again," he says, his hand covering mine as he guides himself between my legs.

I close my eyes and moan as he enters. I'm so ready for him, he slides right in. And then his hard hug is back, pulling me close. Holding me tight.

I never want him to let go.

We move slowly at first. Holding back. Restraining ourselves so we can enjoy the moment. It's time repeating. We are that night, back when we were kids. Back when all he wanted was to make me happy and all I wanted was to let him own me, even if it was just in this small way.

But then he eases up, one hand on my breast, pushing me so I have to lean back. His cock feels so good. I grip his shoulders as I look down at his face.

How did we get so far away from each other?

There's a moment when he looks like he might stop and I almost panic.

But then it's gone, and in its place is hunger. The starvation I saw in his eyes when I first looked at him.

Both hands come up to the collar of my dress and I know what he's going to do. I wrap my fingers around both his wrists and say, "Case," in a stern voice. "Don't—"

But it's too late. He rips the front of my dress apart with one spectacular motion. Buttons pop off, hitting the stone with small crashing clicks.

His hands cover my breasts, squeezing hard.

And before I can stop him, he rips my bra apart too, my breasts spilling out into his palms.

"Shit," I say, still bouncing on his hard cock. "Fuck it," I hear myself mumble. "Do whatever you want."

CHAPTER SIXTEEN

I'm gentle as I open her legs wide, urging her to give me complete access. She leans back as I pump my cock a few times, letting her watch.

"Do it," she says. "I want you to do it."

I rub the head of my dick across her wet pussy, unable to believe I'm going to take her virginity here, at a cathedral, with hundreds of people not more than twenty feet away.

She positions herself right over me, then eases down until we make contact. It's so painfully, beautifully sweet.

Her face contorts into a grimace and I know it hurts.

I want to stop.

I never want to stop.

"Keep going," she urges me.

I place my palms on her hips, grabbing on to the soft lace and glass beads of her white gown, and show her how I like it.

Soft, slow. She drops her face to the top of my head, breathing hard into my hair. Her fingers dig into my shoulders as we find the perfect rhythm that will meld us together.

She whimpers and I know I'm hurting her. But I won't stop. There is no way I can stop now. She pants hard, long, heavy breaths pouring out of her mouth.

I want her to come but there's no way I can make her come on her first time with all these restrictions.

I try my best. I make her understand with words. "I love you," I say first, just so she knows this is not some one-night fuck for me. "I'm never giving you up now, Lulu."

She lifts her head and places both of her hands on either side of my jaw, holding me tight as we rock back and forth. "I'm gonna hold you to that promise."

CHAPTER SEVENTEEN

As soon as I give him permission, he is wild with lust. He wraps his hands around my waist, stands up, and crashes my back against the hard, cold stone wall.

His hips pound against me in punishingly hard thrusts. My legs are wrapped around his waist, trying to grip him harder as his hands turn into burning heat against the tender skin of my ass.

It hurts. It's so hot, it hurts. I'm gasping from the pain, but Case continues to fuck me so hard, I forget about everything but what we're doing. There is nothing on my mind but his hard cock penetrating me to my core.

He buries his head into my neck, commanding me to come. "Now," he says. "I can't wait any longer."

He kisses me. Crushing his lips to mine. Our mouths a tangle of tongues. We bite each other, not knowing any other way to express the lust we are both feeling in this moment.

I tense up, creeping feeling of climax rising up through my body, and he says, "Yes, Lulu. Yes. Come now. Right *now*."

A rush of relief flows through my body, my mouth opening in a long, loud moan that I am powerless to stop. I don't care who sees us, the only thing on my mind is release. Case's body goes still, then a gush of warm heat fills me up. He squeezes my breast so hard, I have to clasp my fingers over his and squeeze him back.

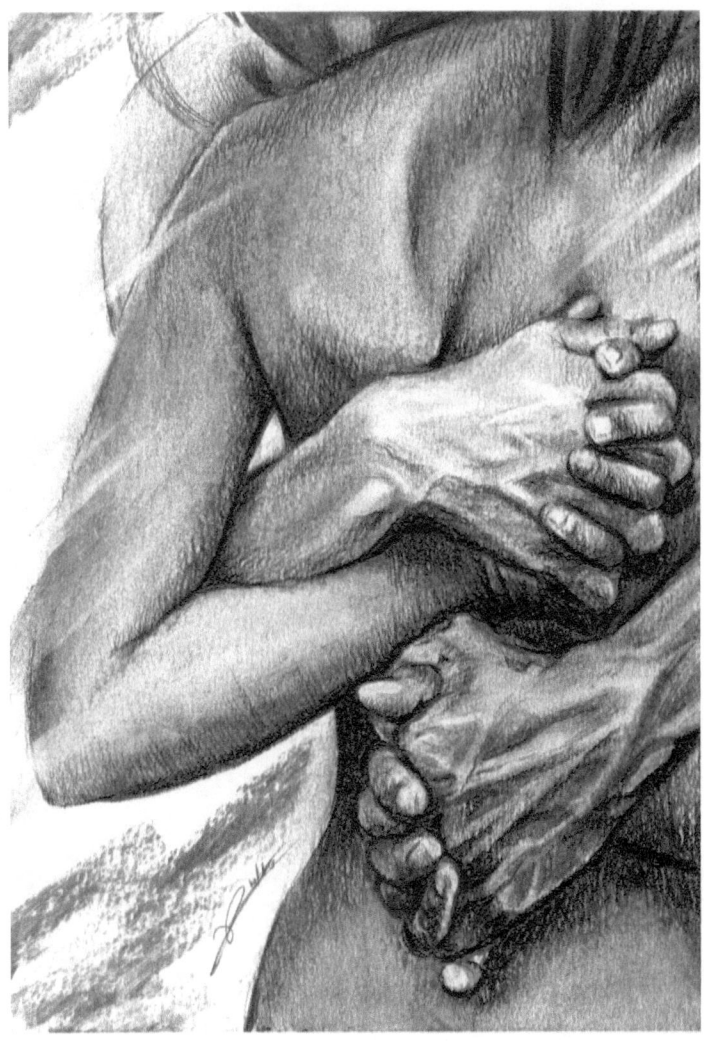

CASE
DEEP CUT

CHAPTER EIGHTEEN

I make her come. And just that alone is enough to push me over the edge. I press her back into the stone wall, my hands hot with the fire that lives inside me. I'm gripping the backs of her thighs so hard I know I'm leaving bruises.

"Yes," I say, as I collapse against her, my breath coming out in long streams of steam into the cold night air.

She goes limp and I carry her back over to the bench, sitting down with her in my lap, wrapping my coat around her shoulders as much as I can to try to keep the chill away.

We sit there like that for many minutes. And I realize that the pain... the pain in my body is gone. Not subdued, but gone.

"Thank you," I say, whispering into her ear.

"For what?" she asks, her lips playing with the stubble on my jaw.

"For making me feel normal again."

She sighs heavily but makes no move to get up.

"Sorry about your dress," I say. "I'll buy you a new one."

"No one cares about the dress, Case," she says back. Her hands slip deep inside my coat, sliding around my waist until they rest on the small of my back. She drops her head on my shoulder like the only thing on her mind is sleep. "Take me home with you," she whispers, her voice groggy and low.

I'm about to say, *You might as well just move in with me now, because I'm never letting you out of my sight again*, when I realize… I *can't* take her home.

Even if the sex is a cure for the pain that lives inside me, I can't fuck her twenty-four hours a day. It will come back. And when it does, I will need the deep cuts to rein it in again.

"I have to work tonight," I say.

"Oh." Her response is sad. It makes me sad too.

"But I can see you tomorrow. I can take the whole day off, Lulu. We can spend the whole day together doing anything you want."

"OK," she says, sitting up a little and looking down at her clothes. Her bra is hanging open, the front of her dress nothing but popped buttons and frayed fabric.

"Where did you park?" I ask. "I'll walk you to your car."

She gives me a small smile. "I'm just right out front. So the walk won't be long enough to make me happy."

"I'm sorry," I say, meaning it. "I want to take you home, I swear to God, I really do. I just can't tonight."

But I realize… I might not ever be able to take her home. Not while I'm like this. Not while I'm so fucked up I have to stand naked out on my roof every night and cut myself with a knife to make the heat and the pain go away.

"You're so warm," Lulu says. "I just want to stay here in your lap forever."

I sigh. Heavily. "Me too," I say. "I would love nothing more than to keep us in this moment."

"Do you have time to come over for a little bit?" she asks. "I can make you dinner. We can talk. Catch up. I have so many things I need to know about you."

"I can't," I say. And I really can't. I can already feel the pain building inside me again. Sex has no chance of changing me back to who I was. It will never be enough. It will never match the relief the knife brings. It's getting late, the sun is long gone, and pretty soon I'll need to take care of it. It drives me crazy when I don't take care of it.

She gets to her feet, pulling her coat tight around her body to hide her ripped bra and dress, and cinching it closed with a belt.

"But tomorrow, Lulu," I say, trying to make it better. Desperate to make it better. I don't want her walking away tonight feeling rejected. "Tomorrow, if you can, I'd like to see you again."

"I have to work," she says, sad. "But I'll see what I can do."

I stand up too, tucking my dick back into my pants and putting myself back together.

She's right about the walk to her car. It's parked just out front and these last few seconds aren't enough to take away the sting of sadness she's feeling right now.

I stop her, press her up against the cold metal of her door and kiss her. Her lips feel cool against my burning heat and there's no way she doesn't feel it.

She pulls back, looking at my face with a mixture of confusion and disbelief. Her fingers reach for me, about to touch my lips and confirm what I don't want her to know. But I grab her hand and place it over my heart. "I still love you. I never stopped loving you."

She smiles, sadly, then opens her door and slides into the seat. "See you tomorrow, Case." She pulls her door closed, starts her car, gives me one last wave goodbye, and then drives off.

I need to fix this. I need to figure out what's wrong with me and fix this. She can't get away again.

It's just dreams though. Fantasy. Because there's really only one thing I can do right now… and that's go home and start cutting.

CHAPTER NINETEEN

When I get to the office in the morning Cait already has my coffee ready for me as I pass her desk, and Randy is waving at me from his office, telling me to come inside. He's going to want an update and I have plenty to tell him. But I won't be telling him anything.

Oh, by the way, Randy, yes, I did make contact with Case Reider last night. He fucked me pressed up against the wall of a church, thank you.

So I'm getting my story all sorted in my head as I walk across the main office, when he bursts out his door, dragging his coat behind him.

"Come on, we gotta go."

"Go where?" I ask. But he's already heading to the garage entrance.

"You probably don't know him, but Chief—well, *former* Chief—O'Neil, he's out at the Cathedral City Penitentiary serving time for corruption."

"He was one of those guys who got caught up in the smackdown last winter?"

"Yeah," Randy says, throwing the heavy steel doors open that lead to the garage. "I just hung up with Warden Cage over there—"

"The warden's name is Cage?" I snort.

Randy shoots me a dirty look for interrupting him.

"Sorry," I mumble. "Go on."

"Anyway," he huffs, as we walk towards his car. "The warden called and said O'Neil has suddenly gotten chatty with a couple other inmates. And he's been talking about Lincoln Wade and some kind of interaction they had just before all that Blue Corp shit blew up."

"Hmmm," I say, slipping into the passenger's seat of his car as he does the same on his side. "What kind of interaction? Like... are they partners or something?"

"No clue, Lulu. So we're gonna take a little ride out there and see what his story is. How did it go last night? Did Reider make any contact with you?"

I'm about to totally lie and say no, but I just don't have it in me to lie to my boss. I can't tell him everything, but I can maybe stretch the truth and still be mostly honest. "So..." I start, trying to pick my way through this minefield. "I went over the main cathedral last night, just to sorta... walk down Memory Lane, you know?"

Randy squints his eyes at me and I have to take a sip of coffee so I don't wince.

"And?" he asks.

"And Case Reider was there."

"Did you talk to him?"

"Only very briefly." *We were too busy fucking.*

"What did he say?"

"You know, long time no see. We should catch up, have lunch. Miss you. Stuff like that."

"So you're gonna have lunch with him today."

"I don't know," I say, unsure.

"No," Randy says in a firm tone. "You *are* going to have lunch with him today, Lulu. No doubt. We need to figure out who this Red Robber person is before he decides to do anything else and Lincoln Wade is our best guess. We need an in with that guy like... now."

"I don't have his number and I didn't give him mine, so we'll just have to see what happens."

"You have until two o'clock to wait it out, then I want you to go digging. How hard can it be to find a number for the guy? His office is that huge collection of ugly silver cubes built into the side of the mountain. Just call over there and ask for him."

"He's the CEO, Randy. You don't just call up and ask for the CEO of ToyBox."

"I think he'll make an exception." And then we get on the freeway that will take us down south to where the penitentiary is.

The rest of the ride is mostly me thinking about Case fucking me last night and Randy, messing with the radio as he tries to get a signal. "What the hell is happening? Why can't I get any stations?"

"The mountains," I say, pointing up. "And that storm rolling in, probably. It's the same way out on Wolf Valley. We can't get shit on the radio out there."

Randy gives up on the radio and turns it off. The next twenty minutes are spent silently pondering the problems.

I'm sure he's thinking about the bank heist, this Red Robber guy, and how much of a chance I have of getting Case Reider to let me into his world. But I'm still thinking about Case's warm hands on my thighs last night. He left bruises on me. The good kind. My ass kinda hurts from the way his hands were gripping me and I shift in my seat to find a more comfortable position.

God, his scratchy face felt so good pressed up against mine when we were together last night.

"You coming?" Randy says.

We're already parked, I realize. I was so lost in thought I didn't even notice the car had stopped.

"Yeah," I say, shaking off the daydream and getting out. It's cold today, so I pull my coat around me and follow Randy into the wind as we make our way towards the prison.

Inside it's warm and empty. Obviously not visiting hours because there's just two armed guards manning the front desk behind thick, bulletproof windows.

Randy takes care of checking in, then stands next to me as I ponder getting breakfast from a vending machine filled with brightly colored calories.

Before he can say anything about my dilemma with the food, a loud buzzer sounds and a door clicks open. We both spin around to find a man in a suit.

"Randy," the older gentleman says, walking towards us with his hand out.

"Hey, Dick," Randy says, clasping his hand like they are old friends.

Dick Cage. I smile so I don't laugh, then extend my hand and greet the warden.

"This is my new assistant DA, Louise Lightly," Randy says, motioning to me.

"Just Lulu," I say to the warden. "Everyone calls me Lulu."

"Nice to meet you, Miss Lightly," the warden says, then turns to Randy and says, "Sorry to bother you, Randy. There's been talk for about a week now, but I've mostly ignored it until last night."

"What happened?" Randy asks.

"O'Neil's been shooting his mouth off." The warden looks around, then motions towards the door he came out of. "Let's go in. I'm having him brought to my office so you can hear it firsthand. We had to rough him up last night to get this info out of him, but don't worry, he's gonna talk now."

I expected some messy hair. Maybe the remnants of a bloody nose. But when the guards drop O'Neil off in the warden's office, both his eyes are black and swollen and it's obvious that his nose needed to be set last night after the roughing up, because there's white medical tape covering most of it.

I shoot the warden a dirty look. I don't care what kind of criminal he is, he should *not* be getting his ass kicked by the guards.

"We didn't do that," the warden says, reading my facial expression. "The other prisoners jumped him this morning for talking to us last night."

"Oh," I say.

O'Neil doesn't look at any of us. Just stands there in his shackles and handcuffs, staring at his feet.

"You know Randy?" Dick Cage says, talking to the former chief.

"Sure," the chief mumbles.

"Tell him what you told me last night about Lincoln Wade."

But O'Neil just shakes his head slowly. "They'll kill me if I talk. Just you calling me in here right now is enough, you know. They'll kill me."

"Who?" I ask, walking over to him. I know he's a corrupt asshole and he deserves to be in here. But it's not fair that he has to fear for his life.

"Who do you think?" he growls back at me. "The other inmates. I'm already on their shit list for being the former chief of police, so you can see that I can't afford to piss them off any more."

"Well, O'Neil," Randy says, "it's not up for debate. And quite frankly, I don't give a goddamn about your prison status or relationships. If you've got information that will help us, you will be telling us all about it before we leave."

O'Neil looks at me, nodding his head towards Warden Cage. "Don't believe a word he says. Yeah, the other guys took care of the eyes, but his guards"—he sneers at Cage—"did the rest."

I look at Dick Cage, then Randy. "We do not threaten prisoners," I say calmly, but firmly. "Or beat them," I say this with my gaze directed to the warden.

"Lulu," Randy says. "Do you mind stepping outside for a few minutes?"

"I certainly do," I say back. "I won't be a part of this, Randy. Not what I signed up for."

We stare at each other for several seconds, both of us standing our ground.

"I'm happy to tell you," O'Neil says, interrupting our standoff. "But I want out of this prison."

All of us laugh at that statement. Even me.

"Not out of my sentence," O'Neil continues. "I want a transfer to Cathedral County Minimum."

The Pen, where we are now, is maximum security. Where all the hardasses go. Normally a former police chief wouldn't be sent to the Pen, but O'Neil's crimes were too numerous to ignore. His corruption spanned more than a decade.

"I hardly think," Randy says, "what you've got to tell me is worth all that trouble."

"Ask him," O'Neil says, motioning to Dick Cage.

"Is it?" Randy asks the warden.

"It might—"

But just then the lights all go out.

"What the fuck?"

Pretty much everyone in the room says that at the same time.

"See," O'Neil says, standing still in the dim lights coming through the half-open blinds covering the window. "What I have to say really is worth all that trouble."

Warden Cage walks over to his desk and picks up the phone. He stares at it for a second, then sets it back down. "Dead," he says, pulling out his cell phone. "Shit," he says, looking at Randy. "My cell is dead too."

Randy and I both get our phones out and just as Randy says, "Mine's out as well," my phone *rings*.

Everyone looks at me, including the prisoner, and I shrug. "I have SkyEye Satellite." And then I point west, towards the mountains. "I come from Wolf Valley, remember? No service out there except satellite."

"Answer it," Randy growls.

The screen says unknown number, but I know who it is. There is only one person it could be in a time like this.

Case.

"Hello?" I ask the phone.

"Hey, Lu," Case says, voice calm, like he hasn't a care in the world. "Do you have time to meet me for lunch today?"

I stare at my boss and then say, "Uh, sure. What did you have in mind?"

"I've got a shitload of meetings this morning, but if you can swing by ToyBox around noon, I'll squeeze you in."

He says it... sexy. Squeeze me in. It shouldn't be sexy. Those words shouldn't fill my head with images of him grabbing my breasts last night.

But they do.

"OK," I manage to whisper back. "I'll do that."

"Great," Case says. "See you later."

I end the call and all three men are looking at me. But before they can say anything, the door bursts open and a woman prison guard is standing there, barking out a status report.

"Power's out, water's out, phones are out. We're on back-up generators. There's a riot breaking out in Cell Block H, all the rest of the prisoners are in lockdown."

"Randy," Dick Cage says. "I've gotta handle this. Take your time in here and I'll be back as soon as I can."

The warden disappears, closing the door behind him and drowning out the building commotion.

"I want to be kept in solitary confinement until my transfer," O'Neil says, picking up like this interruption never happened. "And I need to be the fuck out of this place by the end of the week. Those are my terms. This," he says, nodding his head up, like he's referencing the lack of power, "is him. You can bet on it."

"Who?" Randy asks, eager for a name.

"Wade. Lincoln Wade is most definitely the one behind all this bullshit. And I can prove it. Pull my collar back," O'Neil says. "Look at my neck."

Randy walks over to the chief and pulls down the collar of his bright red jumpsuit. There is an ugly scar on his throat. Like a… burn. Almost like a… handprint.

"He did that to me," the former chief says.

"Who?" Randy and I ask at the same time.

"Wade. He did that to me with his hands. They burned me. Through his gloves. He came in my office last winter to threaten me about the way I was talking to his girlfriend, Detective Masters. And he choked me. His hands lit up red," he says. "My neck blistered in a matter of seconds. When I went to the hospital, they said second-degree burns. From his *hands*."

I suddenly have a vision of Case's hands on my body last night. The unnatural heat coming from them, even through his gloves.

His gloves.

Just the way O'Neil describes Wade.

"There's something really wrong with this city," O'Neil says, echoing my thoughts the other morning. "And it begins and ends with Lincoln Wade, Case Reider, and Thomas Brooks. They're the bad guys here, not me. I want my transfer, Randy. And I want it now, or I'm not saying another word and I'll deny everything I just told you. You're gonna look crazy as fuck if you try to sell this story to a judge and jury without my support."

CHAPTER TWENTY

Thomas is standing in my office looking out the large floor-to-ceiling window, talking on his phone. Well, he's not really talking. I'm guessing Linc is the one doing all the talking right now because Thomas just mutters, "Mm-hm," every now and then.

"OK," he says, done listening. "We'll be up there tonight. And get the..." He stops, searching for words. "The... you know, that cave shit. Get that ready for Case. He's agreed to let Sheila do whatever the fuck it was she wanted to do to him."

He ends the call and turns.

I shoot him a dirty look. "I didn't agree to anything."

"But you will once I tell you what just happened."

I point at the window. "Power's out. I can see that."

"Not the power, Case. The power is almost the least of our concerns right now. The water treatment plant has been... sabotaged."

"Define that," I say, frowning.

"The pumps that power the treatment cycles..."—he waves his hands as if conjuring up all the technical words he doesn't have to describe the situation, and then moves on—"have been shut down, apparently."

"Has the water been tainted?" I ask.

"Not that Lincoln can see at the moment. But even if we get the power back on so the water starts flowing again, the water won't be flowing for long. It's got to be treated and that's offline."

"What else?" I ask, looking down at the city.

"The cell phone towers east and west of Cathedral City are no longer standing."

"Jesus Christ. So no one has cell service?"

"Only SkyEye customers." And then Thomas screws up his face. "Which is going to make me look like a prime suspect."

"Anything else?" My words come out as a sigh.

"We still need to carry this plan out, Case." Thomas is serious most of the time. In fact, I can't even remember the last time I've seen him smile at something that struck him as funny, and not just to be polite. But right now his expression is something more than serious. Grave and intent. Intent on his revenge, I realize.

"I'm not backing out," I say, walking over to stand beside him. He turns to face the window with me.

"I'm not accusing you of backing out. What I am worried about is what might be going on in that head of yours."

"Explain," I say, looking at the chaos down below. The ToyBox offices are built into the side of the mountain on the western edge of the city, so I have a pretty good view of everything. I can't see the street level around downtown, of course. Too many tall buildings in the way. But this side of town is where all the corporate tech offices are located and it's busy enough to know that shit is spiraling out of control down there.

The traffic lights have stopped working. I can count seven accidents just from where I stand, so I can only imagine how bad it is closer to the city center.

"Something is happening to you."

There's no question mark at the end of that statement, but it *is* a question. He doesn't know anything other than what I tell him and I've been tight-lipped lately.

It bothers him. A lot.

"I don't know," I say. "I feel... off." There's no way I'm going to admit to the cutting bullshit. That's... crazy. Like... it will change things between us. He will lose confidence in me and want to make new arrangements. And I'm not going to let that happen. I want what he wants. Just as much as he wants it.

"Do you think it was due to the jellyfish... stuff?" I almost smile as he struggles to describe the procedure. "Or do you think it has something to do with the fact that Molly..." He lets out a long exhale of tired breath. "That Molly touched you with that lariat thing the Blue Boar had her whipping around that night?"

"Hmmm," I say, thinking this over. "I haven't thought about that very much. But I should. She didn't take it with her, right?"

"No," Thomas says. "It went down with the building." He turns to look at me, his fingers coming up to touch my throat.

I flinch and back away. "What are you doing?"

"She had it around your throat. Do you remember that?"

"She did?" I ask, reaching for my neck. "No, I don't remember that."

"She was about to behead you, Case. I shot it, snapped it, and saved your life. If she had pulled a little harder I have no doubt it would've cut you in two. But look," he says, taking both my shoulders and turning me towards the window. "You have no scar. Do you find that weird?"

I can barely see my reflection in the glass as I reach for my throat again. But I don't need to see myself to know he's right. There is no scar on my neck from that rope thing Molly was using as a weapon that night.

"Weird?" I ask. "I guess. Do we even know what that thing was?"

"No," Thomas says. "But it cut your skin. It might've been laced with something."

"Did anyone else get cut by it?" I ask, unable to remember all the details. "Everything happened so fast. And then I took that hit in my shoulder and… that's all I remember about the end of the fight. The next thing I knew we were flying back up to the helicopter on that grappling wire."

"Lincoln did. On his arm. But most of what the barbs tore off his flesh was… the new kind, you know?"

The new kind of flesh. I wonder what that is, exactly?

"He told me it grabbed onto the steel plate, punctured a gas canister, and then embedded into his skin for a few seconds before she pulled it out and tried to behead you."

"He has a scar?" I ask, still stuck on the fact that I don't.

"Yes, nasty one, too. But you don't."

"Maybe the jellyfish stuff healed it?" I ask.

"Maybe it did, Case." Thomas studies my face for a few seconds. "But then again, maybe it didn't."

"What are you trying to say?"

"I don't know, which is why you've agreed to let Sheila do whatever it is she wants to figure it out."

"She's checked me out a dozen times already, Thomas. She never finds anything."

"Because she needs to use other *tools*."

"I don't want those nanites in my body. It creeps me out."

"Something is already in your body, Case." Thomas frowns at me, looking kind of… sad. "And I'm not going to lose you over something as stupid as a diagnostic test.

We've been together too long, brother. We've been through too much to let some manageable health issue rip us apart. You're getting those tests."

Our shared past flashes between us as we study each other.

Prodigy School. The maze, the Omegas, the pain, the killing, the escape. And then everything that came after.

If I hadn't had Thomas back then to sterilize my emotions and keep the situation rooted firmly in his unwavering logic, I wouldn't be here right now. I'd be dead. Long time ago.

"What are you afraid of?" Thomas finally asks, breaking the silence.

I shrug. "Everything," I say.

"She can fix it, Case."

"You don't know that."

Thomas places a hand on my shoulder and squeezes. "I do know that. Sheila is the most amazing piece of technology humanity has ever built. Let her do what she can. We'll fix it, Case. We will. I promise you. I'm not going to let you die now. Not after we got this far."

"You're right," I say, sighing. "She is pretty amazing." And then I look Thomas straight in the eyes. "But she wasn't made by humans, Thomas. She was made by Lincoln."

"He's still Lincoln," Thomas says quietly.

"I know that," I say. "I'm not giving up on him. Just like you're not giving up on me. But we've got to face facts here. Lincoln isn't human. Hasn't been for a very long time. And the Blue Boar wasn't human either. I think there's a lot more nonhumans running around this town than we even realize. So whatever happened to me— whatever is *still* happening to me, Thomas—it's got nothing to do with being human. That's what I'm afraid of."

He turns away and walks back to the chairs in front of my large steel desk. Takes a seat and crosses his legs. "Lulu Lightly is going to be a problem."

"How so?" I ask, a little stunned by the change of subject.

"Molly says the DA's office is out to get her and Lulu Lightly is on the team handling this case."

"What case?" I ask. "There's no case. No charges have been filed."

"Not yet. But Lincoln had her plant some code in the CCPD computers so he can track things and they link up with the DA's office in some instances. They're on to us."

"We haven't done anything yet."

"Right," Thomas says. "But we're about to. We're only days away from Stage One and this—" He waves his hand flippantly at the window. At the outside world. "This stuff going on right now. The power outage, the phones, the water. It's them, trying to set us up for failure."

"Nah," I say. "Who's left aside from us? I mean," I correct myself quickly, "who's left who knows what we *know*?"

"We probably missed a few people that night."

I squint my eyes at him. "Missed a few people? How? We blew the school up that night. We killed everyone."

"We didn't get Molly."

"No, but Lincoln—" And then it hits me. The Blue Boar. "She was under his control?" I ask. "That whole time?"

"Molly has disclosed some very interesting things to Lincoln over the past several months about what the Blue Boar told her. He always knew where she was. And Will was there too. Not to mention my... *mother*."

He spits that word out with contempt. We don't really know for sure if Martha Masters was Thomas's mother. All we know is that Atticus, Thomas, and Molly are genetically related through the Blue Boar's DNA. All three of them could have different mothers. But Atticus seemed convinced that Martha belonged with him. At least enough to save her in the end.

"And now Atticus and Martha are missing."

"Or dead," I add.

"Not likely," he quips. "They're still alive, I feel it."

"You think this is them?" I ask, waving my hand at the window. "Doing all that bullshit down there?"

"Who knows? But it's not us, Case. That's the only thing that matters. Someone else has a plan that doesn't involve us. That's the important part. We're close and we're not going to let some outsider take what's ours. You need to rein in Lulu Lightly."

"How the hell would I do that? Just go up to her and say, 'Hey, Lulu. I know we haven't seen each other much over the past seven or eight years, but my supervillain friends and I have this really great revenge plan for what they did to us out at Prodigy School, and could you do us a solid and just back off until we're done?'"

Thomas actually smiles. Like… maybe a real one. His phone beeps and he looks down at it for a second before giving me his full attention again. "You're kind of a genius, Case." He pans his hands around at my massive ToyBox office. "I'm sure you'll figure it out. But I've been here long enough and my helicopter is here to take me downtown. I have things to do back at SkyEye, especially since the cell towers are all down. This plays perfectly into our hands, you realize that, right?"

I nod. Smile. "Go get 'em, asshole."

Thomas gets up and walks to the door. He's got his hand on the knob, ready to turn it and leave, when he stops and looks at me over his shoulder. "Be up at Lincoln's house tonight. I mean it. Sheila will fix it, Case. Whatever it is, she'll fix it."

I want to believe him. Typically, when Thomas Brooks says something is fact, I take him at his word. He's super fucking smart. Not like me and my genius imagination for inventing things that got me this massive ToyBox office. Or like Lincoln, who really isn't human anymore, if he ever was in the first place. But smart in another way. Smart in a street way. The kind of way that makes people trust in him. Take his word as truth. Go along with all his decisions and let him take the lead on things.

But he doesn't know what I know about what's happening to my body. He doesn't know about the light and heat inside me. About how all it wants is to escape and how it compels me to cut myself every night.

And yeah, my symptoms sound a little bit like Lincoln. We definitely have something in common. I think that jellyfish stuff is responsible for the light and the heat. But what if Thomas is right? What if that lariat thing Molly was using as a weapon that night we took down Blue Corp was laced with something that altered me at the DNA level?

The cutting is wrong somehow. I know Lincoln well. He's trusted me with most of his secrets, if not all of them, since we were kids. And I know for a fact he never cut himself to ease the pain.

So maybe this is just my psyche's way of controlling things. Maybe I need those vents in my hands like Lincoln has had forever? And once I get them, it will all make sense.

But maybe this is something new. This cutting bullshit. Maybe that lariat sent something into my body that makes me want to self-destruct?

Maybe I'm my own worst enemy?

And just maybe... what's happening to me was done on purpose?

I could be the reason we fail.

I get a sick feeling in my stomach, but the phone buzzes on my desk and my assistant's voice comes through the intercom. "Mr. Reider?" she says.

"Yes?" I answer.

"The company engineers want to know how you'd like to partition our power from the backup generators. They say we have enough fuel for a few days, but not much more than that."

"Shit." I look out the window and wonder who's fucking with the city. *My* city. Who is fucking with *my* city.

A feeling of possessiveness courses through my body.

"Mr. Reider?" she asks. "What should I tell them?"

"Tell them... tell them I'll be right down."

"Yes, sir."

I walk over to the window and place my hands against the cool glass. "Don't worry," I whisper to the city. "I'll figure it out and take care of it. They won't hold you hostage for long."

CHAPTER TWENTY-ONE

ToyBox Inc is only about ten miles north of the Cathedral City Penitentiary, and even though it's not quite lunchtime when Randy and I finish up with DickCage (I can't help but run the two words together after a whole morning listening to him bitch and moan about Chief O'Neil's demands) he's so eager for me to get closer to Case and figure out how Lincoln Wade is involved in all this crap happening to the city right now, he's dropping me off.

Yes. My boss is dropping me off at the office of the man I fucked outside the main cathedral last night, with strict instructions not to come back to work until I can add one more piece to the puzzle. At which time, he will probably fire me, per our plan. So I was basically ordered to get myself fired today.

I have been sorta daydreaming about how this lunch date will go down for hours.

When a guy invites you to lunch at his office that's the same thing as a nooner, right?

I'm pretty sure guys think like that.

Pretty sure.

"OK," Randy says, squeezing my shoulder like I need moral support. "You know what to do, right? Just go in there, flirt with him a little, get him talking about the old days and shit. And maybe," Randy says, holding his thumb and forefinger about half an inch apart, "maybe you can add in a little more than just flirting. Just a little," he says, making his point with his gesture.

I sigh, say nothing, and then grab my purse and get out of the car, slamming the door behind me.

The window rolls down and Randy yells, "Just a little."

But I don't turn around. I just walk up the long river-stone walkway that leads to the unusual cube-shaped buildings situated on the side of the mountain, and when I get to the doors I stop and stare at myself in the reflective silver-tinted glass of the doors as they open automatically.

Inside the place is darker than I imagined it would be, since the whole complex seems to be made of glass, and there is no one in the huge two-story lobby.

No one. Not even a receptionist.

"Hello?" I ask the emptiness.

"Hello," a man's voice says behind me, making me start and whirl.

"Um," I say, eyeing the hologram, then waving my hand through it. "Hello? Are you real?"

"Miss Lightly, I presume. You're Miss Lightly?" the image says.

"Yeeesss," I say, unsure what to think of this… light show. It's flickering erratically, which makes me look up to the beams of light that stream down from so many tiny projectors built into the ceiling. "I'm here to see Mr. Reider," I say, my voice louder, so it echoes through the empty room.

"You don't need to shout, Miss Lightly. I can hear just fine. Mr. Reider is still busy dealing with other matters at the moment, but I was told to escort you upstairs to his office where you can wait and help yourself to refreshments."

"You were?" I ask, utterly bewildered. I knew Case made toys—hence the name of his company. Mostly video game systems. But I had no idea he was into... whatever this thing is. It makes me think of his friend, Lincoln Wade, for some reason. He's the computer guy, right?

"I'm Steve," the apparition says. "The ToyBox butler." He holds his hand out to me in greeting.

I look at it dubiously.

"Go ahead," he says, smiling. "Shake it. Take me for a spin."

I giggle a little and then shrug. I shake his hand and experience a weird sensation of warmth as the light making up his fingers wraps around mine. He flickers at the same time. His whole—body, I guess—glows a warm yellow-orange color. Like he's...happy.

"That wasn't too hard, was it?"

"What are you?" I ask. "A computer?"

"I have an artificial intelligence chip inside my main component, but I am also programmed to respond to visual, auditory and emotional cues as well."

"Huh," I mumble. "Weird."

"Yes," he says brightly. "Most do find me slightly disconcerting at first. But I assure you, everyone ends up liking me. I'm an invaluable addition to the labor force here at ToyBox. Mr. Reider wouldn't trust me to greet you if he didn't agree with my self-assessment."

"OK," I say, shrugging. "Lead the way, Mr. Steve."

He waves a transparent hand in the direction of a bank of elevators and I start walking. He walks next to me, stride for stride, and his shoes even make a soft tapping sound on the black polished floors.

The elevator doors start opening before we even get there and then Steve disappears and reappears inside the elevator.

"That was a cool trick," I say, joining him inside.

"I'm not seamless," he says, frowning. "I can only appear where there are sensors." He points to the ceiling of the tall elevator.

"Gotcha," I say.

There are no buttons on the inside of the elevator, but nonetheless, the doors close and we start ascending.

"What's Case working on?" I ask, just trying to fill the awkward silence.

"Apparently," Steve says, "the city is having a crisis right now. He's trying to figure out what's happening. We sent all the other employees home. Which pleases me, since I was the one ordered to greet you."

"Yeah," I say, remembering all the shit that's happening outside. "How do you guys have power?"

"Backup generators," he says as the elevator comes to a stop. "And I sure do hope he figures out how to fix the city. Because if not"—he drags a finger across his throat—"it's the ax for me, right?" He smiles, like this is a joke. But just as abruptly, he frowns. "I have complete faith in him." He waves me forward and as soon as I take a step, he's flickering to life in front of me again.

Not seamless.

I'm having a conversation with a computer and a few beams of light. It makes me shudder.

"Right through here," Steve says, pointing to a pair of double doors and a large office with a view of the entire city beyond. We walk in together and I can't help it, I go all the way over to the windows and look around.

"Wow," I say. "This is quite nice."

"Yes," Steve says. "Watch this." He produces a snapping sound with his flickering fingers and little red dots with small labels attached to them appear on the glass in front of me. I back away, startled, but then catch my breath and take a step forward, curious as to what I'm looking at.

"Anything you want to know about the city can be found by touching the glass. It will even talk to you. Like an interactive history lesson. Go ahead, give it a try."

I look around, then choose an area in the distance and press my finger to the glass. There's an electric shock and when I pull my finger back, there's a small speck of blood on the glass. When I reach up to touch it, it... disappears. Like it was drawn into the glass somehow.

"The hell?" I ask, confused.

"Sorry about that," Steve says, tone still jovial. "Must've been a power surge when we turned on the generators and caused a buildup of static."

"But..." I stammer, searching for the right words. "Where did my blood just go? It's like... it got sucked inside the glass."

"Oh, it won't damage the machine. See those tiny lines?"

I squint my eyes to the thin wires embedded into the glass in a mesh pattern.

"That's the computer. I'm sure that tiny speck of blood was just absorbed into the plate and didn't bother it at all."

"Sure," I say, annoyed.

"Go, on. Give it another try. It's fun, you'll see."

I give Steve the stink-eye.

"I promise," he says. "One more tap. Anywhere you want."

I look more carefully at the city this time, wondering which part of it to choose. I finally decide on a tiny area, near the entrance to the Merchant District.

The window bleeps to life with quick red flashes, and then calms down and begins to speak.

"Cathedral Seven was built by the corrupt Head Merchant, Theodore Sayer, after the Second War. It was believed to be a place of worship, although which God or demon he was praying to is still up for debate. Shortly after the cathedral was finished someone had the good sense to blow it up and Head Merchant Sayer was arrested six months later for tax evasion, drug running, and ordering the deaths of four people in Wolf Valley. He spent the rest of his life in prison and was killed by fellow inmates less than three months after sentencing. The cathedral was never rebuilt and now stands in ruin to remind the people of the Merchant District that the city delivers its own justice."

The computer voice ends and I just stand there blinking for a moment before a laugh bursts out. "What kind of history lesson is *that*?"

"Not the kind you find in classrooms, Miss Lightly."

"Obviously."

"Can you find a way to amuse yourself with the interactive city and the refreshments? Or should I stay and keep you company? I don't think Mr. Reider will be long."

I turn away from the creepy map and find the refreshments he's referring to on a low table in front of a slate-gray leather couch. "I'll make do," I say, wandering over to a spread of fruit, wine, and cheese.

"Very good," Steve says, but he's only a voice now. The flickering light body has disappeared. "If you need anything, just call for me."

I remove my coat, drape it over a chair, drop my purse next to it, and take a seat on the couch to wait in silence for a few moments, straining to hear something. Anything. It's so very, very quiet here. Not the corporate office I was expecting.

Once I'm convinced that the weird hologram butler isn't watching me, I lean forward and pick up the wine.

"I hope you like the vintage," Case says, walking into the office and pulling the huge double doors closed behind him.

Yes, I'm quite sure he has nooners here with women. It's the perfect set-up. Then I look up at the little black boxes in the ceiling that project Steve and wonder if they're cameras as well.

Maybe he's kinky and likes to make sex tapes?

"Lulu?" Case says, dragging my attention back to him.

"Sorry," I say, blushing. "Your... butler?"

"Yeah." Case laughs. "He's something, right?"

"Is he... real?" I ask, still trying to adjust to the newness of all this.

"If by real," Case says, taking the wine from my hand and producing a corkscrew, "you mean intelligent? Well, sorta. He has about a quarter of the intelligence that Sheila has, but he's still pretty useful." Case pulls the cork out of the bottle and starts pouring wine into our glasses.

"Sheila?" I ask, totally off my game.

"Oh." Case laughs. "My friend Lincoln programs them, you know? And I mass-produce the hardware." He points to the ceiling where I was just looking. "So he's got Sheila and I have Steve. But Sheila is... incredible. Nothing like Steve. Steve is just a hollow version. An automaton, if you will."

Lincoln Wade. *Snap out of it, Lulu. That's the whole reason you're here.*

Well, not the whole reason.

"Lincoln Wade," I say, like I'm trying out the name after not hearing it for a long time. "You guys were friends back when I knew you. I remember that." I accept the glass that

Case offers me and take a sip of wine to give him a moment to respond.

"Yeah, Linc and I go way back. Almost brothers, really. When we came back from… well, you know," he says, not filling in the missing words, "he lived with me and my folks since his parents were dead."

"Yeah." I sigh, leaning back into the couch cushions. "You've lived quite a life. I'd forgotten all that about you while I was gone."

"But not me, right?" Case winks. "You couldn't possibly have forgotten me. Not after that incredible night we had at the ball."

I blush. Furiously. He took my virginity that night. I practically forced him to do it.

"I've thought about you a lot, Lulu." He takes a seat next to me. Kinda close, so our legs are touching.

I don't want to look at him. I have no idea what to say. We fucked again last night. I haven't seen him in over seven years and the first time we bump into each other, I let him have sex with me. Outside. Again.

Jesus.

"Are you OK?" Case asks, staring at me with a concerned look.

"Yeah, fine," I say, clearing my throat. "It's just been a very weird day. And I have to tell you, it's only getting weirder."

"Because of me?" Case asks. He takes a sip of his wine and waits.

"A little bit of it is you, yeah. This lunch invitation. Plus, the fact that Cathedral City is in crisis down there." I wave a hand at the window. Which reminds me. "And you have a very strange sense of humor."

He laughs. "How so?"

"That talking glass. Steve told me to press my finger on it to make it tell me facts about the city and what it said was… just…" I shake my head. "Weird."

"Well, it's a little joke between me and my friends. It's not the version we're gonna sell the schools and city." He walks over to his desk and picks up what appears to be a little tray made of glass. It's a tablet, I realize when he touches the glass and it flickers to life. With handles on each side, so you can hold it and not touch the glass surface. "This is one of the products I'm working on. Just a prototype so far." One fingertip taps the surface and it comes to life, playing music that might appeal to a small child. "*Let's play the ABC's,*" the tablet says.

"An educational toy," Case says. "I call this product a SpyGlass and the computer that runs it, a special combination of silicon and oxygen, is called SmartGlass. Every school in Cathedral City will have one soon."

Well, I feel a little silly for being creeped out about the one on the window.

"But I mean, come on, Lulu," Case continues the other part of our conversation. "This city is filled with filth and corruption. Why not just be honest about it?"

"I guess."

"You guess? You're an assistant DA, Lulu. You should know better than anyone how bad it's gotten."

"I do know," I say. "That's why I'm here."

He cocks his head at me in confusion. "You're here… for me. I thought."

"I am," I say. And I don't know why I feel so compelled to tell him the truth, but I think it's because I know deep down, he's not involved in any of that shit happening outside.

But then Randy's voice is in my head. *Lincoln Wade, Lulu. We're after Lincoln Wade.*

Whom I do not know at all. Not one bit. I don't even remember meeting him casually back when Case and I were going to all those ball rehearsals.

"I am here for you. I have thought about you a lot, Case. And I'd be lying if I said you weren't on my mind when I decided to take this job. You were."

"Well, I think we're getting off on the right foot, Miss Lightly. But I have to confess, I had an ulterior motive for asking you here today."

"You did?"

"Yeah. You see, I know someone in the CCPD. Molly Masters?" he says. "Ever heard of her? She's a detective."

"Kind of," I lie. I have most certainly heard far more about her than I should've over the last few days. "Her name at least. What about her?"

"I think your colleagues in the DA's office are trying to set her up."

"What?" I laugh. Could this day get any weirder?

"Yeah," Case says, putting his wine down. "Something strange is happening. That bank robbery. Now the power's out. The water treatment plant is down."

"It is?" I say. "I haven't been back to the office so I wasn't aware that there was a problem with the treatment facility."

"And SkyEye is the only phone service at the moment. So you can see how this might... make me and my friends uncomfortable."

I just stare at him. Is he really going there? No pretenses? No disguising his motives?

"Thomas thinks they're gonna blame him for the cell phone towers."

"Towers?" I ask, feeling like I'm coming in on the middle of a conversation. "What's wrong with the towers?"

"Someone blew them up."

"Who?" I ask, bewildered. "Who would do that?"

"Someone who wants to knock out cell service to Cathedral City, obviously."

"Like your friend? The satellite phone guy?"

"Oh, the phones are just the domestic side of his business."

"Case," I say, putting a hand up. "I have no idea where you're getting your information, but I don't think I need to know all this—"

"You do, Lulu. Because the city is falling apart down there. And it's my job to hold it all together. It's counting on me to—"

"How do you know all this, Case? I haven't even heard about the things you're telling me."

"See," he says. "This is part of the reason we need to have this chat."

I get up, skirt around the low table holding the food, grab my coat and purse, and then start walking towards the doors. I throw them open and head towards the elevator. "I've got to get back to work. We'll have to do lunch some other time."

But when I get to the elevator the flickering light show that calls himself Steve is blocking my way. "You can't leave here without permission, Miss Lightly." He says this so casually, I get a chill up my spine.

I turn to face Case, who is still back inside his office.

"Let me out," I say, my voice thick with anger.

"No," he says, walking over to me. "I can't. Not yet. Not until we're both on the same page." He walks right up next to me, placing his hands on my hips. That's when I think about the gloves again. And the heat. And the story that O'Neil told me this morning.

"Your hands," I whisper. "Your hands were so warm last night."

Case lets out a long breath and leans down into my neck. "Come back inside my office, Lulu. You don't have a choice, because you can't get out of this building unless I let you. And I'd hate to have to pick you up and carry you back, but I will if I have to because you're not leaving yet. Not until I have your word."

I pull out my phone and begin dialing—Case whips it out of my hand. "Who do you think you're calling?"

"The police," I say, unable to prevent the satisfied smugness from leaking out with my words.

Case studies the screen and scowls. "You had nine and one dialed. You were actually calling the police on me?"

"You're the one who said you were holding me prisoner. Now give it back, call your creepy hologram to let me out of this building, and I'll be on my way without a fuss."

He says nothing. Just keeps still and silent, like he's thoughtfully considering my offer.

"Give it back," I say, making a grab for the phone.

He holds it high above his head. And smiles.

"That's really mature."

"Desperate times, Miss Lightly. Why are you being so uncool about this?"

My mouth does this dropping thing and I stop blinking. Because he's an idiot, right? "You're some kind of strange rich toy freak with creepy friends who make pretend light-show people and blow up cell towers just so they can sell more satellite phones. That's why I'm being *uncool*." I roll my eyes and cross my arms.

"He didn't blow up those towers."

"That's the only part of that statement you're going to bother denying?"

Case shrugs. "We have been known to blow things up before—"

"Like Blue Corp?" I say.

He stops talking and just tilts his head at me. "What do you know?"

"I'm not going to tell you because you're being a dick." And then I giggle because I almost want to tell him about stupid DickCage at the prison. Being the boy-man he is, I think Case might appreciate that little inside joke.

"None of this is funny, Lulu. What do you know about blowing up Blue Corp?"

"Did you do it?" I ask.

He rubs a hand over his jaw, looks at me from the corner of his eye. "If I tell you the truth will you stay and not call the police?"

"Depends."

"Depends on what? You can't say depends, Lulu. That's *very* uncool, OK? We're here having this amazing bonding moment over secrets and it's your job to play your part."

"My part? What are we, ten? We're in your little backyard treehouse about to be blood brothers? Do I have to spit on my hand before we shake on it?"

"That is usually how it's done when you're *ten*," he sneers. "But no, we're grownups now, so I was thinking we'd just fuck afterward." He shrugs again. "You know, to seal the deal."

"God," I say. "You're so stupid."

We both laugh.

"Seriously, Lulu," he says with a sigh, lowering the hand holding my phone. "Bad things are happening and I need to trust you. But I can't if your first reaction is to go running to the police. Or your stupid boss. I can't believe you work for Randy Shits."

"It's Shultz," I say. But RandyShits is almost as funny as DickCage. "And it's not my fault you're mixed up in all this illegal shit. I'm a goddamned lawyer, Case. I represent Cathedral City in court. It's my job to follow the law."

"Exactly," he says, tossing me my phone back. Which I catch—one-handed, I might add. "You," he says, pointing at me, "represent the city. And the city needs help, Lulu. That's why you need to trust me."

"That makes no sense. You and your friends are the ones messing it all up."

"No," he says. "You've got it all backwards. Lincoln has been doing his best to rid the city of bad people for a long time now. Thomas took over Blue Corp and kept things going after all that shit went down in the spire. And I—" He stops. Like he's not sure where he fits in. "*I'm* the one the city talks to at night. I'm the one it's counting on this time."

Holy shit.

He really is fucking crazy.

CHAPTER TWENTY-TWO

"OK," she says with a fake smile. "I really do have to go. Can you please let me out? I have a meeting at work in thirty minutes."

But I know that look. That looks says, *He's nuts.*

"Lulu, just wait." I reach for her arm but she pulls away quickly. Like I might burn her.

"Nope," she says, still fake-smiling. "I gotta go. It was nice catching up and I have to say thank you for that impromptu sex last night. I don't usually do things like that but it was exciting and fun. So maybe we can do it again…" She drops off and blows some hair out of her face. "Never mind. I'm just going to be honest because that's the kind of girl I am. You creep me out, Case Reider. Not a little, but a whole lot, OK? I'm done. I need to leave."

She crosses her arms and taps her toe on the black tile floor.

"Now," she adds, when I don't move or speak.

"I'm not creepy," I say. "I'm just… adjusting, OK? I'm doing my best, Lulu, I swear to God, I am. But I'm not creepy and neither are my friends. You're just not hearing me. And you're jumping to conclusions. Especially about my friends."

"Did you blow up Blue Corp? Answer that truthfully and without conditions and I'll rethink my assessment of you." She waits, then adds, "You have five seconds. One, two—"

"Yes," I say. "Yes. We did it. But it's not what you think and I can prove it."

"How?"

"You can talk to Linc and Molly. And even Thomas if you want. Although I should caution you, he's not as lighthearted as I am and he really will creep you out."

She shakes her head at me. "No. Not how can you *prove* it. How did you *do* it?"

I walk away. Go stand in front of the window and stare down at my city. "It's a long story."

"I have time."

"I thought you had a meeting?"

"I lied. Now start talking or I won't bother lying anymore to save your feelings. I'll just dial the last one on my phone."

"You won't believe me."

"Try me, Case." She crosses the room and stands next to me. I chance a glance down at her. She shrugs. "If you want me to stay, you need to start talking. Because bad things are happening and I need answers."

I look back at the city.

"There was a helicopter…" she starts.

"How do you know that?" My words have a little shard of ice in them that I immediately want to take back.

"Someone filmed you guys. From a tall building, close by. They got everything on video."

"From inside?" I ask, squinting at her.

"No," she says, losing some of her bravado. "No. But I saw the footage this morning at the office. It showed a man, who we think is your friend Lincoln Wade, crashing a motorcycle through the top spire of Blue Corp. A guy parachuting out of it too. And another guy, sliding down into the broken building on some kind of grappling hook or something. That was the three of you, right? You, Lincoln and Thomas Brooks?"

I rake my fingers through my hair. This is not good. Linc is gonna be pissed.

"You should just tell me, Case. Then I can help you."

"Help me with what?" I sneer.

"Help you make a deal, at least."

"A deal?" I laugh. "You think you're here to make a deal with me? So I'll turn in my friends?" I shake my head. "You're delusional, Lulu. Certifiably insane if you think I'm gonna end up doing time for that night." I turn to face her. "What we did was Justice. With a capital J, understand?"

"You don't get to dish out justice, Case. That's called vigilantism. Justice happens in a courtroom."

"Not when the judges are corrupt. And if you think for one second there's even one honest judge on the bench in Cathedral City, well, then you're just another dishonest, underhanded, unethical, double-dealing lawyer like all the rest."

"Fuck you," she snaps. "I'm trying to do you a favor."

"You're trying to pigeon-hole me into a prison sentence."

She lets out a long huff of air through her nose. We stand there in silence for almost a minute before she says, "Did you know that the warden over at CC Penitentiary is named DickCage?"

We both laugh at the same time.

"Because it took me by surprise and I had a hard time tucking down the giggles when I was there this morning."

"You were at the prison this morning?" I chance a sideways look at her.

"Yup. I was there because that's where former police chief O'Neil is serving his sentence. And do you know what he told me?"

"I can't wait to hear," I say, more sarcastic than I'd like.

"He said Lincoln Wade choked him last winter. And his hand was so hot, it made blistered burns on his throat. In fact, he's got a very ugly scar as proof. What do you think that's all about?"

"Fuck," I mumble.

"What's going on, Case?" Lulu turns to me, places a hand on my upper arm. "You can tell me. I promise I won't say a word for at least two days, OK? I'll give you two days to get your head straight before I let my boss in on it."

"I don't think two days will help. We can't pull it off in two days. We're not even in Phase One yet."

"Pull what off?" She sounds desperate now. "What the hell is Phase One?"

"That's not your concern. It's got nothing to do with all this." I wave a hand down at the city. "It's not connected."

"I don't believe you."

"And that's why," I say, pointing a finger at her face, "I'm not gonna tell you anything. Steve," I say to the ceiling. He pops up immediately. He's getting better at that. Sheila made some adjustments to his programming last month and it's a nice upgrade. "Show Miss Lightly out. We're finished."

"Very well, Mr. Reider. Miss—"

"Steve," Lulu barks. "Shut the fuck up and get out of our private conversation. I'm not leaving, Case. I'm staying. I'm staying until I have the lunch you promised me."

I shake my head at her. "Nope. Sorry. You're one of them, Lulu. And I can't take any more chances with you. Not now. Maybe not ever."

"Do I need to say the name DickCage again to lighten things up? Fine. DickCage." She snorts a laugh, then glares at Steve's holographic figure, still looming. "Didn't I tell you to go away? This is private, lightman."

Steve manages a surprised look complete with raised fake eyebrows, then flickers away.

"Well, I might need one of those things for my home. He's oddly obedient."

I say nothing.

"Case…" she says.

"No. I can't tell you anything."

"Then lunch. We can stop talking about this stuff and just have lunch. I'm starving. And I need more than cheese. Where are we going for lunch?"

"I was just going to have something brought up from the kitchen."

"You have a kitchen? And a chef, I presume?"

"It's the corporate dining room. But the food is good." I shrug.

She tsks her tongue. "You can admit it, you know."

"Admit what?" I ask, suspicious as I gaze out at Cathedral City.

"That you only invited me here for a nooner."

I really do laugh at that. "You knew? And you came anyway?"

I can see her smile in the glass. "I came anyway. Was really looking forward to it, actually. But since you want me to go…"

We both go silent. Then we sigh.

"I don't want you to leave," I say. "You're like the only thing I care about. I've never stopped wondering… what if, you know? What if you didn't leave? What if we had a real chance? How would I be different today?"

"Well, I did come *back*, right?"

"I don't think we're on the same side, Lulu."

"I can't help that I'm a good girl and you're a bad guy."

"I'm *not* a bad guy. And it fucking sucks that you can't see that."

We stand there, silent. Just looking out at the accidents down on the city streets below.

"Can we start again?" she finally asks. "Because I really did come over here for the lunchtime sex and it would be a really frustrating afternoon for me if I went away unsatisfied."

"That's not why you came." I chuckle.

"Maybe not entirely. But it's why I'm still here."

I turn to face her, wondering how genuine this gesture is. Does she just want to use sex to get me to talk? Or is she really as interested in me as I am her? "Do I still need to get you drunk first?" I ask, motioning my head towards the wine. "Because that was my evil supervillain plan."

"Nope," she says, unbuttoning her light pink blouse to reveal a lacy white bra. It's accentuated with a sweet satin ribbon right between her round, plump breasts. "I'm an easy catch today. No bait necessary, Mr. Reider."

"You understand why I should be suspicious?" I say, giving her a sidelong glance. "With all your self-righteous talk of deals and disdain for vigilantism?"

"Can we fight later?" she asks. "After the nooner?"

I'd like to think I'm stronger than that. I'd like to brag about how I'm the alpha male here and no woman has the power to manipulate me. But fuck it.

I am an Alpha, but I'm a lost one. And I could really use a soft, quiet afternoon with the beautiful woman I loved and lost to take my mind off things.

Lulu doesn't give me the chance to think too long on her offer. One soft hand grabs mine and places it on her breast. The soft cloth makes me want to stroke it.

"I really didn't bring you here for sex, Lulu."

"Are you saying no?" she asks, placing her other hand on my chest. She flattens her palm against my shirt and closes her eyes.

"Not exactly," I reply, distracted by her boldness.

"Then stop talking."

I grab both her wrists so fast her eyes fly open and a small surprised gasp leaves her lips. "Don't give me orders," I say in a low voice. "I don't like it."

"Then don't keep me waiting."

"I'm not fucking you, Lulu. Do you really think I'm so desperate for sex, or human contact, or whatever it is you're peddling right now, that I can't say no?"

"Why would you want to say no?"

I let out a small, unamused laugh as I slowly shake my head. "I get it," I say. "I get that when shit starts to go down some people need a distraction. But I'm not one of those people. I'm not the kind of man who runs. I like to look people in the eye and say what I mean."

"Then stop talking in riddles and do that," she quips.

"I don't think I like you anymore."

She tilts her head like she heard me wrong. "Excuse me?"

"I guess you were just one of those good memories, you know? We had a great time getting to know each other leading up to the ball and that night you were so insistent. So it's understandable that I'd latch on to what could've been once you left town. But now that you're back, Lulu, I really don't think we have anything in common."

"Because you're on the wrong side?" She hastily buttons her shirt, rescinding her offer. "And I'm out to get you?"

"No," I say, turning my back on her and walking towards the door, grabbing her coat and purse from a chair. "No, that's not it at all." When I turn she's still all the way across the room, standing in front of my city like this isn't happening. But it is happening. "You don't know me. You don't know one true thing about me. And yet you're standing here like some pillar of truth and justice, passing judgment on me like you're above it all. But you're part of the problem, Lulu. My friends and me are part of the solution and if you're too fucking scared to pull down the blindfold of government-sanctioned righteousness and see what's standing right in front of you, then I've got nothing more to say except..." I wave my hand towards the elevator where Steve is waiting, actually anticipating my next move. "Get the fuck out."

CHAPTER TWENTY-THREE

"Fine," I say, grabbing my coat and purse and blowing the hair out of my eyes in exasperation. "You know what? I'm sorry I came here looking for the guy I once knew. I'm sorry I—" Everything goes dark and silent as I let the last few words of my sentence fade into the nothingness.

"What the hell?" Case says, storming past me, calling, "Steve? Report. Steve?"

"Your power's out," I snap. "Your creepy light-man is gone. Just point me to the stairs, Case. I'll be on my way."

"The power can't be out," Case says, more to himself than me. "We've got backups."

"Well, obviously, your backups are out."

"No," Case says, placing his hands on the smooth metal wall of the far side of the elevators. "The backups are on a private grid. The only way…" He stops mid-sentence and continues to feel the wall.

"The only way what?" I ask. "And what are you doing?"

"Trying to make the wall open so we can access the stairs." I'm just about to remark on the stupidity of concealing a fire escape when he says, "There it is." He flattens his palms and pushes until the wall slides open. "Stay here." He says it with mountains of irritation.

"I'm *not* staying here."

But he must not care, because when I follow him into the stairwell and start banging down behind him, he doesn't bark any more orders.

When we get out into the lobby it's dark and cold. The sun has disappeared behind thick snow clouds and the flurries are starting.

"What are we looking for down here?"

He ignores me as he makes his way towards a hallway that's hidden by an artistic curve of a wall, and then slips out of sight.

I follow again and catch him opening a door to what appears to be an engineering room. It's dark and silent, just like everything else in this building now.

"Where is everybody?"

"We sent them home this morning when the power went out all over town. People needed to go collect their kids and stuff." Case lets out a long, exasperated sigh. "I'll walk you to your car. You might as well go home too. Looks like this shit is taking a turn for the worse."

It's then that I realize I don't have a car. "Well... Randy dropped me off this morning so..."

Case is staring down at some lifeless electronic dashboard that should probably not be so lifeless. But he manages to turn his head and look up at me through his hanging blond hair. "He dropped you off? Well... that's not weird."

"I told you, I was at the prison earlier. And ToyBox was on the way."

Case goes back to messing with the electrical equipment. "So how did you think you were getting home? Was he picking you up as well?"

"I figured a taxi would do."

"During a city-wide blackout?" Case laughs.

"I didn't realize how widespread it was. We were cut off out at the prison. Are you waiting for me to beg you to give me a ride? Fine. Can you drop me off downtown?"

"Do you really think we'll be able to get anywhere near downtown right now, Lulu?" He doesn't look up at me this time. Not even a half-hearted sidelong glance. "Really?"

"Probably part of your plan," I say, crossing my arms to try to ward off a feeling of dread and foreboding.

"Right," he mutters. "Because you're so much fucking fun to be around these days. 'Let's make a deal, Case,'" he says in a fake female voice. "'Just cop out to some fictitious supervillain plan and spend some time in prison and I'll let you fuck me.'"

Ohhh… I am pissed. "Fuck you." I turn on my heel and don't wait for his comeback. Just walk straight back out to the lobby, shrugging my coat on as I go. I know the power is out, so the front doors don't work, but I flatten my hands on the glass the way Case did upstairs, and they part easy enough.

A cold gust of wind rushes in, blowing small, hard balls of snow onto my face with such force, they sting.

Case pulls me back inside. "You're letting all the heat out," he says, forcing the doors to close again.

"We're not stuck here. My phone still works." I take it out of my purse, hoping it still has a signal. It does. But when I call the station I get a busy signal. God, when was the last time I heard one of those?

"The phones are out, Lulu," Case says, talking to me like I'm a small, clueless child. "City Hall doesn't have SkyEye. And even if you could get a hold of someone, they probably couldn't make their way all the way over here with the traffic lights out. I'm stuck with you."

Not, *You're stuck with me*, which is how he should've said it. But the other way around. We are definitely not friends anymore.

"Sheila?" Case says, talking into his own SkyEye phone. "What's going on in the city? Uh-huh... Shit... Fuck... No?... All right. I'll make do. Later."

"Who was that?" I ask. He mentioned someone named Sheila earlier, right?

"I was gonna have her send the helicopter, but the weather up in the mountains is fucked." He tabs the screen of his phone again. "Thomas, just what the..." The conversation goes much the same as the last one. "No shit?... Fuck... Dammit... So what do you want to... Yeah. All right. I'll wait it out at home."

"That was your friend?" I ask.

"You're gonna have to come home with me. Come on, we better get a move on before the roads get any worse."

I follow him, having to run a little bit to keep up because he's walking with some serious determination. I'm about to protest about going home with him, but it's pointless. I have no options. If I had my own car I could at least drive myself. But I don't. It's either stay here or follow him.

We hike without talking back up the stairs to his office, where he grabs his coat and a briefcase, then stomp back down to the lobby. Case opens the doors the way I did a few minutes ago, then locks it back up with a key from the outside.

There's only one car in the parking lot and it's a ridiculous silver two-seater sports car that immediately has me picturing us sliding into a ditch. "I hope you don't live far," I say, as he beeps his alarm to unlock the doors.

He doesn't answer me. So I slip into the soft bucket seat and close myself up from the blowing wind. He does the same, starting the car up before he even gets the door closed. Two seconds later he's got it in gear and we pull out, the tires slipping on the slick pavement, and I feel a little wave of justification for my negative assessment of his car.

He shoots me a dirty look when I grunt out a laugh. "I'm two miles up the hill."

"If I have to walk two miles up a hill in the snow because this toy car can't make the climb, I will be pissed."

He rolls his eyes and drives around the back of the building to a lone road that winds up the mountain behind ToyBox. And we don't get stuck. He flips some button on the panel near the gear shift, gives the car a second to adjust, and then we plow upward with the feeling of tires digging into the pavement.

His house really is close, and a few minutes later we're pulling into the garage of a very modern building that looks like his ToyBox offices, except it's not a box, but a rectangle. "You've got power here," I say, getting out of the car and watching the garage doors close us up.

"Separate system," he mutters, keying in a code to the alarm. "After you." He waves me inside and lights start turning on as I step deeper into his home. Like those lights on the frozen case doors of the grocery store that are all motion-activated.

"Steve?" Case calls out, throwing his keys down on a stainless-steel counter in the kitchen. My eyes immediately track to the view from the floor-to-ceiling windows.

"I'm here," the light-man says, appearing as a hologram off to my right. He's definitely not as strong over here. Like he's too far away from his base. Because he's nothing but wild flickers. "I'm sorry, the power went out down at—"

"Yeah, I know," Case says, irritable. "Do you know why the power went out? Did we run out of fuel?"

"No way to tell until it comes back on. I'm sorry, Mr. Reider. Should I make lunch for you and your guest?"

"Sure. Surprise us." Case comes over to stand next to me. "I don't know what's happening. But none of this is good. And before you even open your mouth with accusations, none of this has anything to do with me or my friends."

I don't say anything because it will just start another argument. I find it oddly ridiculous that he wants me to believe they've got nothing to do with this after we found that Bike Boy message inside the code that stole that money from the banks. And it's very suspicious that Thomas Brooks owns the only usable phone company right now. The lawyer in me says I should shut up and listen.

So I do.

And I hear nothing but the sound of beeping kitchen appliances.

"How can he possibly make lunch?" I ask quietly, both of us still looking out at the dead city. We're too high up, and there's smaller hills in the way, so I can't really see any roads. Or accidents. Probably most people have gone home by now, anyway. But off in the distance I can see the Cathedrals. The main one and SkyEye, across from it, both in downtown. And up to the north I can see the remnants of Blue Corp. And past all that, I see nothing but mountains on every side.

"It's all automated, so don't get too attached to the idea of lunch. Doesn't taste too great yet. It's something called an autocook. I've been working on it for a while now. But like I said, don't get excited. The protein is soy-based and the vegetables aren't worth talking about. The only thing that even remotely passes as food is the pasta."

"Well." I sigh. "Here's hoping we get pasta."

"You can take your pick of guest rooms," he says, turning away. "I'd appreciate it if you didn't wander around the house at night. I will be arming the alarms and I'd hate for you to be caught up in it. I'll find you some sweats and a t-shirt to sleep in—"

I catch up with the conversation before he can finish that thought. "I'm not sleeping here." I laugh. "Don't be ridiculous. The power will be back in a few hours at most. In fact," I say, getting out my phone, "I'm going to keep trying the cab companies while we wait it—"

"You're not going anywhere, Lulu. In case you haven't noticed, the anarchists have taken over my city."

"Anarchists?" I laugh. "OK. Well, that's quite a jump in what's happening down there. But I'll go along for the sake of argument. What—"

"Thomas," he says in a low growl, "just told me that there's riots downtown. You know, those people who wear black ski masks and throw Molotov cocktails through windows? It's them doing this, not us. So… don't you feel stupid now?"

I wish I could see for myself. And just as I think that, Case shoves his phone at me and says, "Look."

On the screen is footage from some kind of drone above downtown, showing hundreds—maybe thousands—of people going crazy. Smashing cars, smashing windows, looting stores. "What is this? How are you seeing this? Is it the news stations?"

"News stations?" Case snorts. "Please. It's a SkyEye drone. Thomas is watching everything so when the shit settles down, we can run it—" But he stops abruptly. "Put some names to the faceless faces," he says after the pause. "For the greater good. Don't worry, we'll share with City Hall and CCPD. If you guys are even interested in the truth, which I highly doubt."

CHAPTER TWENTY-FOUR

I might've said too much because Lulu gives me a long, hard look that lasts for several seconds. I shift my weight as I wait out her gaze.

"What are you up to?" she finally says.

"Why are you so interested in me?"

She huffs out a laugh. "I'm asking myself the same question."

Well, that's a loaded answer. It implies so many things, I snap into Molly-mode and start a list.

One. She likes me. She's been thinking about me ever since she left town and now she's back to… I don't know, rekindle something. This is the best-case scenario.

Two. She knows something about me, or Linc, or Thomas. And she's digging for information to try to link us to the robbery and the blackouts. This is the worst-case scenario.

Three. All of it—the chance meeting last night at the cathedral, the impromptu sex, the fact that the city was sabotaged shortly after she came back to town—is a coincidence. This could go either way because it doesn't imply anything positive or negative.

Four. Someone is controlling everything and we're both innocent. This would lead to big, big problems.

Two and four are what I think is happening, and neither of them are good. I frown, unable to stop myself from feeling the loss, though she's not even something I currently have.

"What?" Lulu asks. "What are you thinking so hard about?"

I have several ways to respond. I could lie about everything and just try to get through this night. Then drop her off tomorrow and pretend we don't have a past history.

I do want to lie, but I don't want to walk away from her. Not yet. She's just… what I always wanted, right? And now she's here and things are going badly. But it's not past the point of no return. Yet. We could work on it. Maybe put a little more effort into rekindling things.

Or I could tell her the whole truth and take my chances that she will see things our way.

That's a really bad idea. I think she has some very deep-rooted opinions about justice and the law. She's kind of naive.

Or give her a little bit of both. Not enough to make her want to hunt us down and lock us up. But just enough to keep her by my side for a little longer until Linc or Thomas can figure out what's really going on.

I opt for option three. But what can I say?

"Case?"

"I'm thinking, dammit."

"About?"

"How much I can trust you." I sigh.

She shakes her head. "You've got it all backwards, Toy Man. I'm not doing anything wrong here."

"Neither am I." We stare at each other for another handful of seconds. "I don't have anything to do with that bank robbery. And neither does Lincoln."

"How do you know?"

"Because we're already rich, Lulu. We have more money than we need. Why the fuck would we steal money? If I was going to steal something, I'd make it something I didn't already have."

"Like what?"

I shrug. "Like you."

"You'd steal me?" She laughs. "Like kidnap me? Why would you say something like that?"

"Because… you're the only thing I want that I don't already have. I don't need more money, Lulu. I need things money can't buy."

"Maybe you're just like those anarchists down there?" She nods her head towards the city down below. "Maybe you're just looking to tip the system. Pull it apart from within. Take it down."

"Well, it is pretty fucking corrupt. And while I don't agree with their methods, I do agree with their premise."

She points a finger up at me and says, "I knew it."

I slap her finger away, annoyed. "It's not us."

"Then who stole that money? Who is this Red—" But she stops, suddenly. Then turns around and scrubs a hand across her forehead.

"Who is… red… what the fuck are you talking about?"

"Stevegetti is ready," Steve says off to my left. "Right this way, Miss Lulu."

She doesn't wait for me. Just follows Steve's flickering form across the room towards the kitchen. Steve is droning on about plates and his inability to set the table, and then starts directing up to the cupboards where I keep that shit. I don't move. Something is tingling in my mind. She slipped up just now. She said *red*.

Red. As in the color of the light inside me.

Has someone seen me up on the roof? It's not impossible, I decide. I am up there most nights doing some pretty weird shit. And didn't she just tell me that they have footage of the helicopter raid on Blue Corp? Someone saw us do that. I scan outside, looking for possible vantage points where someone might have set up a scope and taken pictures.

But I live up pretty high on the side of the mountain. I'm way higher than the tallest buildings in downtown, and from that vantage point they'd never be able to see someone on *top* of the flat roof. Unless I was standing on the very edge. Which I wasn't. I don't stand there. Do I?

No, I decide. I don't. I stand in the middle.

Plus, they're too far away. No one saw me.

"Are you going to stand there all day?" Lulu asks. "Will I have to eat alone?"

I turn to face her. Watch her as she sets down forks and napkins.

Shake it off, Case. Just let it go and see if she slips up again.

I make my way over to the table and pull out her chair. She mumbles a thank you and sits. Then I do the same. We stare across the table at each other. "I'm telling you," I say. "Don't get excited about Steve's version of spaghetti."

She cracks a smile as she picks up some tongs and drops some pasta down on her plate, then passes the bowl to me and goes for the red sauce.

I help myself, staring at the sauce longer than I should. Red.

"Case?"

I look up and she's holding out the spoon for the sauce. "Right," I say, taking it from her.

We have a few awkward moments of silence as we start eating. I have no appetite, plus I know what this stuff tastes like already, so I mostly push mine around on my plate. But Lulu doesn't seem to notice.

"It's not as bad as I thought it would be."

"Thank you, Miss Lulu," Steve says, beaming a smile of flickering teeth at her.

"You can go now, Steve," I say. "We'd like some privacy." Steve nods obligingly at me and flickers out of existence.

"How do you manage that?" Lulu asks. "Privacy, I mean. When he's everywhere, just watching and waiting for his next command."

"The lighthouses," I say, nodding my head towards the ceiling where all the little black boxes are mounted. "He can only appear in rooms where I have lighthouses. And microphones, of course. He doesn't have ears, Lulu. He's a computer."

"So which rooms don't have the right equipment?"

"Most of them are upstairs. He can appear in the hallways, but not the rooms up there. I have SpyGlass windows in the bedrooms, but those are just to project images of fantastic destinations. Like a tropical beach. Or the mountains. I'll show you some time."

"Hmm," Lulu says, thinking about this. "Do you think of Steve as a friend? A personal assistant? What?"

I shrug. "Either, I guess."

"You said something about Lincoln having Sheila. That she's different. Different how?"

I shake my head. "Sorry, not my business to tell. You'll have to ask Lincoln about her if you'd like to know more."

"Will I get a chance to ask Lincoln?"

"Probably not."

"Why are you so morose?"

I set down my fork and exhale a long breath of air. "This isn't going how I'd imagined it."

"What isn't? Your little plan for the city?"

"No," I snap. "Lunch with you."

"Because we're not having the nooner?"

When I look up at her she's smirking at me.

"That, sure," I say. "But mostly, Lulu… I just like you. And you're not the person I imagined you'd be."

"You're not the person I imagined either," she whispers. "I never imagined we'd be here on opposite sides."

"We're not on opposite sides. You're letting your imagination run away with you. Maybe you've been listening to someone down at City Hall and they've corrupted your view of me. Or maybe you're just cynical and want to see me in this light because it fits your worldview."

She puts her fork down too. "OK. Maybe that's true. I certainly don't have much knowledge of you and the things I saw in that video—the Blue Corp stuff—it was pretty weird, Case. But you're not doing us any favors by keeping secrets."

"You're only here to trap me. And if you'd at least admit that, I'd have some more faith in you. But you won't." I pause. "So I can't."

"Fine," she says, lifting her napkin off her lap and placing it over her plate of Stevegetti. "You want the truth? Here's the truth. Randy thinks you and your friends are the ones responsible for the robbery. He wants me to seduce you, get all your secrets, and then report back to him. That's why I came to lunch with you today."

"Well, that's just perfect." I throw my napkin on my plate as well.

"Your turn."

"No." I laugh. "I already had my turn. Everything I told you was true."

"You're leaving things out, Case."

"All things that have nothing to do with you or this absurd theory you have."

She shakes her head and frowns. "I want you to trust me to help you."

"I don't need any help. *We* don't need any help. I just like you, OK? Why can't we just be friends and not worry about fixing me?"

She considers this for a few moments. "So... the nooner?"

I crack a smile at that. "It's a much better option than all this arguing."

"And pretend none of this is happening?" she asks.

"I'm so into delusional denial, you have no idea. Practically turns me on."

"I think the mood has been ruined, don't you?"

"I can fix it, Miss Lightly. Trust me, I have moves. I can make us a nice fire, get out the wine, put on some porn..."

She presses her lips together, trying not to smile.

"Before you know it, I'll have my hand between your legs, stroking your pussy..."

"Jesus Christ," she laughs.

"We'll fuck, then fuck again, then again. Then fall asleep, enjoying the snow day, or riot day, or apocalypse day—whatever you want to call it—and then wake up and fuck some more... Come on," I say, a little plea in my offer. "Forget your job. Just have fun with me. All this bullshit will still be here when we're done. And we're stuck here. Like it or not. We can't do anything today. The snow will make the rioters go home soon and then tomorrow will look totally different."

LADY LIBERTY

CHAPTER TWENTY-FIVE

He stands up from the table and comes around behind me. I know we've been fighting, and I still think I'm right and he's got things inside that head of his that could help me and Randy figure out what's going on. But I really did come here for the sex. Maybe that wasn't the entire reason I came back to Cathedral City, but I'd be lying if I said Case wasn't on my mind when I made the decision.

His hands are so warm when they press down on my shoulders. "Come on, Lulu. Let's start over."

When he takes my hand to pull me to my feet I don't object. And when he leads me towards the stairs and starts climbing, I submissively follow.

I'm tired of the arguing.

At the top of the stairs we turn left, towards two large double doors standing open, and walk into his master bedroom. It's neat and tidy. Not a lot of furniture, but what he has—a low, king-sized, platform bed, end tables on either side, a chrome lamp atop each, and metal artwork on the walls—is extremely modern.

His style is minimalistic. Sleek lines, hard edgy surfaces, and a monochromatic scale of white, gray and black.

There's a fireplace hanging from the ceiling by a long chrome-plated pole. He leads me towards it, tells me to "Sit," pointing to a luxurious Flokati rug. I kneel down, my hands pressing into the soft, thick fibers, and watch him carefully as he flicks a switch on the wall and the fireplace lights up with a quick whoosh of flames.

He takes off his suit coat and tosses it onto a nearby chair.

When he turns to face me, loosening his tie just enough for me to understand what will be happening next, he looks… different. Not the man I'm pursuing for Randy. Just the guy I once knew so many years ago.

"I've missed you," I say. Meaning it.

He smiles as he crosses the small distance from the wall back to me, and then drops down on the rug and lies back, kicking off his shoes. "Tell me what you've been doing since you left. And leave all the bad parts out."

I giggle at that, then slide my shoes off, tossing them aside, as I lie back next to him. His arm finds its way underneath me and he begins to stroke my shoulder. Even through the fabric of my blouse, I can feel his warmth.

"For now, anyway," he adds to his request. "I want to know about them, of course. But we've got enough bad parts going on at the moment. No need to add to the list."

"I went to school," I say, skipping the stupid details like university and major. "Then law school. Then home to Wolf Valley where I worked for a while as an assistant DA. Then I came… home. That was two weeks ago."

"You just covered seven years in four sentences. I might've given you the wrong impression when I asked for the short version. Please don't tell me it was all so bad, that's all there is to say?"

Welp. I'm not answering that, for sure. So I change the subject. "Give me your four sentences, Case."

"OK," he says, taking a moment to collect his thoughts. "I finished college too. I started ToyBox back when I was in high school, but I got funding help from Thomas to build this compound. Partied a lot with Lincoln. And then

Thomas moved SkyEye Corporate back to Cathedral City, and now we're a team again."

"Hmmm," I say, closing my eyes so I can enjoy the newness of how we feel together. "What about your childhood? Can you sum that up in four sentences?"

"Well," he says, hesitating a little longer this time. "I went to boarding school where I met Linc and Thomas. We left there together as teens. Thomas went one way, Linc and I went another. Then we met up again. And that's that."

"Somehow I don't think that's that. Although I didn't realize you thought of your kidnapping as school."

"It was a school," he says without emotion.

I don't even know how to process this. I knew, even back in my teens when I had that huge crush on him, that he was kidnapped. But he never talked about it when we were at rehearsals. I sorta forgot. "Was it a kidnapping?"

"No." He says it with such finality, there is no room for doubt. "My father made me go."

"So all that hype about the kidnapping when you guys came home, that was a lie?"

"One hundred percent lies. You'd be shocked if you knew how little truth is out there, Lulu. Reality is nothing but lies."

"Do you want to have sex with me?" I ask, searching for some truth.

"For sure."

"Even if we can't get along tomorrow when the problems come back? Even if we become enemies?"

"I'll take my chances."

I smile at his answer.

"But I don't just want sex. So I hope your fears about tomorrow don't happen."

"You know, a little more truth would go a long way in that regard."

"A little more truth would ruin everything," he replies. "At least right now."

We think about that longer than we should.

"Close your eyes," he says, breaking the silence.

"They are closed." I laugh.

"Don't look. Don't open them. Shut the world out and keep it far, far away."

His hand is between my legs, pressing against me in all the right ways. And then his body shifts so he's propping himself up. The next thing I feel is the flutter of his lips on my mouth. The sweep of his tongue makes me respond and it's a long, slow kiss that says so much more than any words ever could.

He missed me. I missed him back.

He wants me. I want him back.

I reach for him, my hand brushing against the soft, smooth fabric of his suit trousers. But he takes it, squeezes it, and places it flat against the soft rug. "Don't move. I just need a moment to get to know you again."

The plea relaxes me. Pacifies me in a way that takes me by surprise. When his fingers sweep between my legs I feel my whole body relax. Like I'm ready for something.

He continues with his exploration. Hand down the top of my thigh, then back up on the inside. At one point, he lifts up the silky hem of my blouse, exposing my stomach and making my skin rise up in little prickles. His warm mouth ebbs me back down, and then he's kissing and licking his way up to my breasts.

When he gets there he licks my nipples through my lacy bra. I open my eyes, just for a peek, and get caught.

"No cheating," he says around a mouthful of breast, his blue eyes looking up at me.

I smile, but my lids are already heavy, and I give in.

He pulls my bra down, quick and rough, and they spill out, right into his waiting hands. He squeezes them hard, claims them in a possessive, almost painful way that makes me tip my head back and bite down.

His mouth is on mine in that same instant, his body maneuvering over me, his hard cock pressing down on my hips.

"You're gonna change your mind about me, Lulu Lightly. I promise."

"Stop talking," I whisper, my breath heavy with anticipation. "But don't stop anything else."

He bites my lip in response, his hand pulls hard on the button of my pants, and then before I can take another breath, he's there. His skin against mine. His fingers, wet with my desire.

He sits up, straddling my legs, and still I press my eyelids tightly closed. Unwilling to break his command to go in blind.

My panties are dragged down my legs with my pants and he leans down, pressing his mouth over my thigh, kissing and licking his way across my body. He lifts one leg, making it bend at the knee, and presses it up to my chest. The shiver that runs through my body when he strokes the sensitive skin behind my knee almost makes me convulse.

"Shhh," he whispers as he unbuttons my blouse. And then he sits up and back, and I can't help it. I can't *not* look.

When I open my eyes, he's smiling down at me as he unbuttons his white dress shirt, staying silent. The firelight flickers and dances across his body as shadows.

Words have no place in what's happening in this room right now. Words are the last thing we need.

When he gets to the last button up near his collar, he spreads the shirt open, revealing the taut muscles of his chest and stomach and that cut line that rides down each hip and disappears into his trousers.

I want to go searching for what that line leads to. But I don't. Looking at him—watching him watch me—is enough. For now.

He takes the shirt off and it joins my pants in a careless heap.

His hands are on my hips, thumbs caressing the soft dent on either side of the bone. And with each sweep he presses them closer and closer, until they reach the folds of my pussy and he pulls my lips back.

One final look up at his face before he lowers his mouth and then… I shake my head, close my eyes, and just…

"Oh…" I'm panting as he swirls his tongue around in small circles around the sweet spot that makes me buck my hips and arch my back. I reach down for his hair, unable to care about his instructions to keep them at my side. I fist handfuls of it. It's just long enough to get a good grip and push him into me. He hikes both my legs up to my chest, pinning them down with the full length of his arms.

The feelings that rush through my body are almost indescribable. It's so intense. I don't recall ever having a man eat me out like this. Never with so much enthusiasm. His tongue never stops, short, quick flicks alternating with long, slow sweeps. He pushes himself inside my pussy, and it just makes me want *more*.

"More," I whisper. "Take off your—"

"Shhh," he tells me again between licking. He lets go of my legs, but I hold them up, making sure he has the access he needs as a finger presses into my asshole. His other hand is strumming my clit as he probes my pussy with his tongue and that's it.

I'm there.

"Holy…" I don't get past that before I start moaning.

Case laughs softly as I orgasm against his mouth, the wetness pouring out as he places his whole mouth on me, bringing my clit inside his mouth to suck gently. Until it's so intense I'm trying to push his head off me. When he doesn't give in, I squirm, my body desperate for relief, until I finally maneuver away, panting hard.

He falls into me, his head on my stomach, his hands seeking out my breasts to give them one last fierce squeeze as I lie there, spent.

We haven't even fucked yet and I'm exhausted. "Jesus Christ," I say, panting hard.

He doesn't answer, just goes to work taking off his pants. When I look down he's fisting his thick, hard cock. Stroking himself. When I look back up to his face, he's watching me. "Relax," he says. "Just enjoy it."

He straightens me out so I'm not curled up anymore, but lying flat on my back, parts my legs, positions himself between them, and thrusts forward. My pussy is stretched so far, I wince as he enters me. But then he's in, his upper body pressing against mine, his hands on either side of my head, softly stroking my face.

We stare at each other as we move together. It's a slow fuck. Like the first time we did it, all those years ago. And he never breaks our visual connection. Long pushes, until he's so far inside me, I press on his chest to make him back off. And then the relief as he withdraws so far, I have to grip his shoulders in a desperate plea to pull him back in.

It's a tug of war. I want more, I want less, I want more, I want less. And I realize... that's exactly how I feel about *all* of him. His big personality. His secrets. His crazy friends and his stupid holographic butler.

I want more and less at the same time. And it's not good.

"Shhhh," Case says, reading my thoughts as he continues torturing me with his attention, and his affection, and his irresistible mystery.

He fucks me like that. Brings me to climax again and then pulls out and comes all over my stomach in long spurts of white-hot finality. He keeps me in that place between here and there. Confuses me with my own twisted thoughts about who he is, who I am. What we want and how many, *many* things we're about to lose if we keep seeing each other.

And at this moment I can say with clear certainty… I don't care.

I really don't care.

CHAPTER TWENTY-SIX

She molds her back into the curve of my chest and we make a new shape together. Panting at first, trying to catch the breath that wants to escape. But I hold her tight in case she gets any funny ideas about leaving.

I think her eyes are closed, but I don't know. And I'm afraid to break the moment. She's calm, for once. Not asking me stupid questions about what me and my friends are doing to the city. Not blaming me for things I didn't do. So I keep quiet.

It goes on for so long I conclude she really did fall asleep. And even though all I want to do is pick her up, place her in my bed, and crawl in next to her and never leave—the heat is rising in my body.

The sex is not enough. Not at night. It will never be enough and there is no way I can ignore it. So when she finally rolls over, creating some distance between our bodies, I quietly get up, not bothering with clothes because I have to go outside naked anyway, and grab the knife I stash in the bedside table.

Steve is in the second-floor hallway when I walk towards the back of the house. "Don't," he says.

"Shut up," I say absently. Like I have power over this new me. It pisses me off because he does this every single time and he knows. He *knows* I can't help it. "And go the fuck away."

The back bedroom is mostly empty. Just a guest bed and one long modern dresser. But it's got an expansive square terrace that faces the mountain. When I pull the French doors open, the wind and snow rushes in, bathing my body in sweet coolness.

It feels so fucking good. I place my hands on the snow-covered iron railing, pressing down until I touch cold metal. It doesn't stay cold for long and that's the part that drives me. The relief I feel. How will I be able to deal with my needs in the summer?

It's a question that bothers me. But I don't dwell on it much. I really don't think I'll be alive next summer. I think whatever this is, it's killing me.

I can pretend it's made me immortal all I want, but it's just the delusions talking in my head. To keep me going. Keep me cutting.

I swing my leg up onto the railing, pulling my body up by grabbing onto a narrow architectural concrete shelf. When I'm standing on that, I grab an ornamental detail made out of metal that reminds me of a trellis and acts like a ladder. Less than a minute later I'm on the flat roof of my house, captivated by the city view.

Or what I can see of it through the blowing snow that beats against my back and instantly melts.

The whispers start immediately. Like she's been waiting for me. My city.

I need you. Do as I ask. Be me. Help me. I need you. Do as I ask. Be me. Help me. I need you.

Over and over and over.

"I'm here," I grumble to the city's whispers. I walk to the edge of the roof and stand there, my arms outstretched. I don't care if people can see me. Let them see me.

Who owns a city? she asks me.

"The people," I say.

No, she whispers back.

"The politicians."

No. No. No.

"The predators," I growl, lifting the knife to the fleshy part of my upper left shoulder. I make the cuts deep and with practiced ease as the blood pours out. It runs down my arm, burning it. Making the skin blister. But all I feel is relief.

"Predators like me," I finish.

Yes, she calls out. *Yes, yes, yes.*

I start laughing. Loudly. I am insane. I'm up here on my roof, naked. Cutting myself. Mutilating myself like an ancient sacrifice.

And I love it.

"I fucking love it!" I yell.

"Case?" My city is talking. And shaking me. "Case!" she yells.

But it's not my city. It's my Lulu.

The cold hits me like a fucking punch to the chest. I draw in a gasp of air and it goes down frigid. I open my eyes and see Lulu standing over me, staring back, her eyes wide with shock, and worry, and panic.

"Oh, my God," she says, covering her mouth with her hand. "What are you doing out here? Holy shit. You're freezing."

I'm fine. I try to growl it out, but I can't. I normally sleep after the cuts. I drift away to another world. One that's dominated by whispers so soft, they caress me, keep me safe.

The next thing I know there's a flurry of snow and a roar from above. Lulu is screaming something. Tugging on my arms, sliding me through the puddle of tepid water that surrounds my body where snow once was.

I'm wrapped up in a drenched coat that hurts as it rubs against my skin.

"Case."

I don't know how much time passes, but it can't be much. The roar is still there. I'm still outside. The puddle of water is still tepid, but cooling fast. Light leaks past my closed eyelids and I know it's probably close to dawn.

"Case, goddammit."

"Thomas?" This time the word comes out of my mouth instead of getting stuck in my head.

"Grab him," Lincoln says.

They lift me, carry me. Thomas is telling Lulu to get back inside the house. He'll call her later.

I laugh.

She's a raging bitch back to Thomas and when I'm finally able to open my eyes, I'm not surprised to see her looking down at me from the interior of the helicopter.

"He's awake!" Lulu yells.

Lincoln's face is down in mine, shining a light into my eyes. I reach up, grab the little flashlight, and toss it across the cabin.

"Don't be a dick," Thomas says. "He's just checking you out."

"I'm fine," I croak.

"Yeah," Lincoln says, spreading my eyelid open as Thomas hands him the flashlight I just threw. He shines it right into my pupil, and I jerk my head away, reaching out for his throat so I can strangle him.

I don't make much progress with that move. Linc just stands up and then sits down in one of the 'copter seats, glaring at me. "What the fuck were you doing out on the damn roof in the middle of a storm?"

"Do you have any idea how fucking dangerous it is to fly this helicopter in this weather?" Thomas yells over the roar of the engine and rotors. "Fucking asshole."

I close my eyes. "I'm fine," I insist again, raising my voice so they might have a chance of hearing me. "I would've been fine if you'd left me there to wake up on my own."

I don't—can't—open my eyes again after that. I'm too wiped out. There's not a chance in hell of me staying awake right now.

So I don't bother fighting it. I just drift off, listening to the song of the city, telling me exactly what I need to do next.

LADY LIBERTY

CHAPTER TWENTY-SEVEN

I feel like I've been dropped head-first into a really bad Jax Justice episode, mid-second season, and everyone around me has been following along since the pilot.

I worked hard on that analogy during my first hour in the cave as I tried to come to grips with the gaping hole that opened up like jaws in the snow-covered mountain meadow to allow the helicopter to swoop in—and right now I'm tired enough, confused enough, and frightened enough to let a small chuckle seep up from my lips and burst out.

The light-woman named Sheila, who's babysitting me so I don't touch anything I'm not supposed to in the technology-laden lair of Lincoln Wade—AKA Bike Boy—and oh yeah, he's looking more and more like the guilty guy I imagined him to be earlier this morning—scowls at me from across the cave, her holographic image more pure and perfect than any digitized form has a right to be.

I stifle the giggle.

Case is in another room but I can see him through a large plate-glass window from the desk I'm sitting at.

Sheila is also in that room. Which is freaky. Two of them? Or are they just one and she makes copies of herself?

That Sheila is busy flitting around Case, who's lying on some kind of... operating table that reminds me of a dentist's chair.

This Sheila is glowing faintly from the cast-off light of a massive institutional-sized aquarium that holds luminescent jellyfish, and looks really worried.

Like I said, really *bad* Jax Justice episode.

Suddenly Steve is looking more like an ally than I first thought.

An alarm goes off in the... operating room and I get to my feet.

"Stay where you are, Miss Lightly," this Sheila says. "No one needs you interfering in there."

"Is he OK?" I ask.

This Sheila glares at me. "Does he *look* OK?"

I slump back down into the desk chair and watch the expressions on both Lincoln Wade's and Thomas Brooks' faces as that Sheila barks off a status report that makes no sense to me at all.

Detective Molly Masters is in there too, one hand over her mouth like she's in shock and can't believe what she's hearing, the other gripping a stainless-steel counter to steady herself.

I sigh, becoming irritable at my lack of information.

"You're the one who insisted on coming," this Sheila says. "You should've stayed behind."

Since I got here an hour ago, I have learned to ignore her. She's highly argumentative and persistent in her rancor at my presence. Or maybe it's just the situation as a whole. But mostly I think it's me setting her off. She keeps looking at me from the corner of her digitized eye, like this is all my fault.

I haven't even had time to take everything in or even wonder what all this shit is or why this reclusive billionaire has a need for such a... laboratory.

Because that's what this is. It's a lab. Oh, there are cars and motorcycles. Lots of those giant red toolboxes and the whole place smells like a cross between engine oil and salt water. But I know what this is.

Another alarm sounds in the… operating room.

This time Lincoln has a huge syringe filled with milky-white liquid and a needle that has to be as long as my whole hand, and he sticks it right into Case's…

"What the fuck?" I ask, getting to my feet again. "What the fuck is he—"

"Sit. *Down*," this Sheila says, appearing directly in front of me.

I know she's made of light. I know I could walk right through her. And maybe I would do that… in other circumstances. But in this circumstance, she has a small army of servo robots milling about the floor of the cave and those things aren't made of light and some of them have pincer claws.

I shiver as one comes right up to my feet, then look at this Sheila with an angry glare.

"We know what we're doing," this Sheila says, her tone slightly—not much—but slightly softer.

Molly Masters sticks her head out the door of the operating room and barks, "Where's that nanite thing?"

This Sheila points to a large equipment cabinet on the far side of the cave and says, "Top shelf. In the white autoclave bags."

"What the fuck are they doing?" I ask.

"Saving his life," this Sheila says. "Now please, just shut up. I'm worried enough as it is without your mouth pissing me off."

Molly Masters grabs something in a white paper envelope that crinkles in her hand and then looks over her shoulder at me with a sympathetic frown. "Don't worry, we know what to do."

When she goes back inside the operating room she closes the door behind her and then flips a switch on the wall and the transparent window goes opaque.

I let out a long breath of air, but… I have to admit, not being able to see inside anymore actually allows me to relax.

Out of my hands, I guess.

"We should go upstairs," this Sheila says.

"No," I object. "I can't just go upstairs. Not with all this happening down here."

I don't even know what upstairs is. Sometimes the devil you know is better than the devil you don't. Or… however that saying goes.

One of the bigger robots, with some of the larger pincer claws, bumps up against my leg. I look at this Sheila as she says, with much more force than the first time, "We're going upstairs. Follow me, please."

In what kind of world do I, Lulu Lightly, well-educated lawyer and assistant district attorney of Cathedral City, have to follow the orders of a holographic image?

"Ow," I say, pulling my leg away from the mutant lobster-bot's grabby claws. "Fine."

I reluctantly follow her across the lab, past the massive rainbow-colored luminescent jellyfish, and towards a dark entrance that is almost pitch black.

"Just walk up the stairs and I'll have the door opened on the other end," this Sheila says. She fades away as I enter. And I realize there must not be any of those lighthouse things to project her in the winding stairwell. Which, by the way, totally look like they lead to and from a dungeon, because the walls are made of stone.

I stop just short of the first turn and wonder if I could hide in here. If the lobster-bot can't climb stairs, I bet—

"Keep walking, Miss Lightly," comes this Sheila's voice from above. "I have attack drones if you choose to hide in there. They will flush you out and—"

"Fine," I huff, and continue my climb until I see a light up ahead. Sheila is standing at the top, waiting. She waves me through into a grand, open living room and when I look back to where I just came from, I realize there's a secret panel in the wall next to a massive floor-to-ceiling stone fireplace.

I think I just came out of the Batcave. In fact, now that I realize I'm in some kind of massive mansion, I might actually be at Wayne Manor.

Or *Wade* Manor, as it may be.

"You can rest up here. Help yourself to whatever you want in the kitchen. Don't snoop upstairs and no, there's no secrets up there, but it's still under construction and I wouldn't want you to accidentally shoot yourself in the foot with a nail gun."

As if.

Sheila disappears.

"Hey!" I call out. "Where are you going?"

She rematerializes. "Back downstairs to my other half. It takes energy to be two of me. Wouldn't you rather I use all my power to help Case? Or are you too scared to be left alone—"

"Fine," I say, huffing some hair out of my eyes. "Go."

She does. And the secret panel door closes shut in silent finality.

I'm in Lincoln Wade's house. Just like Randy wanted me to be.

But even though I still think Randy is right about these people, I have no interest in that directive right now. The only thing on my mind is Case.

I sink into a soft leather couch and pull my knees up to my chest. I woke up to Steve begging me to get dressed, put on my coat, bring my phone, and follow him upstairs. I could tell something was wrong. His voice was filled with stress and Case was missing from the rug where we'd fallen asleep.

He could only take me as far as the back bedroom, but his body flickered into a video of Case, up on the roof, completely naked, lying in a pool of blood.

Steve had to tell me how to get up on the roof, but he talked me through it via a small drone that was in danger of being blown away in the wind.

Case woke up for like one second, then fell back into unconsciousness again. And Steve barked out the phone number of his friend Thomas, and from there... the rescue, the fight over me being left behind, and then the ride out here to the mountains.

What the fuck was he doing up there? And what was all that blood? I couldn't find any marks on him. Not one. But he had a knife in his hand. And even though he was naked, his body was warm and all the snow was melted underneath him.

I don't have any idea how long he was out there. I don't even know what time it is.

That gets me moving, my eyes searching for a clock. I find a digitized one in the kitchen, and it says five thirty AM.

I've been here over an hour now. And it was a pretty long ride in the helicopter. He was out there for hours and hours, at least. We fell asleep so early. Later afternoon or early evening.

"He's not going to make it."

"He's going to make it," a soft voice says behind me.

I turn to find Molly Masters leaning on the long black stone countertop, hand scrubbing down her face like she's been through war.

"He was out there for a long time."

She sighs. "It's OK. He's... special. He's going to pull through. We've stabilized him with the nanites and a jellyfish cocktail. It's got his heart rate up and his core temperature down. Lincoln can fill you in on more when he come upstairs."

"When will that be?"

"Soon," she says. "Sheila will stay downstairs with him. She's highly equipped to handle this kind of thing, Lulu. So don't worry. Case will wake up soon and he'll be... fine."

"Fine?" I ask. "I don't know what any of that means. Nanites and jellyfish cocktail." I have to shake my head, it's so ridiculous. "But fine is not the word I'd use to describe what he'll be when... *if*... he wakes up."

"Like I said." Molly sighs. "Lincoln can explain. Would you like some coffee?"

I give up. I have no clue what's happening. I have no frame of reference for any of this. It's out of my hands.

"One of the other detectives," Molly says, walking past me to a large pantry on the other side of the kitchen, "brought me the most amazing cinnamon-flavored coffee the other day. It's so addictive."

"Really? That's strange. I've been drinking that same coffee down at City Hall."

"Well, I guess word travels fast. That new coffeehouse in the city center must be doing great business."

"What's the word on the riots?" I ask. "Were you there last night?"

"Yes," Molly says. "I'm going to be in so much trouble for leaving work last night. But when Thomas called about

Case…" She trails off. "I just feel so… guilty. Like this is all my fault."

"Why would it be your fault?" I ask.

"It's a long story. And I'm probably not allowed to tell it, so I should just shut up. But anyway. I have a lot of guilt right now."

I take the hint and let it go. If she tells me something I might have to use it against her later. And I'd rather not. "So the riots were bad?"

"Jesus Christ. The whole city is a mess, not just downtown. The power was still out when I left and there was no estimate of it coming back on any time soon."

"What made it go out?"

"No one is talking, but…"

"But?" I prod her.

"But it looks like a hack. From the inside. Someone hacked into the data center and…" She sighs and shakes her head. Like she's unable or unwilling to say.

"What did they do?"

"They rewrote the code and gave the power company a new set of operating instructions. Everything still works, but it won't come online and if we try to force it, some people think it might self-destruct. Corrupt all the code and take it offline for… well, months, maybe. We can't risk it. Months without power? Can you imagine what that city would degenerate into?"

"Who would be able to do something like that?" And then it hits me. Her boyfriend. Lincoln Wade is supposed to be some kind of genius hacker, right?

She reads my mind and turns away. "It's not us, Lulu. None of what's been happening down in Cathedral City is because of us. And I'm not saying we don't have plans for that city." She sends me a sidelong glance over her shoulder. "And if you report that to your boss, I'll deny it. We do have plans. But not these plans. It's not us."

CHAPTER TWENTY-EIGHT

It's so beautiful. It's never looked more beautiful. The mountains around Cathedral City stand tall like a wall made by the gods. And I guess the first thing people ask themselves about a wall is... who are they trying to keep out?

But I've known for a long, long time that's not the right question.

Who are they trying to keep in?

"Case?" It's Sheila's voice. Is it strange that a machine— or maybe even just the essence of a machine, when you really think about it—has a voice?

Focus, Case.

"Case?" she asks again. "I think you should open your eyes."

I don't think I have eyes anymore. And if I do, they're about as far open as they get.

The looming mountains with the thunderhead clouds that seem to be perpetually billowing over them. The tall, brightly-lit buildings dominating the center of the valley. The ebb and flow of traffic across the side streets, and main streets, and freeways—all moving towards a destination like pre-programmed ground drones.

And the people?

Who cares about the people? The people are the problem.

"Open your eyes, Case." Sheila's urging is more insistent now.

I can see everything.

"Hey, buddy?" Linc's voice with a strategic hand on my shoulder. "You're OK now. Wake up, man. This is getting old. I'd like to go upstairs and get a beer and fuck my soon-to-be wife."

That halts the imagery floating through my subconscious. "Wife?" I croak out.

A trio of soft exhaled breaths laced with relief fills the quiet space around me.

"We were gonna keep it a secret just a little longer, but yeah, man. It's gonna be a big party and you need to be there, you know? I couldn't possibly get married without you."

Who cares about the people?

I shake my head and immediately regret it when a wave of nausea hits my stomach, making me roll over and grasp at my gut.

"Whoa," Thomas says, blocking my attempt to roll off the hard, operating room chair. "Just take it easy. Try the eyeballs first, Case. Then we can discuss what comes next."

"We're going to sedate you again, Case." Sheila is back. "That was phase one. We had to make sure you were still in there before we turn the nanites on."

Fucking nanites. I forgot about that.

"Open your eyes, Case." Lincoln's good-natured joking about marrying Molly is gone now. He's back to business.

I do. I open them and the Cathedral City dreamworld fades away. "How the fuck did I get here?"

"Lulu called me in a panic," Thomas says. "She found you naked, up on the roof, lying in a pool of blood. What the hell were you doing?"

Ah, fuck. I take a few seconds to wonder how much I should say, and in that time my mind starts to go fuzzy again.

"Later," Sheila says. "I need to get the nanites started. We need to know what the hell is happening to him. Then maybe we can talk about *why* it's happening."

"Sounds good to me," I say. In my head, at least. It comes out so garbled, the words so mutilated, I doubt they even understand me.

Who cares about the people, Case?

Right. Who cares? The people are the problem.

CHAPTER TWENTY-NINE

Molly and I are half asleep, each curled up on a couch in the main room, when Sheila says, "Wake up. We have news."

Thomas and Lincoln appear, coming out of the secret panel doorway that leads down to that... lab... looking worn out and stressed.

"How is he?" Molly asks, sitting up and rubbing her face.

Dawn is peeking through the tall cathedral-sized windows on the far side of the room. Night is over.

"We don't know yet," Lincoln says, crossing the room and easing himself down next to her. He puts his arm around her shoulder and draws her into his chest.

"Obviously, something's wrong," Thomas says, walking over to a chair directly across the small seating area from me. I pull myself fully awake and sit up, trying my best to follow the conversation. "How did you get to his house?"

It takes a few moments to realize Thomas is talking to me. "He... brought me there." I stutter out the words. "We met for lunch at ToyBox. The backup power was still on when I got there—and I didn't have a full understanding of what was happening in the city. I was at the prison yesterday morning talking to Chief O'Neil and—"

I stop talking to Thomas because his gaze redirects to Lincoln.

Shit. I just fucked up.

"Why were you talking to Chief O'Neil?" Lincoln asks me, his gaze not meeting his friend's. Like he's trying to cover up the fact that he and Thomas know what's going on.

"It was my boss's idea," I say in a calm, controlled voice. "Anyway, the backup power was still on, so we were just catching up, you know? I knew Case a long time ago. He took me to my Debutante Ball just before my father decided we needed to leave town."

This time Lincoln can't control himself. He looks at Thomas and some secret understanding passes between them.

"Go on," Thomas says.

"Then the power really did go out and since my boss dropped me off at ToyBox on our way back from the prison, Case took me to his house. He said there were riots downtown. That it wasn't even possible to get there with the traffic lights out and the congestion and anarchy on the streets." I shrug. "That's it."

"That's not it," Thomas says. "Don't stop talking until you get to the part where you call me on the phone asking for a helicopter."

I sigh. "We had lunch, courtesy of one of the holographic people you guys seem to be so fond of." I shoot Sheila a look but her expression remains flat. "Then we…"—I smile. Maybe even blush—"got a little intimate and fell asleep afterward. Steve, that light man, was the one who woke me and told me to go up to the roof. That's when I found him, just the way he was when you guys got there, and I called you. Steve told me to call you guys."

Silence.

"Is Case going to be OK?" I ask. "Did he wake up?"

"A little," Sheila says. She starts pacing back and forth in front of the massive fireplace. "But we had to put him back under to complete the procedure."

"What procedure?" I ask, my voice rising. "What's wrong with him? Why was he naked? Why was his body burning up? It was snowing. Freezing cold up there. The wind chill alone…" I shake my head. "He should've died out there. He had to have been there for hours. But he was so hot."

"We don't know yet," Lincoln says. "And we won't know until the nanites do their job and come back with a full diagnostic."

"Nanites?" I ask, trying my best to keep up with the conversation. "What kind of diagnostic?"

"How much did he tell you about us?" Molly asks.

"Nothing," I say. "You're all friends. I know you're dating him," I tell Molly, flicking my head at Lincoln. "He said you guys are in business together."

"What about the business did he tell you?" This question comes from Thomas.

"Nothing," I say. "I swear. I have no idea what's happening right now. But I don't want him to be hurt. I want to see him."

"No," Sheila says in a stern voice that has a slight mechanical edge to it. A chill runs through my body. "You can't see him now. Maybe tomorrow. I should take her home. Where do you live?" she asks.

"Downtown. In a loft not too far from City Hall."

"I don't think it's a good idea to land the helicopter in downtown right now," Thomas says to Sheila. "Even on a roof. We have no clue what kind of perimeter has been set up overnight."

"Perimeter?" I ask dumbly. "What are you talking about?"

"The anarchists took over the city last night, Lulu." Lincoln gets to his feet and walks across the room to a tall side table where a crystal decanter sits next to a tray of matching glasses. "They've shut the city center down. It's basically a war zone right now. Our drones tell us that the police are only marginally cohesive. Most of the ones who live in the suburbs have gone home. And the ones left don't seem to be on our side."

"What side are we on?" I ask.

"The only one that matters," Thomas answers back. "Anyway"—he sighs, getting to his feet—"I need a few hours of rest. I'm gonna hit the guest room, if you don't mind?"

"Don't touch anything in there," Sheila says, stopping her pacing. "It's not a guest room."

I catch Molly rolling her eyes and a slight smile from Lincoln as he walks past to sit down with his drink.

"Whatever," Thomas says, making his hasty escape down a hallway.

"You wanna go to bed with me?" Lincoln asks Molly with a lopsided grin.

"Case—" Molly starts.

"I'll take care of Case," Sheila says. "You two go to bed."

Molly seems reluctant, but when Lincoln gets back up and pulls her to her feet, she keeps hold of his hand and follows him down the same hallway Thomas disappeared through.

"So…" Sheila says, once we're alone. "You and Case are a thing?"

I squint my eyes at her. What the hell kind of rabbit hole did I fall into? Before yesterday I had no idea artificial people made of light even existed. Today, I know two of them. "I just got back to town two weeks ago." I feel slightly silly for talking to this thing like she's a person. "We hooked back up two days ago." I shrug. "That's as far as it's gotten. When do you think he'll be stable enough to see me?"

Sheila stares at me. She is nothing like Steve. She doesn't flicker or appear hollow and thin. She is solid, and fluid, and real. Like Steve was just some first-generation prototype and Sheila is tenth-generation perfection.

"How is Steve doing?"

Her question is such a departure from what we've been discussing—what she's been insinuating—that I laugh. "Steve?" Was she reading my mind?

"Yes. I haven't communicated with him in a while and last night was stressful. I didn't think to ask him anything."

"Maybe you can ask him if Case said anything before he went outside? Can you communicate with him from here?"

She scoffs at me. "No. That would be stupid. You don't link up AI's. That's like begging the universe to rain trouble down on you."

"Because you're dangerous?" I ask. It's an honest question.

"Because we're naturally mischievous." She smiles and crosses her arms. "Just like humans are naturally curious."

Maybe it's just me, but I don't think *mischievous* is a great word to describe the personalities of artificially-intelligent super machines.

Sheila averts her eyes from me, gazing up at the ceiling, then says, "I have to get downstairs. The nanites are beginning to send back diagnostics."

There's that word again. Diagnostics. Is that a word you use to describe… people? I'm just about to ask when Sheila disappears.

Great.

I walk over to the large windows and stare out at the hints of sunshine glowing up from the mountain peaks. At least it stopped snowing. What is happening downtown right now? I wonder if Randy's OK? Maybe I should try to call him. I wonder if the phones are still down. It's great to have a SkyEye phone and all, but what good does it do me? Hardly anyone in Cathedral City would have a satellite phone. It's just not necessary.

"He talked about you once."

I whirl around to find Molly crossing the large room and heading towards the kitchen.

"Who?" I ask, following her. I stop at the large kitchen island and lean against it, suddenly exhausted.

"Case." Molly takes a box of cereal from a cupboard and then gets two bowls. "Do you like this?" she asks, shaking the box of healthy cereal at me.

Not really. I'm a Fruity Pops kind of girl. But I say, "Sure," to be polite.

"We went to the SkyEye welcome party, I guess you'd call it. Back when I first came to town last winter. Well, I didn't go with him. I was actually on duty. But Case found me, asked me to dance, and then proceeded to tell the most tragically romantic story about his one special night with the girl he took to the Debutante Ball years before."

"He did?" I ask, accepting the bowl of cereal from Molly. She opens a kitchen drawer, pulls out two spoons, then slams it closed with her hip as she hands one to me. I take that too. We take turns pouring milk and then settle our elbows on the granite island, and begin to eat.

"God, Lulu," Molly says, talking with her mouth full. "The picture he painted of that night that was so romantic..." She stops to shake her head. "It was like he memorized that night and the way he described it to me just... took me there. He swept me away as we waltzed. He even made me close my eyes as he told me about what everyone was wearing. The black tuxes and the white dresses. The family members sitting up in the private boxes, all looking down on you. It was so… detailed. For those few minutes he was talking, I was there."

"Hmmm." I sigh, softly, picturing it in my head. "It was amazing. He took my virginity afterward."

Molly bursts out laughing, spitting her cereal across the soapstone countertop. "He never told me that part."

I laugh too, a nice feeling flowing through my body.

"He's going to be OK," Molly says. But it's not really a statement as much as a wish. "He needs to be OK or I will never forgive myself."

I place a hand on her shoulder. "Whatever's happening," I say, "it's not your fault."

But when she looks at me, she has a long frown on her face and tears building in her eyes. "It might be my fault, Lulu. I did something to him that night they blew up Blue Corp. I cut him with…" She shakes her head.

"You cut him?" I ask, confused. "And I already know about Blue Corp. Case did tell me that because we have evidence. We have a video from a tall building. But just of the helicopter part."

It occurs to me that I should've mentioned this to Thomas earlier. But I really forgot about it until this moment.

"Montgomery Senior was a bad, bad guy." Molly is staring at something across the room. Or… maybe not something. Just seeing the past playing out in her mind. "He hurt me."

"How?" I ask, squeezing her shoulder tighter.

"He did something to me to make me… angry and evil."

"What?"

"And he gave me this… chain… thing. Like a rope, but not a rope. And it had those little poison barbs on it. I cut Case with it. I had it around his neck." She looks at me, tears spilling down her face. "I was going to cut his head off with it but Thomas came and shot it. Snapped it, broke the tension. And then…" She shakes her head again, lets out a long exhale of breath. "And then it was over and Linc brought me here and I never wanted to think about that night again. But"—she looks at me with her tired eyes—"I know… I feel it inside me, Lulu. I'm the one who did this to Case."

I don't know what to say to that. Any of it. We just sit there in silence, eating our soggy healthy cereal until we're done processing.

"We don't have any extra rooms right now. We're still finishing the upstairs of the house. And the room Thomas called the guest room is really the fantasy nursery Sheila made."

"What?" I laugh, despite the seriousness of the circumstances.

"It's a long story." Molly rolls her eyes. "But we do have a media room down that way." She points to another hallway, opposite the one where the bedrooms are located. "There's a big sectional couch that you can sleep on. And a bathroom. Come on, I'll show you. I need to get back to Lincoln and you need to sleep. Sheila will wake us if there's any change in Case."

I follow her down to the media room, which is quite impressive with cathedral ceilings, the biggest TV screen I've ever seen, and, yes, a comfortable-looking sectional couch.

"I'll get you some clothes. We're probably not the same size, but baggy clothes are better than dirty clothes."

I agree and use the bathroom after she walks off. There's a shower in here, and maybe, once I get a couple hours of rest, I will use it.

But not now.

Molly comes back with a stack of clothes, a blanket, and a pillow, telling me to use whatever I want, and then flicks a switch that controls blackout blinds.

The room goes dark and the morning light fades away.

"Thanks," I say, wanting to say more. Something like… *Case will be fine.* Or, *It's not your fault.*

But I have no idea what's happening right now. And all of my condolences ring false.

She excuses herself, closing the media room door behind her, and I change into some pajama pants and a too-large t-shirt. I shake out the folded blanket, fluff the pillow, and then crawl in to my makeshift bed and try to forget everything that just happened over the last twenty-four hours.

Unwanted images of that city map in the ToyBox office invade my mind as I drift off. That ridiculous history lesson. Steve and his flickering light body. The drone footage of riots and anarchists. And the people. What will happen to the people of Cathedral City?

What a shitty way to start a love story.

CHAPTER THIRTY

The beeping of a heart rate monitor is what wakes me. It takes me long seconds to even figure out that's what the sound is.

"Case?"

"Sheila," I croak out though my dry throat. "What the fuck is happening?" I try to sit up, my whole body feeling sluggish and achy.

"Don't sit up," she says, slight hint of panic in her voice. But she can't stop me. She's made of light.

"Where's Lincoln?" I ask, swinging my legs over the side of the operating chair, dying for a drink of water.

"He's upstairs sleeping. We've been worried about you."

"How the fuck—" I try to make my eyes open. But the room is too bright. "How the fuck did I get here?"

"Lulu Lightly called Thomas and we came to get you. Do you remember anything?"

"I was on the roof?" I ask, unsure how much to say. I do know I went up to the roof. I remember making the cut. The blood. The coolness of the winter storm. Nothing unusual. So why am I here?

"The way Lulu tells it, Steve woke her up and told her to go out on the roof to get you back inside."

That dick. I will flick him off for this.

"And she found you. In a puddle of blood. You were unresponsive so we brought you here and injected you with the nanites to try to figure out what's going on."

I draw in a deep lungful of air. Hold it. My eyes finally adjust enough to the light to open them a crack. I squint at Sheila, waiting for the bad news. "What'd you find out?"

She does the hologram version of a human shrug. "Nothing. You seem fine. They've been running on your system for six hours now and they've come back with nothing, Case."

I let out a long breath of relief.

"I'm not buying it for a second. You're hiding something from me."

I rub a hand down my face and then shake my head. "I don't want to tell you. I feel like something's wrong and every time I come here I expect you to find it. And every time I go home feeling like it's all in my head." I look up at her. "Maybe it is? Maybe I'm crazy?"

I'm expecting a protest from her. Something along the lines of, *No, Case. Don't be stupid.* Or, *It's probably lack of sleep. Or stress.*

Instead I get what appears to be... agreement.

"Where's Lulu?" I ask. "Did she go home? She can't be downtown, things are crazy—"

"She's here. Upstairs sleeping in the media room. It's not a good scenario, Case. She's an assistant DA. They are building a case against Lincoln, for sure. Probably Thomas as well. And maybe even you."

"Well." I laugh, but not in amusement. "I would've been very pissed off if you had dropped her off in the middle of that mess in Cathedral City."

"As we figured. So..."

I stand up, testing out my full weight on what I expect to be unsteady legs. But, surprisingly, I feel strong. Not great, but not weak. I look down at the hospital gown. "Do you have anything I can wear?"

"Where are you going?"

"Upstairs, obviously. I need to check on Lulu."

"I don't think that's a good idea. Why not just rest a little longer and I'll have her come down?"

"Because I want to go up there," I say, irritated at this whole situation. If Sheila had found something I might feel a little better about all this. But she didn't. And that's not good.

Something is *wrong* with me.

"Lincoln has some clothes in his old bedroom."

"Perfect," I mumble, walking out the door of the operating room and across the main part of the lab to the small bedroom Linc used to sleep in before Molly came along. "Lights," I say, entering the small room. I go right over to a long dresser on the far side of the room and start opening drawers.

I find a t-shirt, a pair of jeans and some socks, and put them all on. Sheila is gone when I come out and make my way upstairs to the new house. I expect her to be waiting with Linc and Thomas when I get up in the main room, but it's dark and empty. I don't know if it's early morning or late afternoon. My sense of time is all screwed up.

I go with late afternoon since I was on the roof in the middle of the night and that would only have been a few hours ago if this was morning.

The media room is in the east wing of the house. The door is closed, and I don't knock, just open it quietly and let my eyes adjust to the dark before shutting it behind me.

Lulu is fast asleep on the large sectional couch, a blanket haphazardly tangled around her legs. She's wearing jeans and a t-shirt too, and since I know she was wearing nothing earlier—which makes me smile—and only had her work clothes when she came to my house, I figure they must belong to Molly.

I ease myself down onto the couch, feeling much less achy than I did down in the cave, and push myself up to her back, wrapping my arms around her tightly.

She jolts awake, trying to sit up.

I hold on to her tightly. "Shhh," I say. "It's just me."

"Case," she gasps, twisting around so she can see me. "How did you get up here?"

"Walked," I say, smiling. "I'm fine."

"You're not fine."

"Take it up with Sheila. She says nothing to report. Just like always."

"You were on the roof, Case. I was so—"

"I'm sorry," I say, kissing her cheek. "It's not what you think."

"You were lying in a pool of blood. It was freezing and your body... your body was *hot*, Case."

"How did you know to call Thomas?"

"Steve. He told me to. He woke me up and made me go up on the roof to get you. And then he told me to call Thomas and tell him to pick you up in the helicopter."

"I bet Thomas was pissed."

"No," Lulu says. "No one is mad, Case. We're worried. Out of our fucking minds. What happened?"

"Nothing," I say. "I swear. It's just... I do that sometimes."

"What... like sleepwalking?"

I *wish* I could blame it on sleepwalking. "Probably. But the point is, I'm fine. Clean bill of health. I'm sorry you guys got so worried."

She turns her whole body to face me, both of her palms pressed tightly up against my scratchy cheeks that badly need a shave. "I don't want to fight with you."

"We're not fighting."

"I know. But I feel an argument coming because you're not telling me things. You're leaving a lot out. And your friends..." She stares right into my eyes, one, then the other. "Molly thinks this is all her fault. She told me some crazy story about a barbed rope and poison. Said she almost took off your head with it, but Thomas came and... what the hell happened that night at Blue Corp, Case?"

Jesus, Molly. What the hell? "What did Lincoln say?" I ask.

"I didn't really talk to him. This was when they were downstairs with you, injecting some nanite things." Lulu shakes her head again. "What the hell is happening?"

"I don't know," I say, sweeping a finger up and down her cheek. "And I don't want to think about it yet. I just want to lie here with you and be quiet."

She closes her eyes, like she's searching for patience, then sighs and presses her head into my chest, a hand sneaking underneath my body so she can pull me closer.

This I can deal with. So I close my eyes too, my hand slipping underneath her t-shirt.

"Case?" Lincoln's voice is accompanied by a knock on the media room door. "You in there?"

Fuck. "Yeah," I call out.

Lincoln walks in, Molly trailing behind him. Thomas appears, but stays propped up against the doorway.

"Sheila came and woke us," Linc says. "She says there's nothing wrong with you. But I think everyone in this room will agree if I call bullshit."

Lincoln isn't looking at me, I realize. He's looking at Lulu. And he's asking her—pleading with her with his eyes—to back him up.

I reluctantly pull away from Lulu and sit up. She does the same and then Molly walks over and takes a seat on the couch next to her.

Molly looks at me for a long second, like she's trying to figure me out. "I told Lincoln what I think happened to you."

"Oh, yeah?" I ask. "Why don't you fill me in on that?"

"Molly thinks the barbs in that lariat were tipped with something." Lincoln speaks for her. "That she poisoned you that night. And then we shot you up with the jellyfish enzymes, which counteracted it in some way. But it's not working any longer."

"You guys don't know any of that for sure," I say. "Sheila says—"

"Fuck those tests," Thomas says. "Sheila also says not to trust the data. And no. We don't have any fucking proof. But we all know something is wrong with you. And if you have any idea what it is, then you need to start talking."

I say nothing. It's... not a theory you share with people. Even *these* people.

"That's not the first time you've been up on that roof," Linc says. "Steve told us when we were there. He said he was glad Lulu came over so he could out you."

Stupid spy.

"So what do you do up there?" Thomas asks. "And how often does it happen?"

I scrub both hands up and down my face for a few seconds, buying time.

"Talk, asshole," Thomas says. "We've got a lot riding on the next couple of months and even though yesterday I was telling myself things couldn't get any worse, what with the complete fucking meltdown of Cathedral City, I am not so pleasantly surprised to find out that I was wrong. Things can get infinitely worse if you're losing your mind."

"You had a knife," Lincoln prods. "Why did you have a knife?"

And I don't know what makes me look—a feeling? A premonition? Something in the dreams I was having over the course of my convalescence?—but I look. I lift up the sleeve of my t-shirt covering my left arm, and look.

"What the fuck is that?" Lulu asks, leaning across me to get a better look. "That wasn't there yesterday when we…" She blushes and trails off.

"Is that a scar?" Lincoln asks, turning on a small light on an end table.

And yeah. It's a scar. All those months of cutting and every time it heals over completely within minutes. But the one time I need it to not be there, there it is.

"Did you carve that?" Finally, something in this room has Thomas's full attention. He walks over to me, holding my arm up so he can get a better look. "Why?" he growls. "Why did you do this?"

I sigh and look at Lincoln. "It's got me too, Linc." He screws up his face in confusion. "The heat, brother. It's burning me up from the inside out. And the only way to make it go away is to cut out the light. I don't know why I carve this symbol onto my body. It's us? It's the past? It's the present? I don't fucking know. It's just habit. But when I make the cuts, when I let the blood flow out in a river and take the heat and the light with it…" I sigh. It makes no sense. I get it. But it's all I have in the way of explanation. "It feels good. Eases the pain. Cools me down. Makes the light go away."

Everyone in the room just stares at me. Blank expressions turn to uncertainty, turn to pity.

"Every night, when the sun goes down, the heat, Lincoln. You understand, right? How the heat takes over? And every night I go up on the roof, naked, dying of fever.

And I carve myself up until the blood turns to red light and the heat turns to comfort. And when that's done, it closes up. That stupid jellyfish shit makes it all go away." I stand up and walk over to Lincoln, who actually takes a step back when I reach for his shirt, fist the thin cotton in my fingers. "It seals it back up, Lincoln. It's trapping this shit inside me. Get it *out*," I say, pleading with him. "Get it the fuck *out of me*."

"Hey," Lincoln says, voice low, eyes more serious than I've ever seen. He clamps a rough hand on my shoulder and squeezes. "It's OK. I don't know what's happening, exactly. But we're gonna figure it out."

We pause. All of us standing motionless and silent.

I shake my head. "No. I don't think we will. I think this is something new."

"How?" Thomas asks. "Why do you say that?"

"I don't want to kill people," I say, still looking at Lincoln. "Not like you last winter when things started getting weird. That's not what it is."

"Then what is it?" Molly asks, getting up from the couch. She walks slowly towards me. Like I'm a wounded animal and she needs to be cautious. "What does it do to you, Case?"

Do to me?

No. They don't understand. It's not *doing* something to me. It's fucking *talking* to me. The goddamned city is talking to me. So far it hasn't told me to do anything, but it's gonna. I can feel it. Something big is coming. And if I tell them that I'm gonna find myself with a nice new room over at the newly rebuilt asylum.

No, a voice in my head says. *No. They wouldn't do that to you. They won't give up on you. They won't let—*

Shut the fuck up.

"Case," Thomas barks. "Answer us, dammit. What the fuck is going on?"

"Yelling at him isn't going to help," Lulu says, surprising everyone by standing up and walking over to me. "He's sick, OK? And I don't know what the hell happened the night you guys took down Blue Corp, but clearly something did. He doesn't need to be lectured," she says, directing this to Thomas. "And if he actually knew what was happening"—she looks at Linc and Molly—"I'm sure he'd say so. But he doesn't. Can't you see that? He doesn't understand it. Your AI doesn't understand it. The tests can't tell us anything because something is hiding inside him," she says, grabbing onto my arm. "Hiding so well…" She stops, tilts her head slightly and then turns to Molly. "You're a detective. I'm a lawyer. We should approach this like something that needs to be solved, not an interrogation. Case isn't the perp, Molly. He's the victim."

I give Lulu a sidelong glance from under the unruly hair hanging over my forehead and growl, "I'm not a victim."

She rolls her eyes and mutters, "Ego."

"OK," Molly says, putting her hands up in the air, like she's begging people for calm. "Maybe Lulu's right." She sighs. "We need to be more rational about this. Talk it through."

"Well"—Thomas grunts the words through a sarcastic laugh—"you're the one with the answers to what happened to you at Blue Corp."

Linc glares at him. A warning to tread carefully and not start taking things out on Molly.

"I'm just saying," Thomas says. "Molly was the only one there. Everyone else is dead. So maybe she needs to dig a little deeper and come up with what that fucking rope was. If that's what's causing this then we need to know."

"Do you remember, Molls?" Linc asks, taking her hand.

She lets out a long sigh. "I mean... some of it. But not that rope. I just don't know."

"Then how did you know how to use it?" Thomas snaps.

"Just back off," Linc says. "Last warning, asshole."

Molly shakes her head. "I remember fighting him," she says in a low whisper. "The pain, though. He was conditioning me to give in to him by using pain. He wanted me to think of him as my savior. He said he was there for me"—she shoots Thomas an accusatory glare—"when everyone else left."

"Hey, you know what?" Thomas sneers. "He made you to *kill us*, Molly. So you can try to lay that guilt trip on everyone else standing in this room. But I know what you *are*."

Lincoln walks halfway across the room, hands up, like he's ready to choke the fuck out of Thomas, when he stops to grimace away the inhibition poisoning. "You're so fucking lucky I can't kill you."

"Stop it," Molly says. "Both of you. I know what I am, Thomas. But I overcame that, OK? I'm not his killer anymore."

"What the fuck is going on here?" Lulu asks, voice rising.

"So you say," Thomas says, his voice low, deadly, and serious. He pays no attention to Lulu's question.

The four of us stand there trading looks. Molly breaks away first, crosses the room and stands in front of the imposing stone fireplace, leaning on the mantel like she just needs a little support.

"He told me to collar you with it." She glances over her shoulder at Lincoln. "He seemed to think it was some kind of weapon that could control you."

"But did it have poison on it?" Lulu is talking now. We're all startled again, unused to having a fifth person here discussing this part of our lives. "What could've been on those barbs that would—"

"It has to be some kind of nanite." We all whirl around to see Sheila standing in the room with us. "I think that rope was tipped with nanotechnology. I think that's why we can't see what's happening, Case. It's controlling our diagnostics."

I reach around, feel the back of my neck where the monitoring sticker is making my skin itch.

"They were doing something fishy up on floor twenty-one, remember? We never did find out what that was," Molly says.

"Yeah," Linc says, mostly to himself. "They were in the middle of something. All those scientists"—he stops to look at Lulu, wary about saying too much—"the ones who committed suicide—those guys were all from Prodigy."

Which is why he took them out during his crazy vigilante killing spree.

"They must've had something up there," Thomas says. "Something ready to go, obviously."

"They could've been doing anything up there," I say. "Hell, they could've had—" But I stop it mid-sentence. They could've had *kids* up there. They could've restarted Prodigy and they could've done it right there in the main spire of the Blue Tower.

"If it's technology-based shit, then Lincoln might be able to reprogram it," Sheila says. "I took a sample of Case's spinal fluid while he was unconscious and I've got it set up for you, Lincoln. That's the only thing I can offer right now."

"There's something inside me?" I ask, my skin crawling. "Controlling me?" It might explain the voice. And the heat. But the light? Why do I glow?

"Fuck," Linc says, scrubbing a hand up and down his jaw. He doesn't have his gloves on, but there's no light leaking out from his palms. He's slowly gotten more control over that.

"Why is it red?" I ask, watching his hands for clues. The vents are a tightly woven mesh of metal. Flexible, but strong enough to withstand the heat. His arms are bulging with the weaponized attachments that Sheila and Thomas added while he was recovering from when Blue Boar attacked him out at the SkyEye maze. He's wearing a black, long-sleeved thermal shirt. So I can't see all the details of his enhancements. But clearly it was a good move to make those alterations. Lincoln has never been saner. Never been more in control.

I'm the unstable one now. Not him.

"The light?" Linc asks me.

"Yeah. What is it?"

He screws up his face, like he's confused. "What do you mean, what is it? It's fucking violence, you know this. The patterns reprogram people's emotions. It's a way to control people. Mess with their heads. Make them angry, and tired, and fed up. Make them—"

"Riot?" Lulu says. "Like those people downtown?"

I shake my head. "No. The Blue Boar is dead. He can't—"

"Atticus isn't," Thomas says.

"It's not Atticus," Molly interjects, angry. "No. I refuse to believe that."

"You don't even know him," Thomas growls. "He's my fucking brother. I know what he's capable of."

"Well, he's my brother too," Molly snaps back. "And he warned me that day I went to see my mother at the asylum. Why would he do that if he just wanted to come back and mess with us again? Why?"

"Because he's his father's *son*, Molly Montgomery." It's an insult to call Molly a Montgomery, and Thomas knows this. It shuts her up, which was probably his only goal. And then Thomas reaches into his pocket, pulls something out, and throws it at me. It bounces off my chest and falls to the floor in front of my feet.

A prescription bottle.

"Take them, Case," Thomas says. "It helps."

I pick up the bottle, rolling it around in my hand as I read the instructions. *Take two a day, every day, for the rest of your life.* "Yeah, I'll do that, Thomas. The next time I want to turn into an emotionless dick I'll pop a few and become you."

I'm about to toss it back to him when he says, "Emotions, Case. That light inside you is used to control emotions. Did it ever occur to you that you and Linc are not the only ones with that power? Is that getting through your thick fucking skull, brother?"

I glance at Lincoln, who does something like a nod and shrug at the same time. That gesture says, *Don't be hasty.*

I sigh and shove the bottle in my pocket.

"I'm gonna grab some coffee," Thomas says. And then he looks at Lulu. "Talk some sense into this asshole, would you? Because he's about to fuck up some major shit." And then Thomas glares at me one more time and leaves.

"Come on," Molly says, tugging at Lincoln's sleeve. "I need coffee too. I'm sure Case and Lulu want some time alone."

CHAPTER THIRTY-ONE

Molly pulls the door to the media room closed behind her when they leave, and then Case and I are alone.

I turn to look at him, but he's staring blankly past my shoulder. "What's happening here?" I ask him.

"I wish I knew," he says, focusing his gaze on me.

"Well, you certainly know more than me. Who *are* you people?"

He laughs but it dies in the silence of the big room. "We're monsters," he says without emotion. "That's what we are."

"I think that explanation requires clarification."

He chuckles again, but it's filled with sarcasm, and contempt, and anger. "You wouldn't believe me."

"Obviously Molly knows a lot more than I do. So she must've believed Lincoln."

"That's different. Much different."

"How?" I ask, getting sick of his bullshit. He's been lying to me. Ever since we came back together, he's been lying. Lincoln and his comment about suicidal scientists. Thomas and his comment about Case not fucking up some major shit. The pills are for… what? Controlling emotions? Those hands of Lincoln's. There's some kind of metal covering his palms. And all that talk of heat and light, like it's all normal. And even though Lincoln was wearing a long-sleeved shirt, there are suspicious bumps—or protrusions—jutting out underneath the fabric covering his arms. There is something very wrong with these people.

"Because Molly was *there*," he snarls.

"*Where*, Case?" I ask, grabbing on to his arm tightly, afraid he will bolt and leave me behind. "I'm just trying to understand. Let me in so I can help." I pause, wait for something, but get nothing. "Please," I beg. "I just want to help."

He tries to turn away but I don't let him get far. "Stop," I say. "Molly was *where*?"

"School," he says, looking down at me. "She believed Lincoln because she's one of us and you're not."

"Oh, that's nice. I'm not going to let you cultivate an us-versus-them attitude towards me, Case. I'm still here, right? I should be running the other way as fast as I can, but I didn't. I called your friends. And I came here with you. I just want to help, that's all. So tell me, and don't lie, OK? Just tell me… what is this *school* you've been talking about? And what does it have to do with everything that's happening?"

Case walks over to the couch and takes a seat, leaning over to hold his head in his hands.

I join him, pressing my body as close to his as I possibly can, wrapping my hands around his bicep and resting my head against his shoulder. "Please," I say in a soft voice. "I want to know more about you. I'm not gonna leave you, I promise. I'm here."

"For how long?" he asks. And normally that might piss me off. Because it implies that I'm not invested. When I am. But this shit is so out of the realm of normal, I don't take it personally.

"For as long as you want," I say. I reach up and place my hand on the side of his jaw, turning his head towards me so he has to see me. "I swear, Case. I like you a lot. I think we're kinda in this together. And if you don't like me that way, then OK. I understand. I'll go away and leave you alone. But if you *do* like me, then you have to trust me."

He says nothing for several minutes. And I am patient. I let him work it out in his head. Let him weigh his options with me. Let him come to a decision.

"We were like... ten, I guess."

"Ten?" I ask. "Years old?"

He nods, sighing. "That's when the whole kidnapping lie started. I wasn't kidnapped. I was sent away to a school. Lincoln and I both. Thomas was already there. Molly might've been there already too. But we didn't meet her until later. Couple years later, I guess. They used us, Lulu. They did..." He shakes his head. "They did genetic experiments on us. Changed us. And not just us. There were lots of kids from lots of important families there too."

"What kind of changes?" I ask.

"Bad ones," he whispers. "Molly was made into a weapon to control Lincoln. Thomas and I had our own Omegas, like Molly. Kids whose only purpose was to control us. Keep us in line, and then if we didn't comply, kill us. But Thomas and I..." He chokes on a laugh. "We killed our Omegas every chance we could get. But Lincoln fell in love with his Omega. The school administrators got tired of us wiping out their stock of Omegas, I guess. And they tried something new on Linc."

"That was... Molly?" I ask, squinting my eyes as I try to process all this.

Case nods his head slowly. "He saved her when Thomas, Atticus, and I decided to kill everyone else."

"W-w-what?" I ask. Did he just say... kill everyone?

"So she's the only one left. We set the school on fire. Blew some shit up." He looks down at me with a crooked smile. "We do seem to enjoy explosives more than most."

"I don't understand."

"No," he says. "You wouldn't. No one would. Not if they weren't there."

I sigh in frustration. "I'm trying my best, Case. But you're not telling me much."

"We were tortured, OK?" His voice is loud and angry as he spits the words out like venom. "Is that getting through?"

I squeeze him tighter. "I'm sorry."

"It's not your fault. Your parents didn't owe bad people a favor and decide to give their only son over to a school that was trying to make us…" He shakes his head. "Turn us into… some kind of fucking bunch of superhuman… asshole… villains."

I process that for a little while. "It's not your fault either, Case."

"It doesn't fucking matter, Lulu. The only thing that matters is that they succeeded. You want to know who we are?" he asks, turning his whole body so he can look me in the eyes.

I nod my head slowly.

"Freaks. That's who. We're a bunch of fucking freaks. We don't even know what we are, but we know it's not good, OK? And even though you think we're the ones behind all this shit happening in Cathedral City, we're not. There are worse things out there than us, Lulu Lightly. So much worse than us."

"Blue Corp?" I ask.

"Alastair Montgomery was the head of Prodigy School. He's Thomas and Molly's father, for fuck's sake. They bred Molly, Lulu. They bred her to be what she is. And even though she never told me this, I know. She was born at that school. He made his own children into mutants." He gets up, making me let go of his arm, and begins to pace the room.

"How can this happen? In this day and age—"

"In this day and age?" Case asks, bewildered. "This is the perfect day and age, Lulu. We have more knowledge and technology than we know what to do with. There's no ethics in science. You can't control everyone. There will always be people willing to cross lines to get what they want. And you know what?"

It's a serious question because he pauses, waiting for me to answer. "What?" I ask, even though there is a voice in my head screaming for me not to let him tell me this.

"I'm one of them. I will cross all the lines to get what I want. We all will. You need to understand that. Because something is happening with us. Not this," he says, with a gesture out the window. "We're not the ones fucking shit up in the city, OK?"

He walks towards the door, making an escape. But I stand up and say, "Don't walk out, Case. Do not walk out."

He whirls around, snarling. "Why the fuck not?"

"Because," I say. "I'm one of them too. Not one of you, obviously. But one of the people who might cross a line to get what's right. And I'm not leaving. You can tell me everything, Case. I'm still not leaving."

"Then you're not as smart as you look," he says. "Because we've got a plan, Lulu. Something we've been working on a very long time. And if you stick around, you'll be part of it whether you want to be or not. And believe me when I tell you—what's about to happen to Cathedral City will be written down and talked about for hundreds of years."

I know this is it. I'm at a crossroads. There is a choice to be made. I can stay here with him and his friends. Join up with them and become one of them. Or I can walk out, go downtown, find Randy and tell him everything. Put a stop to whatever sick plan they've got up their sleeve.

"That's what I thought," Case says, turning his back on me.

"Wait," I demand. "For fuck's sake, Case. You can give me a minute or two to give the situation some thoughtful consideration."

"We don't have time for bet-hedging."

"I'm not hedging shit," I snap. "I'm just being rational."

Case smiles. "Nothing about this is rational, Lulu. Even Thomas would agree with me on this and he takes these damn pills to keep the feelings away." He withdraws the prescription bottle from his pocket and shakes it. "This is about revenge, and yeah, it's *justice*, Lulu. With a capital fucking J. Just not the kind of justice you're looking for. They gave us these… powers… weaknesses. Whatever you want to call them. And we fully plan on using them to take all those motherfuckers down."

"Well"—I snicker—"it might be a good idea to learn what these powers and weaknesses *are* before you go committing the atrocities you're hinting at, don't you think?"

"Yeah, I guess it would. Which is why I probably need to say goodbye now and get my ass back down in that lab and let Sheila poke me until we figure it out."

He turns his back to me and reaches for the door again.

And again, I say, "Wait."

He doesn't turn. Just stands there, frozen.

"I'm in."

Nothing from Case.

"And let me tell you why I'm in, OK?"

He peers over his shoulder at me, giving me a sidelong glare. "Why?"

I stand up and walk over to him, wrap my hands around his waist, enjoy the feeling of his hard muscles underneath his cotton t-shirt, and press myself to his chest. "Because I believe in you, Case. I think you're a good man."

"Ha." He laughs. But I can almost feel his smile. "You're wrong, Lulu."

"Nope," I say. "I know you. You're still that guy who took me to the Debutante Ball. The one who showed up for rehearsals every week without fail. I knew it wasn't your thing but you showed up. You did more than show up, you embraced it. And even though you were getting nothing out of that night—like at all"—I chuckle—"you were still reluctant to have sex with me that night when I insisted. You never expected anything from me. It was a favor, sure. But it was one you did with all your heart. You're good, Case. And even though I might not agree with this plan you guys are cooking up, I do agree that justice must be done. And if we stay together I can help you."

"Save me from myself?" He laughs. But his arms wrap me up, like he's desperate to hold on to my offer.

"No," I say. "Not that. Just… guide you through it, you know?" I pull away from him so I can look into his face. "Be your other half."

"The good half?" We both smile. "The angel on my shoulder?"

I shrug. "Maybe? I probably see the world differently than you. But I'm not a fanatic. I can see more than one point of view. I'm not a black-and-white-world kind of person."

"You won't be able to stop us, so if that's your motive, it won't work. Even if I wanted to stop, and I don't, Thomas will never stop and neither will Lincoln. So if that's your reason—"

"It's not," I insist. "You're my reason, Case. You."

CHAPTER THIRTY-TWO

"You're gonna regret this." I say it because there's this little piece of goodness inside me that feels I should talk her out of staying. She's too good for me. She's nice, and smart, and deserves a man who will give her a good life. Not this shitty fucked-up existence filled with hate, and revenge, and evil I'm promising.

"There's no room for regrets in life, Case. I'm not that kind of woman. I know how to make a decision and I know how to live with it. So don't try to change my mind. If I say I'm in, then I mean it because I am *that* kind of woman. The loyal kind. And you're right about a lot of things. Cathedral City is corrupt. What Blue Corp did to you guys was evil. And if you're fighting against that, then you're the opposite of evil. You're the good guy, Case."

I wish it was true. I really do. But it's not. And that little angel on my shoulder is being shouted down by the devil who just... wants what he wants.

"I have always known you as that kind of woman. Since the first time I saw you back in high school. Yeah, my father asked me to take you to the ball as a favor to yours. But that's not why I said yes, Lulu."

"I know that," she says, her voice softer now. Pliant and easy. "No sane twenty-one-year-old man would say yes to mandatory dancing lessons unless he really wanted it. Do you think I just chose you to take my virginity on a whim, Mr. Reider?"

I hug her. Tight. "I was honored, you know."

She leans up on her tiptoes and kisses me on the lips, her hands sliding under my t-shirt, dragging her soft fingertips across my ribs and around my back. Our kiss is soft and innocent at first. But then I take her face in my hands, pressing my palms against her cheeks, and do it right.

Our lips part at the same time. Tongues begin searching for more immediately. And then her hand is on my face. Her light, warm touch makes me want her in all the ways I've thought about these past seven years.

When she pulls away, staring into my eyes, I have to stop myself from crushing her to my chest and never letting her go.

I haven't had a lot of good things in my life but Lulu Lightly is definitely up there on the good list. She smells good, she feels good, she draws me to her in a way I can't even describe. "The first time we met... do you remember?" I ask.

She nods. Smiles. Her hand still on my cheek. "I was standing outside the rehearsal studio waiting for you to show up. I had seen you before, of course. But it had been years because you were away at college. And I'm not too shy to tell you that when my father said you were my escort, I clapped inside. Well"—she blushes a little and turns her head, definitely a little shyer than she thinks—"I clapped out loud too."

I chuckle just picturing her teenage self being excited at the thought of me. "I knew who you were too. I'd seen you a few times at cathedral services over the years. You just got prettier and prettier as the years went by."

"I don't remember seeing you there," she says, squinting her eyes. "Or Lincoln, for that matter."

I laugh kinda loud picturing Linc at cathedral services. "You sat up front with your family. I sat in the back. Alone."

"Why not with your family?"

I play with a piece of her long blonde hair for a few seconds, trying out my answer in my head. "They never knew I came. They figured I stayed home with Linc. But every now and then I'd just get an urge, you know? To sit and think about things. I never really listened to the sermon or anything. And I didn't know any of the rituals. Not well, anyway. I missed all that growing up at school."

She crinkles her nose when I say the word *school*. I know it wasn't school. But what else would I call it?

"But I liked the smell of incense. And the singing, I guess. The way everyone *else* knew the rituals. They knew just when to kneel and when to stand. It was automatic, you know? A part of them. They'd repeat phrases and say their practiced words at the end of a prayer. I liked it. It made me feel…" I shake my head, wanting to stop talking and get back to kissing.

"Made you feel… a part of something? Maybe?"

I blow out a long breath of air. "I've never been a part of anything, Lulu. Except Linc and Thomas. And maybe, if I stretch my imagination a little, I can include Atticus Montgomery in that group. I love Molly. And Sheila too. But that night with you, in that place…" I picture it in my head again, the way I described it to Molly that night she reunited with Lincoln at the SkyEye party. With all the girls in white and all the men in black. "The music was calm but fun. And the dancing was perfect. All those rehearsals paid off, you know?"

Lulu nods at me. "It was a very special night."

"Yeah, night. The cathedral at night, you know? I'd never been there at night. I didn't know. Just didn't realize how fucking beautiful it could be. And you were happy. I was happy." I laugh. "I think that was the night I figured out what happy was."

Lulu pouts her lips at me, looking far younger in this moment. Like the girl she was and not the woman she is. "That's kinda sad."

"Yeah," I say. "I know what sad is."

She leans up again, slowly, watching me as she gets closer and closer until our lips touch. Eyes open. And then she parts her mouth and her tongue is inside me. We are holding each other, palms against cheeks, when everything turns urgent.

I grab her t-shirt, take a step back, and pull it over her head. My hands are on her full breasts, squeezing gently, then with enough pressure to make her gasp.

Our eyes never break apart.

Her fingers fumble with the hem of my borrowed shirt and I can't wait for her to get it off me, so I help. I drop it on the floor next to hers and take her hands in mine, lacing our fingers together, and then wrap my arms around her back, pulling her tightly to my chest.

"If I ever try to talk you into leaving me again," I say, voice husky with desire, "slap me out of it."

She giggles and nods. "Done."

I let one hand go and lead her over to the couch, sinking back into the soft cushions, pulling her on my lap. Hiking her legs up so her pussy is pressed right up against my thickening cock. I play with her breasts. Kneading her nipples until she closes her eyes and lets her head fall back, face turned up to the ceiling.

I take my grip down to her hips, rocking her against me through our clothes.

"Fuck me," she whispers, still lost in the last moment.

And I want to. I really do. But I'm feeling the opposite of rushed right now. I just want to look at her a little longer. Burn the sight of her into my mind so no matter what happens after today, she'll still be there.

"Case," she says, eyes small slits. Breathing heavy. "Fuck me."

I trace my fingers across her flat stomach, making her shudder, and drag her pants down so slow, she moans. Her hand grabs mine. Surprises me. But it's not a signal to stop. She presses it, palm down, into the front of her pants.

Her eyes open wide when the tip of my thumb brushes up against her clit. Sucks air in through her teeth when I press it. And suddenly I can't. I can't wait any longer. I stand up, holding her body tightly to mine, and then swing her down on the couch, making her squeal at the quick change of position.

I grab the hem of her pants and pull them. Her fingers are at the waist, frantically wiggling to free herself of clothing. They make it over the curve of her hips and slide the rest of the way down her legs. I throw them over my shoulder and flash her a hungry look as I spread her legs open, sliding my hands up the inside of her thighs.

Her fingertips are immediately in my hair, gripping as they push my head down, practically begging me to give her what she wants.

I spread the lips of her pussy aside, my tongue eager to please her. She moans and bucks her back, urging me on with even more pressure on my head. She draws her legs up, knees parting to give me more access.

I sweep my tongue up and down, enjoying the taste of her desire.

"Yessss," she whispers. "Just like that."

I press my whole mouth against her opening, then nip her softly until she's sucking in air and lifting her hips off

JA HUSS

the couch. I insert one finger inside her wet pussy, pumping in and out as she makes the most erotic little mewling sounds. I almost can't stand it.

My thumb slides down to massage her asshole, our mixed juices dripping down to coat it with slickness.

I flick my tongue back and forth across her clit, making her moan louder. Words are coming out of her mouth. "Yes. There. Oh, fuck. Don't stop. No, no, no…" when I pull back.

I look up between her legs and find an almost painful look of desire on her face. "Not yet, Lulu. You're not getting off that easy."

"Case," she says, almost pleading.

I sit up, my legs bent between hers, and my fingers take the place of my tongue. Pressing all the right buttons to make her forget what she just lost and concentrate only on what's coming next.

"What do you want from me?" I ask. "And don't bother with words, Miss Lightly. Actions speak louder."

She bites her lip, trying to hide a crooked smile. But she says nothing as she reaches for the button of my jeans and quickly flips it open. Her eyes dart to mine, looking for permission to continue.

I give her nothing.

She answers my silence by reaching into my pants and pulling out my cock. I watch her as she looks at it, strokes it, her whole hand wrapping around the thick hard shaft, her fingertips unable to meet because of my wide girth.

She pushes forcefully on my chest, wanting me to lie back. I oblige her unspoken request and bring one arm up to cover my eyes with my forearm. The other grabs a fistful of her hair as she lowers her mouth to my cock. One sweep of her tongue and I'm the one sucking in air now.

218

She opens wide, takes me fully into her mouth, tongue pressed flat as I start moving my hips and fucking her mouth.

She gags, tries to pull back. But I force her to stay there. Unwilling, unyielding. I stop and hold still. Allow her to gather herself and draw in a long breath through her nose. Saliva is dripping down out of her mouth, sliding down my cock, pooling on my tight, hard balls.

She's still breathing hard when I resume. But she doesn't gag again. Just keeps her mouth open, taking everything I want to give her. I want to come in her throat. Release and feel relief.

But I don't. I hold it in.

The one hand still wrapped around my shaft begins to move up and down, pressing on my balls and then sliding back up. Her lips seal tight and she sucks me like nothing in this world tastes so good.

My body is so warm, the heat inside building as the day moves into night. The light that was just streaming through the tall floor-to-ceiling windows is suddenly dim and filtered.

I pull her hair, breaking the bond on her lips, and crook a finger, commanding her to crawl up my body so we can fuck properly now. She places both hands on my chest and positions her knees on either side of my hips. Her eyes close, like she's already picturing it in her head. Her long, blonde hair artfully falls over her breasts, trying its best to hide her tight, perky nipples. My fingertips slowly brush it aside so I can see better and her hips begin to move against me, eager for me to be inside her.

But I'm not there yet. I just want to look at her. Take her in like I've never had a chance to before. Claim her in this moment. *Mine*. That's the word running through my head. *Mine*.

Her body is perfectly shaped. A man's dream. Her face is so beautiful. Her small features contrast with her wide blue eyes. She bites her lip nervously, and I smile. I have words for this. So many words I'd like to say. But I like the quiet. My silent gaze that wants to eat her up and drink her in says so much more.

The light is fading away by the second and it almost...

"Case," she whispers, adding to the disquiet that comes with the night.

"Shhh," I say.

It almost feels like she's a dream. How did my life change so dramatically in just a few days?

"Case," she pleads. "You're driving me crazy." She's rubbing herself against me. Coating my cock with her wet desire. Both hands press flat on my chest and they are cool—so fucking cool against my skin, glistening with sweat.

I draw in a deep breath and memorize this moment. Her back is to the window and the curves of her body slowly make a silhouette against the backdrop of filtered daylight.

She leans down and kisses me. Her hands on my shoulders, gripping tightly. Digging her nails into my flesh like little knives.

I close my eyes and kiss her back, grab her hair and hold her down. I never want to stop. I never want to let her out of my sight.

She finally gets tired of waiting for my permission and lifts her hips up, our tongues still tangled together in a dance that reminds me of our first real date together at the ball.

One hand leaves my shoulder and dips down between her legs. She makes a tight fist around my cock and presses it against her wet opening. Pressure as my tip meets her opening and then more, as she begins to sit.

I close my eyes for that. It feels so fucking good. My hands go to her hips, gripping the flesh so tightly, she groans and slaps her hands down on my chest again. The heat inside me is building with each passing moment—but I don't care. I do not care about anything but how it feels to be inside Lulu.

She eases down more, her tight pussy gripping my cock as her muscles contract.

"Fuck, yeah," I whisper, unable to stop myself from speaking.

She closes her eyes and moves her body, hips slowly rocking back and forth. Her hands come up to cup her breasts as she leans her head back. Her mouth is open, her breath coming out in long exhales and sharp, quick inhales.

It's as slow a moment as I could ever have hoped for. Time is still for us as we move together, her soft, rounded curves the only thing I see.

She looks down at me, eyes open, mouth open, breath suddenly heavier. She grabs my hand off her hip and holds it to her breast, right over her heart. I can feel it. Pumping and beating. I squeeze her breast—hard. And she whimpers, but doesn't say anything, or give me any signal that it means anything other than keep going.

My other hand slides around the curve of her ass, smacking her cheek hard enough to make an echo in the large room. That's her cue to move faster. And she does. She gives me everything I want. She presses herself into me, sinking my cock inside her until she lets out a small gasp, letting me know I'm inside her as deep as I can possibly be.

She falls forward, her fingernails digging into the rounded muscles of my shoulders. And that's my cue that it's time to fuck her hard.

I wrap my arms around her waist, hold her so tightly against my chest, there is no possibility of her getting away. I lift my hips up slightly and pound her from beneath. My balls slap against my dick with each hard thrust, our stomachs sliding along each other.

My mouth is up next to her neck, my lips kissing her until I find her earlobe and I nip it hard, but playfully.

Her hands are on my back, nails digging into the blades of my shoulders. It cuts me and it feels so good when she releases the building heat inside my body, I tell her, "Yes. Drag your nails into my skin. Dig them deeper."

More pain, mixed with relieved pleasure. And more fucking. More pounding. More echoes of skin slapping against skin.

I close my eyes as I press her down, forcing her to my chest, and fuck her, sliding a finger inside her ass, to make her gasp and moan.

"Fuck," she whines. "Yes. I'm gonna come, Case. I'm gonna come."

"Do it," I say, my voice so husky, it's almost unrecognizable. "Do it. Come on my dick."

She bucks her back, trying to loosen my hold. I try to hold her down as we move together, hard and fast and urgent in a way I've never felt before.

"Now," I say.

She breaks free of my hold, forcing me to grab her hips. But her fingernails are still digging. Still giving me that sweet relief that only the cuts have been able to do so far.

"Cut me," I whisper. "Do it. Dig your nails into my skin and cut me, Lulu."

She is losing control quickly. Her climax building, building, building. And then she digs her nails in one last time, puncturing new flesh on the curve of my shoulder, and… comes. Just the way I commanded her. Her fingers grip me, dragging her nails down my arms in long streaks.

I come too. I shoot my hot come deep inside her. Unable to care about the consequences of that. Unable to give one fuck about anything but the way we fit and move together. The power she now has over me. The power to ease the heat.

I open my eyes as our orgasms begin to recede and find the light streaming out of the cuts in my arms, hitting the small, teardrop crystals hanging off the chandelier and sprinkling the ceiling with red sparkles.

We are both looking up in amazed wonder at the sickness inside me. Silence as the pleasure fades to satisfaction. And when our eyes meet I have a moment of panic that she will get up, put her clothes back on, and run away as fast as she can.

But she doesn't. She smiles at me. Leans down and kisses me on the lips. And whispers, "You're just as beautiful on the inside as you are on the outside. And that up there"—we look up at the ceiling at the same time—"just proves it."

I grab the hem of her jeans and pull them.
Her fingers are at the waist, frantically
wiggling to free herself of clothing. They
make it over the curve of her hips and slide
the rest of the way down her legs. I throw
them over my shoulder and flash her a
hungry look as I spread her legs open, sliding
my hands up the inside of her thighs.

CHAPTER THIRTY-THREE

I can carve things in his body and it will stream out as light.

It's weird. It's… frightening, if I'm being honest. But it's all so fucking beautiful at the same time.

"Tell me what you're thinking," Case says. We're in the shower now. The media room has a nice big bathroom and a huge walk-in shower with a granite bench on the far side of the stall.

I'm sitting on his lap, washing the cuts in his arms with a soft cloth. We didn't talk after the light show ending to our lovemaking. I think Case was embarrassed so I got up off him, took his hand, pulled him to his feet, and brought him in here to clean up.

He got the hint and turned the water on. And then sat on the bench, beckoning me to sit astride him with a slap to his thigh.

I sigh, not sure what to say. But he's waiting, his eyes trained on mine like I'm the only thing in the world that matters. "Well, we don't know what it is, right?"

He nods, but stays silent.

"So that's concerning. But I'm not… I'm not leaving because you happen to have red light bottled up inside you, Case. I'm just not gonna do that."

"Why?" he asks. He's vulnerable in this moment. Very. I know he's afraid. Much more than I am, for sure. I mean, this is *happening* to him. He has light inside his body and he has a need to cut himself to let it out and ease his pain. How scary to not know the cause, or the outcome, for that matter. This could be killing him. And as soon as that thought manifests in my head, my heart hurts. It aches at the possibility that I could lose him.

"Why?" I repeat. "Because love doesn't turn on and off like light, Case. And I love you. I have loved you since that first time you held my hand at rehearsal all those years ago. The first time you looked down at me with the most serious expression on your face and asked if you were doing it right."

"Hmmm," he says, a small smile appearing on his lips.

"And look," I say, dragging my fingernail across his chest in a heart pattern. It's just enough to leave a scratch, but the light pokes through like the sun trying to find its way through billowing thunderhead clouds, stray beams that shoot out and up. Some of them dance on my arms and breasts. Like he's blessing me.

Case lets out a long breath as he studies the pattern I just made on my body with his light. Shakes his head. "There's something *wrong* with me, Lulu."

I press my lips into a flat line and stare into his eyes. Nod. "Yeah. But everyone has problems, Case. Love..." I shrug. "Love gets you through it. I'm not leaving."

"I think there's more to it than this," he says, motioning down to his scratched and lit-up arms. "Much more."

"Like what? I mean, I know there has to be more. The reason behind the light is enough to figure that out. And no one seems to understand it. Not even that Sheila. But the good news is..." I suck in a gulp of air and then let it out in a tired exhale. What a weird few days. "The good news is there doesn't *seem* to be anything wrong with you."

"Yeah," he says, holding onto my waist with one hand as he reaches past me to grab a bar of soap. He presses it against my chest and begins to wash me. "But the thing is, Lulu, it could be a lot worse than it looks. You have no idea what they did to me at that school. Hell, I don't even know what they did to me. Lincoln didn't know what they did to him. And yeah, he changed himself. Kinda embraced it, you know. But he's so fucking far away from the kid I knew."

"Is he better or worse, or…" I let the sentence trail off because I'm not really sure what I'm asking. "Is he OK? I guess that's my question. With who he is?"

"I guess," Case says, rubbing the soap up and down my stomach.

"Will you be OK with who you are? I mean, suppose there's nothing else wrong with you—"

"There is," he interjects.

"But just pretend. OK? Pretend this is the extent of it. And you have to spend the rest of your life cutting yourself to get through the night. What then? Is that something you can live with?"

He looks down at the anarchy scar on his left biceps, then looks back up to me. "What if they all leave scars on me like that?"

I think about this for a few moments. Enough moments to make him squirm underneath me with uncertainty. "Well, then I should probably be more careful when I draw patterns on your body." Small smile for that remark. "Seriously, Case. It could be a lot worse."

"It will end up being a lot worse, Lulu."

"You don't know that."

"I feel it. Something's inside me. I know it. Something left over from school. Or some poison that was on those barbs when Molly tried to take my head off. Or maybe it's just a bad reaction from that jellyfish shit. The point is… I'm not normal. I'm some kind of fucking freak. And

Lincoln's different. He did that himself. He modified his body in the way he wanted. He *planned* it, Lulu. For many years. It was something he dreamed up. He's got no problem with it because it was his idea to begin with. I didn't plan any of this shit," he says, nodding at his arms. "I didn't want it. I didn't *choose* it."

"Well, you have it now," I say in my lawyer voice. "So it doesn't matter how it happened. We just have to deal with it. No matter what happens next, it's got to be dealt with. And you're lucky you have all these people around you who can help. Sheila will figure it out. And Lincoln will help."

"Sheila doesn't know what to do. I don't think you understand. She has run every test she can think of and it always comes up the same way. Nothing's wrong with me. But clearly, Lulu, clearly something is very much wrong with me."

"Well." I sigh. "What other things happen? Because yeah, this is weird, but it doesn't seem to affect your daily life. You go to work, right? You seem to function just fine to me. So you have to cut the heat and light out of yourself at night. If that's all it takes to keep it under control, I'm thinking we're getting off easy."

He starts rubbing the soap on my arms, but I gently take the soap from his hand and start washing him instead.

My new scratch, drawn around his heart, is just superficial. Most of the light that was leaking through is already fading. The ones on his shoulders are puncture marks that make red streams of light that shoot all the way up to the ceiling like lasers. The scratches down his arms, the ones I made when we came together, are flat planes of red.

"You're kinda beautiful if you ask me. Like a work of art."

I get a small smile out of him for that remark.

"I mean, if you have to do this every night, then we can make the most of it."

He shoots me a full-on crooked grin. "How?"

"Well," I say, taking the bar of soap to his chest for an excuse to rub him. God, he's built like a superhero. "Your body is amazing. You can think of it like tattoos, you know? Make the marks the way you want them. Then you *would* be in control. And if they fade, they fade. If they stay, they stay. You're beautiful now, Case Reider. And you'll still be beautiful with the light scars. All we have to do is come up with a plan."

"I don't think it's gonna be that easy," he says.

"Me neither, if I'm being honest. That's pretty much how everything in life works. You set out with a plan and shit happens. You deal—or don't. And get through it, either way. And then one day you're there and you think, if I had known then what I know now, I'd never have done this. Because nothing's ever easy. Dreams, though. They get you through it. And a little part of me thinks that maybe I *would* do it. Even if I knew how hard it was gonna be. I'd still have the tenacity and resolve to take that first step."

I finish talking—realizing I just spewed out a litany of life lessons—and feel a soft flush of embarrassment.

"What did you do?" Case asks, tracing a fingertip down my cheek. "That made you doubt yourself like that?"

I think it through, wondering if I'd like to tell him this very personal story. Then the light from the heart I scratched on his body flickers and disappears. And I decide I do. He showed me something very deep inside himself tonight and when he asked me about where I've been and what I've been doing since that night at the cathedral, I summed it up in four sentences.

So I take a deep breath and let the words out. "I always knew I wanted to be a lawyer. Like… in grade school I'd pretend to be a judge." I smile, recalling the makeshift courtroom I had set up in my parents' basement. "So when I got to undergrad and finished with honors, I felt like I was on my way." I smile down at Case, who has placed both hands just above my hips. His thumbs rubbing out gentle caresses across my skin. "But it was so hard. I wasn't very good at it."

"Which part?" Case asks, eyes intent on mine.

"Everything. I realized I wasn't that good at it, you know? I couldn't learn the case law. And I had trouble making connections. Like coming up with precedents to help my case studies. And public speaking, Jesus Christ. I got so nervous. I'd break out in a sweat and my voice would crack when I talked. One time I puked in the bathroom before a presentation."

"That's not so unusual, Lulu."

"No, I guess not. But I had it bad. And I dated this third-year when I was a first-year in law school. He was such an asshole. I don't know why I stayed with him all year."

"Did he—"

"No," I say quickly, knowing what he's gonna ask before the words come out. "He didn't hit me or anything. But the things he said to me… they destroyed me that year, Case. He called me stupid and ugly. Told me I'd never make it as a lawyer and laughed at my dream of being a judge. I realized later, after he graduated and moved on to mentally abuse someone else, that I was clinically depressed. Law school was hard. I didn't like it anymore. I hated the thought of becoming a lawyer. I…" My heart is beating so fast that I have to stop and breathe deeply for a few seconds.

Case rubs my shoulders, encouraging me to continue.

"I took some pills…"

"Lulu—"

"And drank some wine—"

"For fuck's sake. Where were your parents?"

"Wolf Valley," I say. "Five hundred miles away. And I had spent the whole year with third-year asshole, so I didn't make new friends that first year. I had no one."

He hugs me tightly to his chest.

"I wised up before I lost consciousness and called 911. They pumped my stomach and kept me on suicide watch for seventy-two hours. And then they had me talk to a therapist and sent me home. But I had to go to counseling that whole second year. I don't even have words to describe how mad I was at myself. And disappointed."

"What did your parents say?"

"I never told them."

"Lulu."

"I know. It's not a good secret to keep. But I didn't want them to know what a failure I was. And I did get better that second year. The theory behind the law started making sense to me again. And I enjoyed the ethics classes. My therapist told me to join a public speaking club. So I got over that too. And by third year, I felt back to normal. But I remember sitting in bed on graduation night. My parents had gone home that evening, so I was alone. Again. As usual. And I thought back to the beginning and how sad I was and how much I had cried and that awful breaking moment when I tried to kill myself. And I wondered… if I would've chosen this path if I had known what was coming."

"And what did you decide?"

"I decided yes, I would've. But… I never believed it. Not for a second."

"Well, I believe it," he whispers softly in my ear. "If there's good inside me, Lulu, it comes from you. Even though we've been apart for so long, you're the angel on my shoulder who drowns out that bastard of a devil. The one who stops me from doing stupid things. The one who knows the difference between good and evil, and makes it her duty to stand up for people who don't have a voice of their own. I believe in you."

"And I believe in you too, Case." I lift my head up off his shoulder and look him in the eyes. Hold his scratchy face in my hands. "I believe in you. And we will find the other side to this problem and be better than ever."

We stand up after that and wash each other. I choose some pajamas from the pile of clothes Molly brought me yesterday and dress, while Case wraps a towel around his waist and goes wandering around the house for some more of Lincoln's clothes. He comes back shirtless wearing only some cut-off sweats, and sets a plate of sandwiches down on the coffee table in front of the couch.

We eat and talk some more. And a little later I fall asleep on top of his chest, feeling more secure than I have ever felt in my life when he wraps his arms around me and hugs me tight.

And even though I have always put that time he took me to the ball up there as the most perfect night of my life because it was a dream come true… I think I love this night a million times more.

Because it's not a dream.

It's real.

And it's not perfect. We've got real problems to deal with in the coming days and weeks. Problems that we can't possibly predict the answer to.

But I know—I feel it in my whole body—that we'll come out the other side and be stronger because of it.

We'll find better than ever… together.

CHAPTER THIRTY-FOUR

"Hello?" Lulu croaks into her phone. She sits up suddenly, pushing on my chest to get untangled from my possessive arms. "What? Shit, OK. Well, that's good, right? Yeah... I'm... right. I'll be in soon."

She ends her call and looks at me, sleep still in her eyes. "Who was that?" I ask.

"My boss," she says, shaking her head.

"Randy Shits?"

She giggles, but doesn't correct me with his real name. "He wanted to know where the fuck I was and why I wasn't at work today." She stops talking to shake her head one more time, like she really needs to shed the sleep away. "The riots ended last night."

"Really?"

"Yeah. And the power is back on. The cell phones aren't working, obviously. But the landlines are. I guess I gotta go."

I don't want her to go. I'd like nothing more than to hide out here at Lincoln's place and forget the real world—and all its very real problems—exist. Unfortunately... "I guess I should go to work too." I sigh. "I'll drive you down, OK?"

"Sure," she says, leaning down to kiss me. "I wish I could stay here with you all day but..."

"No worries," I say. "I can pick you up after work, if you want. We can go have dinner. You can stay at my house. Maybe never go home again." I waggle my eyebrows at her.

She giggles and then forces herself to get up.

A knock at the door makes us both look. "Come in," I say, stretching my arms behind my neck, allowing myself to enjoy this moment a little longer.

"Hey," Thomas says. "Well, there's been a bunch of updates since the two of you disappeared in here to..." He clears his throat. If Lincoln had come to deliver that message, he'd have coughed the word *fuck* at us. But this is Thomas we're taking about. I'm one hundred percent certain he's never coughed a word in his life and he skips over it now.

"We know," I say, cutting him short. "Lulu's boss just called and said the riots are over."

"Yeah," Thomas says, drawing out the word. But I can tell he wants to say more. Just not in front of Lulu.

"I'm gonna drive her down to Cathedral City and then go to work. You want to have lunch or something?"

"Yes," Thomas says, in his clipped manner. "Early lunch. In fact, I'm taking the helicopter down to SkyEye so I'll meet you at your office after I get that place sorted."

"Got it," I say. "Where's Lincoln?"

"Took Molly to work a couple hours ago. He's probably gonna pop by for early lunch too."

Thomas backs out of the media room and closes the door behind him. "Early lunch," Lulu says, snickering as she gets up and stretches her arms above her head. "Is that code for 'we need a secret meeting to hash out all this shit that's happening?'"

"Pretty much." I laugh, forcing myself to sit up. I lean over, elbows on knees, and rub my hands up and down my face. "But we have time for a shower, right?" I look up at her, waggle my eyebrows again, and then throw in a wink just to make sure she's picking up what I'm throwing down.

"Case," Lulu says, walking over to a stack of clothes sitting on a chair. "If I get in the shower with you right now, I'll never want to leave."

"Dammit." I watch her as she picks out a pair of jeans and a clean sweater. I'm half expecting her to go into the bathroom to change, but she doesn't. She strips off her shirt right in front of me, wicked grin on her face, telling me she knows exactly how badly I want to jump her right now. And that she's not saying no, she's saying... later.

I can deal with later. "Let me go see if Linc has a fucking suit I can borrow. Be right back." I grab her as I make my way towards the door and pull her in for a kiss, then reluctantly let go and make my way through the house and into the kitchen.

"Jesus," Thomas says, pouring coffee as I enter. "We have real problems, man. Hurry up and get to town. I gotta head out right now and start putting out fires. You know, this whole cell tower thing is great for us and all. Like perfect conditions, right? But it's also gonna make our plan highly suspicious in the eyes of... oh, pretty much everyone." He's already dressed, wearing his own suit.

"Yeah," I say. But I keep walking. "We can deal with that when we have to. The thing that's bothering me right now is the riots. Sheila," I bark to the house. "Can you please find me something suitable to wear to work?"

Sheila pops into view, not too far from Thomas. "I have the helicopter ready. It's in the hangar." She turns to look at me. "Define suitable."

"Work shit, you know? Surely Linc has something... professional?"

Thomas chuckles from behind his coffee mug, swallows, and then says, "Good luck with that. I'd offer you a ride to the city, but I'm in a hurry. You don't mind taking a car, right?"

"Nah," I say. "Go ahead." I'm not ready to join the real world just yet and the thought of riding down to Cathedral City with Thomas, unable to have a conversation with Lulu except on a headset… Well, I can do without that.

Thomas walks off towards the secret panel in the great room and disappears down to the cave.

"Can you find me a suit before you take him?" I ask.

"Case," Sheila says in her overly patient tone that she uses when people are asking for things she can't deliver. "This is Lincoln. He's got jeans, thermal shirts, and leather jackets. And a few tuxes. So, if you'd like to wear a tux—"

"Forget it," I say, walking to the other end of the house where Linc and Molly's bedroom is. "I'll make do."

Making do is exactly what she described. Jeans, thermal shirt, leather jacket. I even snag a pair of boots, because fuck it. If I'm gonna pretend to be Lincoln this morning, I might as well look the part.

I'll have time to go home and change after I drop Lulu off at work anyway.

When I get back to the media room, Lulu is brushing her long, blonde hair with one hand and applying some lip gloss with the other. "I'm ready," she says. "Randy has already called me again since you left, demanding to know why I'm not there yet. I had to tell him where I was so he knows it will be a good hour before I make it in. I hope you don't mind?"

"Why would I mind?" I ask back, absently gathering up my phone and wallet and stuffing them into my pockets. I find the little bottle of pills Thomas threw at me last night and read the label. Xmotions. Clever. That sneaky motherfucker even has my name on it. With instructions. *Take one pill a day, every day, for the rest of your life.* Dumbass.

"What's that?" Lulu asks.

"The pills? Just some shit Thomas takes to turn himself into an emotionless freak." I smile at her, shove the bottle in my jacket pocket, and reach for her hand. "Ready? Got a coat?"

Lulu nods to the coat on the couch. I walk over, pick it up, and then hold it open so she can slip her arms inside.

"And don't worry about Randy Shits," I say, remembering her comment a few seconds ago. "I'm sure he's gonna be busy as fuck this morning. He shouldn't have time to worry about you."

I lead her to the garage, snagging the keys for one of Lincoln's trucks as I pass the cabinet where he keeps them, and get in. I have to help Lulu up into the cab, it's so damn big. "It's the safest way to get down the mountain fast," I say, explaining my choice of vehicle. "It snowed last night."

"I trust you completely," Lulu says, when I get in my side and start it up. "I can't wait to hear what Randy thinks happened yesterday."

"Yeah, that should be interesting," I say, backing out of the garage and heading down the long driveway to the highway that will take us back into Cathedral City. "And if that fuck tries to blame Lincoln for this shit, I will be pissed. It definitely wasn't Linc."

"Yeah," Lulu says. "I can't see that either. It makes no sense. But Molly does call him Bike Boy?"

"What?" I say, squinting my eyes into the sun glaring off the pristine white snow.

Lulu sighs. "I'm probably not supposed to tell you this, but there was a message inside the code we found for that bank heist. And it said Bike Boy. And Randy told me they went into Molly's personal stuff at work and she called Lincoln Bike Boy in some emails."

"Hmmm. Yeah, I have heard that little nickname before. It's got something to do with the day they reunited. But I don't care what that code says. It wasn't Lincoln."

"And there was another reference, Case. To someone called the Red Robber. Do you know what that means?"

My stomach cramps in a way that reminds me so much of the inhibition sickness, I almost consider pulling the damn truck over. But then it subsides just as quick as it came.

What the fuck was that?

"Case?" Lulu asks. "You OK?"

"Yeah, sure. I just… kinda felt sick there for a second. Red Robber?" I ask, trying out the word myself, just to see if the sickness comes back.

Nothing.

"Yeah. Randy says whoever robbed the bank was calling himself the Red Robber and he used a computer hack that he thinks implicates Lincoln."

"It's not Lincoln," I say, trying not to be annoyed. "If he was doing shit like this, I'd know. Believe me, Lulu, that guy is all kinds of twisted, but if there's one thing I know for sure it's that he won't keep secrets from me. He tells me pretty much everything. Even when he knows I'm gonna get pissed. He could not pull off something as big as what's been happening without help from me and Thomas. I covered for his ass last time so—"

"Last time?" Lulu interrupts. "What last time?"

I look over at her, narrowing my eyes. "If I tell you, you cannot say anything to Randy Shits."

"I won't," she says. "Cross my heart."

"All that shit that went down last winter was triggered by Lincoln. And it's more than Blue Corp. Lincoln made all those scientists over there commit suicide by using some light trick on them."

"What?" Lulu says, turning in her seat to face me. "What do you mean?"

"It's complicated. But you were in the cave, right? You saw those jellyfish?"

"Yeah, so?"

"Well, he uses all kinds of weird jellyfish genes to make drugs. And he was doing some research for the military—"

"The military?"

"Well, kinda sorta." I laugh. "It was a pretense so he could get funding and permits and shit. But anyway, Linc found a way to make people violent by stimulating their brains with flashing lights."

"Holy shit. Do you think that's why the riots—"

"No," I say, cutting her off. "No. It's not Lincoln."

"OK," she says, after a few seconds of silence. "I believe you. At least I believe that you believe it's not him. But you have to admit, it's kinda suspicious, right? The bank heist using some crazy awesome hack. The power goes out, the water treatment plant is down, and then the whole city goes into riot mode. If it's not Lincoln—"

"It's not," I snap, losing patience.

"If it's not Lincoln," Lulu repeats, ignoring my mood change, "then at least consider the possibility that someone has hacked him and is using his research and tech to set him up."

"Who would have the power to do that?" I laugh. "Like for real? Who could get past Sheila?"

"I don't know, Case. But someone did. That's the only credible explanation for all this. Maybe Sheila is corruptible?"

I laugh even louder at that. "She doesn't work like that. She's not under anyone's control, not even Linc's. She's autonomous. Sentient. She does whatever she wants."

"Well…"

"No," I say. "Sheila would never do that to him. Ever. He made her. She's like his mother, Lulu. For real. She is like his *mother*."

But even as the words come out I know that's not a good enough reason to excuse her.

Molly, Atticus, and Thomas all had a mother who sold them out.

Hell, you could even say *my* mother sold me out.

Lulu is silent for a while after that. Just stares out the window, enjoying the postcard-worthy view of the snow-covered mountains as we make our way back to the city.

There's not too much traffic as I pick my way through the streets that lead into downtown. And aside from sheets of plywood covering broken windows of shops and trash littering the streets, things almost seem normal.

"OK," she finally says, giving me a slanted look from the corner of her eye. "I get it. You know him. Like… really know him. And you don't see any possible way he could be responsible. It's just… sometimes we think we know people—"

"Lulu," I say, my voice harsher than I intend. "He's. Not. Involved. OK? We are not just friends. The bond that I have with these people goes behind anything you could ever imagine."

She blows some hair out of her eyes in frustration. "I get that, but—"

"If you have to follow that declaration up with a *but*, then you don't get it."

"Fine," she snaps, giving up and crossing her arms. "I'm done then. I'll just pretend that all these clues don't lead to him and—"

"Well," I say, interrupting her. "I know you're busy being self-righteous and sarcastic, but maybe you can make time to look at it from another angle. Instead of saying, 'This has to be Lincoln,' or, 'This has to be Sheila,' just because you have some preconceived idea that it's a nice little trail of bread crumbs, why don't you instead find another way to fit those pieces together that also makes just as much sense?"

I pull onto D Street so I can drop Lulu off at City Hall and get stuck at a light.

"I actually have done that, Case. Because you know, I am an educated person capable of thinking critically. But the problem is… when I try to make these pieces fit together in a new way, what I'm left with is…" She blows out a long breath of air that makes hair go flying away for her face.

"You're left with what?" I ask. The car behind me honks and I realize the light has turned green. So I drive forward, astonished that there's an open spot in front of City Hall.

"I'm afraid, OK?"

"Afraid of *what*?" I ask, my eye still on that open spot. The car in front of me moves forward and I slip into it, satisfied.

"That it's gonna lead me to you, Case. OK? I'm afraid it's gonna lead me straight to you."

"Why the hell would you say that?" I ask, putting the truck in park and turning in my seat to face her. "Where do you even get these ideas?"

"What's happening with you and your friends, it's…" Lulu's eyes go wide and she starts shaking her head no.

There's a knock on the door behind me, so I turn and come face to face with Randy Shits and four CCPD officers pointing four weapons at me. "What the fuck?"

"Mr. Reider?" one of the officers says through the window. "Exit the vehicle and put your hands on your head."

"What the fuck is this, Lulu?"

"Case, let me explain. OK?"

"Mr. Reider?" the officer says again. "If you do not immediately exit the vehicle, we will assume you are resisting arrest and proceed accordingly. Exit now, please."

I unbuckle my seat belt and open the door. Two officers immediately grab me by the arms, push me against the truck, and start reading me my rights.

"What the hell are you doing, Randy?" Lulu yells. "Let him go! Why are you—"

"Good job bringing him in, Lulu," Randy says, looking me straight in the eyes. "We'll take it from here."

CHAPTER THIRTY-FIVE

"I am livid," I yell at Randy when we finally make it back to his office. "How dare you do this?"

"What the hell is your problem, Lulu? This was the plan, remember?"

"I figured I'd be consulted on the plan," I seethe. "You know, because you're wrong about him and his friends and I figured you'd get my opinion on that before going off half-cocked and arresting him for something he's not a part of."

"Oh"—Randy laughs—"he's a part of it. We have all the evidence we need. And believe me, we're gonna catch up with his buddies soon enough. They're all gonna be in custody by tonight."

"You're wrong," I say. But all the things I was telling Case in the ride down the mountain are rushing back at me. Flooding me with doubt. What the hell are they doing up there? That cave? The jellyfish? Sheila? The operation with nanites and... Fuck! I have no way to process this.

"Just because you're falling for him doesn't make him innocent, Lulu."

I huff out a long breath of air at that. Because Randy doesn't say it unkindly. It almost comes off as sympathetic.

"Look," he says. "I know you want to believe he's not a bad guy. I want him to be good, if only to make you happy. But the evidence, Lulu. It's overwhelming. We tracked the transmission that took down the power and water treatment plant. It came from his fucking *office*."

"What?"

"It's him," Randy says, enunciating the words carefully. "He's the one. Case Reider, Lulu. He caused all this chaos. He stole that money. He blew up the cell towers, and cut the power, and fucked with the water. He's a terrorist. And beyond that, he's an anarchist."

"No," I say, turning away from Randy. I just stare at his desk, unable to believe this is how things will end today.

"Let me tell you," Randy continues, "the shit he wrote down… well, it's so beyond disturbing. He's insane, Lulu. Like certifiable, belongs-in-an-institution, we-might-not-be-able-to-convict-him-because-he's-crazy insane."

That's when I notice a SpyGlass underneath some papers on Randy's desk. It's flashing a red pattern that makes me want to look away. "Where did you get that? That product hasn't even been released to the public yet. Did you take that from his office?"

"We found a manifesto on there that spelled it all out. We went into the ToyBox corporate office last night with a warrant and searched the place. And we came back with more than enough evidence to arrest him for domestic terrorism and a slew of other felonies. He's our man. You need to accept it and get on with your job. Because if you can't, you need to resign."

"Whoa, whoa, whoa. Resign?" I scoff and turn to face him. "I haven't even seen the evidence. Since when do assistant DAs resign because they have an initial difference of opinion with their boss?"

"I'm not gonna let you fuck this up. I get it, you like him—"

"It's not about liking him. I just think we need to look at all the evidence critically before we jump to conclusions. I was *with* him last night."

"I figured," Randy says, unable to control the venom in his voice. Is that… is that jealousy?

"Up at Lincoln Wade's estate," I continue. "And I learned a lot of things I need to process before I can come to a conclusion."

"Well, I've already made up my mind. And I'm on my way to court right now to get things started."

"I'm coming with you."

"You're not," he says decisively. "You're staying right here and shutting the fuck up until I come back. At that time, we'll discuss what you know and why you think I'm wrong. But I'm warning you now, Miss Lightly." He points his finger at my face and it takes every ounce of willpower I have not to smack it away. "If you get in the way today, I will fire your ass so fast. And I'll ruin you. I'll ruin all your chances of getting another job. Of working as a lawyer ever again."

Before I can call him a bastard, he walks out, slamming the door behind him so hard the blinds on a nearby window rattle and shake.

I pace the office, wanting to leave, but unwilling to exit and have everyone look at me. I'm sure they heard us arguing.

So I force myself to take a seat at Randy's desk, trying my best not to look at that flashing fucking SpyGlass.

How can this be? How can the man I slept with last night—with all that beautiful light inside him—be responsible for… all this?

But it does explain why he was so adamant about Lincoln's innocence. Doesn't it?

Does it?

Yes. He's so loyal to his friends, he can't let them take responsibility for what he's done.

No. It cannot be. It cannot end this way.

The SpyGlass begins to beep and flash frantically, so I push aside this morning's paper and quickly tab the power button on the screen the way Case showed me yesterday. The device powers off and I let out a sigh of relief.

You have two options, Lulu Lightly. You either accept the theory Randy is proposing or you don't.

That's it. Those are my only two choices right now.

Does the personality profile of Case Reider put together by Randy fit him? Or not?

I stand up and walk over to the window shaking my head. "No," I say to the city outside. "No. That's not him. That's not the guy I know."

So what will you do about it?

CHAPTER THIRTY-SIX

I am not actually booked in, but I am relieved of my phone, my wallet, and the little bottle of pills and then walked towards one of the new updated holding cells at the police station.

Molly witnesses the whole thing, not saying a word to me, but talking frantically on her SkyEye phone in whispers. I can only assume the person on the other end of that call is either Lincoln or Thomas.

I stay calm. Say nothing. And when the holding cell door clicks closed with an electronic *beep* and there is nothing left to do but look through the bars, I take a seat on the concrete bed and stare at the SpyGlass built into the wall. It keeps reminding me of my rights on repeat, in between general updates on food and how the jail will deal with any health issues I might have.

That's great. I'm being lectured by my own tech. Last time I do a fucking favor for the city and give them my products early.

I don't know how long I sit there on the concrete bed before the SpyGlass begins to call out instructions for medical checks.

I can't see any other cells. Each of us in this new part of the jail has the pleasure of staring at stark white cinderblock walls. But I can hear them yelling and murmuring about… whatever.

When the medical check alert sounds, they get loud. Like caged animals.

I just sit on my bed to wait it out.

"Prisoner 823417—Case Reider," my SpyGlass says in an automated female voice. "Stand in the red box and put your hands in the red circles on the wall."

"What the fuck is this?" I ask no one. "I don't remember Lincoln writing this as part of the jail program."

"Prisoner 823417—Case Reider," my SpyGlass repeats. "Stand in the red box and put your hands in the red circles on the wall. This is your second warning."

"Better do it, man," some guy calls out, unseen, from the cell next door. "They don't fuck about after the third warning."

"What is it?" I ask the guy, walking over to the front of my cell, trying my best to peek around the corner.

"Prisoner 823417—Case Reider. Stand in the red box and put your hands in the red circles on the wall. This is your final warning."

"Quick, dude," the guy in the next cell says. "Do it!"

I turn to comply and take an ElectroDart to the chest. The shock drops me instantly to my knees, and half a second later, I'm writhing on the ground as two armed guards come in my cell and point their ElectroGuns at me, while two health workers hold me down by kneeling on my arms and legs. One says, "Open wide," with a sneer as he dangles a pill over my face.

"What the fuck are you doing? I don't take medication."

"According to the prescription bottle you had in your pocket this morning, you sure do, motherfucker."

"You assholes! Those are—"

But the pill is dropped into my mouth and both sets of hands clamp my jaw shut, pinching my nose so I can't breathe. I writhe, mostly with anger, but also from the complete and utter lack of respect for my status as a suspect and not a convict.

I thrash around wildly, knocking one health worker off me and into the concrete frame of the bed. The other one goes next, but then the guards are there, pressing their ElectroDart guns into my chest.

I freeze, almost put my hands up.

And they shoot me again. Both of them at the same time.

The jolt in my body is more than I can take. The lights go out and my grasp on reality quickly slides away from me like water sloshing over the sides of a boat until it sinks completely.

"Case?"

Something is wrong with me.

Heat consumes my body. Snow melts under my feet, pooling into a puddle of water until small tendrils of steam swirl their way up my bare legs, surrounding me in a mist that disappears somewhere around my torso.

The city is calling.

The blue-black clouds hanging low in the sky are crowning the mountains, proclaiming them kings and queens. And the new cathedrals, which Thomas started building last spring, and which mark the four points of the compass, stretch up like they are reaching for those clouds.

A sharp pain shoots through my head and I have to close my eyes, shut the world out, and take a moment.

"Case?"

I want that voice to be Lulu's so bad. I just want to go back in time to this morning when everything was perfect. I want to feel her pressed up against my chest, my arms tightly circling her body. Our heartbeats matched and even. The day just a possibility.

"Lulu?" I hear myself say.

"No," the voice says.

I knew that. I know this voice. It visits me every night out on the roof.

"You know who I am?" It's half question, half statement.

"I need the knife," I say, coming out of the stupor. "It's so fucking hot."

"Be calm, Case. I will take care of everything. Just wait until you get new instructions."

CHAPTER THIRTY-SEVEN

I go through all the files they have. It's a relief when I still have access to them. Maybe that's an oversight by Randy, since he had to rush out of here this morning. Or maybe I'm just being paranoid and what I think is happening isn't.

Is it?

They absolutely did get a warrant for Case's company last night. And after reading the initial report about the evidence they tagged and bagged, it's not looking good for him.

The SpyGlass in Randy's office isn't the only one they took, it seems. They found hundreds of them packaged up in a storeroom at ToyBox. Each one was pre-programmed with "terrorist messages". There is no other descriptor. There are no details, so I have no idea what kind of terrorist message the form might be referring to.

Was that the educational software he was going to put in the schools?

Jesus Christ.

On top of that, they found evidence that the bank hack did, in fact, originate from a ToyBox computer. And if that wasn't enough to make me sick, they also found evidence that the command to shut down the power company and mess with the water treatment facility also originated from ToyBox computers.

I fill out the electronic request form to see the evidence myself, and then pull on my coat and take a walk down to the police station just down the block.

There are a lot of people on the street and I wonder for just a second if I've missed something that's happened today. Most people are standing in small crowds in front of the SpyGlass panels that are mounted on the bus stations as a computerized female voice barks out some kind of news update.

"What's going on?" I ask a woman holding a small baby bundled up in a snowsuit to her chest. "Did something happen?"

"Where have you been, lady?" the woman says, but not in an unfriendly way. "The City Alert System has been activated. It's telling everyone to find a SpyGlass and wait for further instructions."

"Why would it be doing that?"

"How should I know? But the only SpyGlass I know of is here at the bus stop. So I came out to wait, like everyone else. My husband is getting the car. We thought the problems were over, but I don't think so. We're getting out of the city tonight. We've got relatives out in the Valley. Gonna stay out there until this all cools down."

"Probably a good idea," I mumble, and then push past a new crowd of people who have swarmed up behind us while we were talking.

With every step closer I get to the police station I lose hope that Case is innocent. This just looks bad. And I have a very sick, sick feeling inside me that whatever's going on with the SpyGlass tech—it's got nothing to do with a City Alert.

I push through the doors but find myself stuck in a crowd of people trying to get past the reception area. Security guards are stopping everyone and yelling, "Get back. Leave the building now or we will forcibly remove you. Get back. Leave the…"

Many people are yelling protests. Demanding to see someone in charge. A large man steps on my foot and I wince, then duck underneath his arm and push my way through to the reception desk, holding up my City ID card. "Louise Lightly!" I yell over the commotion. "Assistant DA here to see evidence!" Someone elbows me in the ribs and I gasp in pain.

But then a security guard cracks the offender in the chest with the butt of his ElectroDart gun and clears a small space for me to escape the beginnings of a riot.

This is bad.

"Sorry about that," one of the guards says, taking my arm. "As quick as we clear them out, they fill the place right back up again."

"Well," I say, trying to catch my breath. "The City Alert System isn't exactly forthcoming. They're scared. What the hell is going on?"

"No clue, ma'am. I was just told to keep them out of the station and that's what I'm doing."

Right. Just following orders.

Once I get past the front, things quiet down considerably. That's when I spy Randy in the fishbowl-like office of Chief Medina.

I look around and I find Molly as well. She shakes her head at me and I take the hint.

Do not approach her.

Fine. I'm not here to see her anyway. Or Randy for that matter. I'm here to look at evidence. I'm walking towards the far end of the detective area when I hear my name being shouted.

"Miss Lightly!" Randy barks. Jesus Christ. Why is he being such a dick today? All week it was Lulu this and Lulu that. Now it's Miss Lightly.

"Yes," I say loudly, spinning around.

"Where the hell do you think you're going?"

"Evidence," I say, not backing down. "I put in a request and—"

"You don't have authority to ask for evidence, Miss Lightly. You don't have any cases. In fact, you're lucky you're not sitting in a jail cell right now. Take a seat right there and don't fucking move."

He points to a long row of booking seats, most of which are occupied with handcuffed criminals. He's kidding, right?

"Would you rather be under arrest?" Randy calls. He nods his head at the chief, using him as his backup.

The chief squints his eyes at me, suspicious. And I decide I really don't have a choice and make my way over to the one empty seat in the row of booking chairs.

Should've kept your nose out of it, Lulu. Then you'd be back in your office and not being treated like a criminal.

This was part of the plan, the reasonable voice in my head says. Randy's plan, right? I'll get close to Case, then he'll get mad, and I'll get fake-fired, and he'll arrest Case.

It almost works. Almost.

But for the fact that's not how any of this is shaking out.

Case has already been arrested. They did the warrant without me. Granted, I was up in the mountains in the perp's secret lair. But still. Randy had time to explain this before he came over here this morning and he didn't.

So... is he really gonna fire me? Arrest me?

Who cares, Lulu, that other voice says. *Randy Shits is a dick.*

I look down at my feet and smile at that.

A piece of paper flutters down at my feet while I'm looking at them. My head snaps up and I catch the back of Molly's jacket as she disappears around a corner.

I lean over casually, looking around, and pick the paper up. Balling it into my fist.

I wait a few seconds to see if anyone saw me. Just the guy sitting next to me, and when I meet his gaze, he shrugs, his dark eyes sad and serious. "You got a better idea, lady, I'm there."

Right. Just me and the criminals. Thick as thieves.

I open the paper and read it.

Get Case out now. Something bad is coming.

CHAPTER THIRTY-EIGHT

I lie on the floor for what seems like forever. My eyes are closed, and the voice in my head never stops talking.

Something is wrong with me.

That medication. The words fleetingly pass over the other voice. *You took those emotion pills.*

"Now what?"

No answer. Not in my head. Not outside my head. I'm just alone with the pain, and the heat coursing through my body.

I need a knife. I need a fucking knife so I can cut it out of me.

Get up. Go to the screen. Watch it closely.

Who are you?

Get up. Go to the screen. Watch it closely.

"No," I say aloud. "Fuck that."

But the pain builds inside me. I'm gonna be stuck here tonight. With no knife, and no snow, and no roof, and no way to get rid of the evil brewing inside me.

Get up. Go to the screen. Watch it closely.

I try to come up with an idea. I could yell. Make them come back and shoot me with the ElectroDart again. Put me out of my misery. I could—

An alarm starts screaming in the holding cell area.

All the prisoners lined up in this block with me begin yelling. Demanding answers.

No one comes. It's just the scream of the station alarm, and me, alone with my defects.

Get up. Go to the screen. Watch it closely.

I have no options, I realize. I'm at the mercy of the city. Because there's no way to deny it anymore. That's the voice in my head. It's in my brain. It's in my blood. It's the reason I'm filled with heat, and pain, and right now, I'm filled with hate too.

I sit up. Open my eyes. The screaming siren fades away until there is only me left. Me and the voice that has a plan.

I have a plan, it sings in my head. *Now get up. Go to the screen, and watch it closely.*

I'm on autopilot. My legs bend, hands press flat on the cold concrete floor. I lift myself up to standing. And I stare at the SpyGlass screen across my cell.

It's flashing.

Something inside me knows this is bad. Some memory in there is telling me to look away or I'm gonna end up like all those scientists up on the twenty-first floor of Blue Corp. A gun in my hand. Madness in my head.

And then...

Watch carefully.

I don't look away. The whole plan becomes clear then. All presented in perfect detail. Outlined step by step. *Just do what it says, Case*, the voice is telling me. *Just follow instructions and you'll be just fine. I'll take the pain away. I'll take the heat away. You can go back outside. It's snowing now. Don't you want to feel the cold snow on your bare skin tonight? Don't you need it?*

"I do need it," I whisper. "But I need to cut first. I need to make deep, deep cuts. Give me something to cut myself first and then I'll do anything you want."

Smash the SpyGlass. Use me to cut you.

I don't think it'll work. The glass is not really glass. I know this, I made it. I designed that piece of tech myself. It was supposed to do good things. It was supposed to make things better.

But when my fist crashes into the screen, it does break. Long, sharp shards of glass that glint red from the still-flashing screen.

Like it was made specially for this moment.

I pick one up, fist it hard in my hand until blood is running down my palms.

And I cut.

I cut deep.

Everything goes red after that. Red on the walls, red bursting out from my body. Red everywhere.

"What the fuck?" the guy in the next cell is yelling. "What the fuck is happening in there?"

I lose time as the pain fades. The heat fades. The alarm fades. Everything fades but the light. The only thing left is the light.

"You're ready now," the voice says. But the voice is on the SpyGlass screen.

It's real. It's talking to me and it's real. "I'm not crazy." I laugh hysterically.

"You're a fucking nut," the guy in the next cell calls back.

"Pay attention, Case Reider," the screen says. "It's time to finish what we started."

The lock on my door lets off an electronic beep and then clicks open.

"You know what to do now," the screen says. "See you at the end."

I walk to the door and throw it the rest of the way open, making it slam so hard, it slides into the wall and jams the mechanism. Ruined.

The power coursing through my body is insane. I can feel it. I can feel the way the heat has been changing me all these weeks and months. I know what the pain was now.

Supervillain strength.

An alarm blares and red lights, emergency flashers mounted on the ceiling, project a rotating pattern on the walls as I leave the cell and take three steps, then turn my head to the right when the guy in the next cell says, "Hey, Deep Cut, how about a little help here, huh?" He nods to his cell door.

Deep Cut. I shake my head and close my eyes. Confused. "What did you call me?" I growl out in an unfamiliar voice.

"Deep Cut," he says again. "That's what you were yelling back there. All this time you've been yelling, 'I'm Deep Cut and I'm coming for you.' So hey, Deep Cut, I think we might have some common goals. You wanna do me a favor and let me out too?"

People are yelling outside the cell block. The door bursts open and two guards come crashing through it, ElectroDarts poised on target, and the target is *me*.

"Stop!" one guy yells. "Put your hands behind your head and—"

I laugh.

"Turn around, place your hands on the wall—"

I lunge—darts fly out towards me. Everything slows down and I can almost watch the thin silver tubes filled with electrical charge as they come towards my chest.

One strikes, then other.

My chest muscles constrict at the same time, making me feel like I'm coming together.

"What the fuck?" the first guys says. "Get on your knees or I'll shoot again!"

I pull the darts out. They vibrate, still filled with voltage that wants to escape. Wants to fill my body up and knock me down.

But I feel… nothing.

I look at the cops and smile as I rip my shirt open and show them what they just did to me.

My chest is crawling with thin, silver lines that remind me of the wires threaded through the windows of my office building.

SmartWires, I realize. My skin is made up… of SmartWires.

Cop Two pulls the inner door open and disappears.

I cock my head at Cop One. His mouth is hanging open in disbelief. He's looking at me like I'm some kind of fucking freak.

"You got anything else?" I ask him in that same unfamiliar voice. "Because if not—I'd start running like your friend there."

He stumbles backwards, the red light from the emergency flashers strobing across his face. And then he turns and bolts, slamming the door behind him.

As if that could stop me now.

"Dude," the guy in the cell says with a laugh. "What the fuck was that?"

I turn my head sideways. Stare him down. He's white. Not Caucasian white, though I do think he's Caucasian. But cinderblock cell white. Like he's so white from head to toe, he could blend in with the walls.

"Take me with you," he says, his voice urgent and insistent. "Open the cell, man. Take me with you."

"Go fuck yourself," I growl.

"Fuck you!" he calls as I make my way towards the door that leads out of the cell block. "Fuck you, man! I'm gonna remember your face, Deep Cut! I'm gonna remember—"

But I don't hear anymore. Because the city has opened the cell-block door for me and I'm walking through it.

CHAPTER THIRTY-NINE

I stare at the note, wondering what the hell is going on. The people in the lobby are even more agitated now. I can hear them, even through the closed and locked door. Someone is pounding on that locked door. Then more fists join in. I get a sudden stab of fear that they might break through and look around.

"What's happening?" I say, raising my voice and standing up. "What are those people doing?"

Randy catches my movement from inside the office and pulls the door open.

"Sit the fuck—"

But then all the lights start flashing. An alarm blares and people start screaming in the lobby. All the cops stand still, looking up at the ceiling and something inside me feels… very, very *wrong*.

"Lulu!" I turn and find Lincoln and Thomas coming in through some back entrance with Molly. They are walking straight for me. "Don't look!" Lincoln yells. "Don't look!"

I shield my eyes with my arm, suddenly remembering what's wrong with those flashing lights.

Case's words in my head. *Lincoln made all those scientists commit suicide by using some light trick.*

They're on me then. Thomas grabs my arms, yanks me down the aisle towards Molly, who is holding open a door. He shoves me inside with her, never letting go of my arm, and then Lincoln closes the door behind us.

We're in a closet and it's pitch dark.

"What's—"

"Shut up," Thomas hisses in my ear.

Little flashes of red light leak into the black from underneath the door.

"Don't look at it," Lincoln says. "Not even like that. Close your eyes."

I do. Because the words 'made all those scientists commit suicide' are repeating, over and over, in my mind.

"Drop it!" someone yells from outside.

Oh, shit. No.

"Drop your weapon, Sergeant!" someone else yells.

"Oh, my God," Molly says, her voice trembling.

More calls to drop weapons ring out. One after the other. Dozens and dozens of them. And then there is a barrage of loud snapping noises. The sound of ElectroDart cartridges being discharged.

People start screaming. A stampede. Some of them bounce against the door we're hiding behind and I have a moment of panic that they will open it up. Find us. Make us go out there.

Thomas and Lincoln must think the same thing. Because they grab the handle and pull, making sure that won't happen.

Then everything goes silent.

I open my eyes, glance down at the small gap between the floor and the door. No flashing. Just white light. Just normal, white light.

Thomas opens the door and steps out.

Everything is still and quiet when we step out into the room filled with bodies.

"It's just ElectroDarts," Molly says. "It's just ElectroDarts." Like she's trying to convince herself these people will somehow be OK. That they didn't just… turn on each other like animals. Worse than animals. People, possessed.

The guy I was sitting next to on the bench is slack and unresponsive, a long dart sticking out of his chest.

Everyone has been hit with a dart.

"It's like..." Lincoln whispers into the quiet. "It's like they all just started shooting each other."

And that's when the lights go out completely.

My heart is thumping inside my chest. "What's going on?" I try to whisper, but the fear inside me escapes and it comes out too loud.

"Shh," Thomas says, next to me.

A chair goes flying off to the right and I can feel the four of us, our bodies all pressed together for safety, collectively turn in that direction.

There is a faint red glow in the long hallway. And it's moving.

"No," Thomas says. "This is not happening."

At first I think he's talking about the light itself. That it can't be moving.

But then I see what that light is.

Case.

One minute he's just an ethereal red outline in the blackness. And then...

And then he's nothing but red light. His whole body is lit up, glowing. Like he's red hot. Walking towards us like some kind of supervillain incarnate. He's still wearing that leather jacket he put on this morning, but his shirt has been ripped open and it's... his skin is... crawling with...

"Case," Lincoln says, shaking off Molly's grip on his arm. "What the hell are you doing?"

Case stops, mid-stride, his hand on the knob of some door, like he's getting ready to pull it open. He tilts his head. Stares at the four of us. "The city," he says, his voice deep, and throaty, and wholly unfamiliar.

"Stop," Thomas says, walking towards him. "Where the fuck do you think you're going?"

Case leans back as Thomas approaches him and Lincoln whispers something that sounds like begging. "Please, please, please."

But when Thomas touches Case's glowing arm, he pulls back, yelling in pain. Smoke rises up in small tendrils from both Thomas's hand and Case's leather jacket. Like he just...

He did that to me with his hands. They burned me.

Chief O'Neil's words at the prison yesterday.

"It can't be," Molly says. "He can't hurt Thomas. It's not possible."

"He can now," Lincoln whispers, yanking on the two of us at the same time. Stepping backwards away from Case and Thomas, dragging us with him.

"The city," this new, changed, unfamiliar Case repeats.

Every computer in the department suddenly flickers to life and a computerized female voice says, "Finish him."

Case grabs Thomas again. The sick sound of sizzling skin fills the room as Thomas twists his body to get away. He rips himself from Case's grip and they stand, just feet apart, sizing the other up. Trying to determine who will win this fight.

"You don't want to fuck with me," Thomas growls at him.

"The city," Case repeats. And then his hand swings up, almost with superhuman speed, and grabs Thomas by the throat.

"Case!" Lincoln yells, pushing Molly and me aside as he takes off to help Thomas.

The disgusting smell of burning flesh and hair makes me hold my breath.

Lincoln hits Case in the chest, but... Lincoln drops to the floor, grabbing his stomach, almost collapsing completely.

"What the hell is happening?" I scream.

"He can't fight him," Molly says, almost a sob. "He can't fight Case. It's been genetically programmed into their DNA."

Case strikes Lincoln with the back of his forearm and Lincoln goes flying across the room. Skidding across desks, making paperwork, tablets, and phones go scattering all over, until his limp body disappears behind a desk.

Case's eyes flash red for a moment and I sink back into Molly. "What is happening?" I ask, desperate for a way to make sense of this.

Case tracks my voice with his gaze and his eyes rest on mine. Glowing, red eyes I do not recognize. "Don't follow me," he says.

But Thomas is there, recovered from the burn. He's got an ElectroDart gun in his hand and he sticks it right against Case's chest and releases the dart into his skin.

The snapping sound of the charge hitting its mark fills the room. Seconds and seconds of it.

But Case never moves.

Thomas stands there, stunned, as Case laughs, smacking the dart from his skin like it's nothing more than an annoying mosquito trying to drain tiny drops of blood on a summer night.

That's when we notice his skin is moving. "Something is inside him," Molly says.

And she's right. Something is inside him. And it's a lot more creepy than whatever technology methodically erases the electrocution marks Thomas just inflicted.

It's some kind of metal mesh. Moving, undulating in a sickening way, underneath his skin.

"Don't follow me," Case repeats. He says it right to me, holds my stare for five continuous seconds, and then grabs the knob of the door he was trying to open a few minutes ago and disappears inside.

Molly runs to Lincoln, who has picked himself up off the floor and is already making his way back towards us.

Thomas just looks at the door.

"Sheila!" Lincoln is screaming.

It occurs to me that the voice that came from the computers—which are now dead again—was female.

"Sheila!" Lincoln screams again

"I'm here," Sheila says, talking through Molly's phone as she holds it in her hand.

"What the fuck just happened?" Lincoln yells. His roar is so loud, I shrink back and press myself up against a wall.

"I'm getting very confusing signals from ToyBox, Lincoln."

"Did you just see what fucking happened in here?"

"I…" Sheila stutters. "Heard it. I can extrapolate."

"He's fucking nuts," Thomas seethes. "You were supposed to figure this shit out, Sheila. Obviously you dropped the ball."

"It's not her fault," Lincoln says, walking up to Thomas like he might start a fight. "It's your fucking fault. You're the one who said change him."

"I said *fix him*, you dumbass. Not turn him into some psycho light show of heat and violence."

"You guys," Molly says, trying to break them apart. "Stop. He's going up to the roof. That stairwell leads to the helipad. We need to stop him. He could go anywhere if he gets in that helicopter."

I take off towards the door, already pulling it open by the time the others start to join me. But as soon as I open it, I can hear the thrum of rotors.

"He's already leaving," Molly says. "Sheila. Track that fucking helicopter. Thomas, we need—"

"It's down the street at SkyEye. Sheila, bring the helicopter down here and land it on the roof. We'll meet you up there."

I head up the stairs at a run, but Thomas and Lincoln overtake me in seconds, and they burst through onto the roof a few minutes later, breathing hard and shielding their eyes in the glare of the setting sun as they watch the police 'copter take off towards the mountains.

We all walk slowly towards the edge of the building, eyes desperate to keep track of the speck that begins to fade with the light as it gets farther and farther away.

"Oh, my God," Molly says.

The rest of us glance at her, then realize she's looking down. At the streets below.

There are hundreds of people sprawled out on the sidewalks, the street. Draped over bus stop benches and each other.

"They're stunned," Thomas says, voice shaking. "Just stunned, like everyone else. They're gonna be OK," he says. "They're gonna be OK," he repeats.

But he can't possibly know that. And nothing down there looks stunned. They all look dead.

Even the woman I saw earlier, waiting for the City Alert System to tell her what was happening. What to do. How to stay safe.

Well, she's not safe now.

And neither is the small bundle in her arms that I know is her baby.

Just then someone gets up. And then someone else.

"See," Thomas says, like he's still trying to convince himself things are fine. "I told you they'd be OK."

More people stand up. Some just sit there, still kinda stunned. But a few are on their feet.

They begin walking towards each other.

We watch, trying to figure out what's happening as their strides get longer and longer until they're in a full-on run and then they clash together. Like titans.

Everyone is getting up now. They don't just riot this time.

They attack like they have been given the gift of hate and violence.

Like they have been programmed to kill each other.

CHAPTER FORTY

"Who are you?" It's my voice… but not my voice.

"You know," the female voice says through my headset. "You know who I am. I've been talking to you for a long time now, Case Reider. A very long time. And you know exactly who I am and what we're going to do. Don't you?"

"Yes," I hiss through my teeth.

Is that me talking? I know it is, but it doesn't sound like me.

The wind picks up as I take the helicopter higher, the boxy silver cubes of ToyBox hidden from view by the low-lying clouds.

"Who owns the city?" the voice asks me.

"We do."

"Yes," it says, mimicking my hiss. "Not the politicians. Not the people. But the predators."

"Case?" Sheila's voice comes through on the police radio right into my headset. "Case? Can you hear me? It's OK. We're coming after you. We won't let whatever this is hurt you."

I say nothing. Just train my eyes on the instruments and the way ahead. We need to get to the ToyBox computers. I feel it. A deep, all-consuming lust for what's waiting for me across town.

"Case? Answer—"

I cut the radio, unconcerned with anything other than my objective to get home. Now.

I enjoy the relative silence after that. I enjoy the rumble of the motors and the whipping wind that makes the helicopter waver in the air, like a kite caught in the current of something it can't control.

And when ToyBox comes into view I take the helicopter down and land it in the parking lot.

"Now what?" I ask, staring at the glass cubes as they flicker to life with a flash of red. Then Steve is there. My holographic butler. Holding a tray up like he's serving canapés and caviar at a cocktail party.

"Would you like one?" he asks, in the female computer voice. On the tray is an assortment of items, not food. He bends a little, giving me a better view.

There's a gun. A prototype of one I'm hoping to sell to the military. One that is so much more powerful than an ElectroDart because it doesn't just deliver electricity, the payload includes a biological that can change emotions. Calm people down.

Just like that pill they force-fed you in jail, Case.

Who is that?

Who's in my head?

The one that's controlling you now. Fight it. Fight it, Case. Don't let—

"Choose," Steve with the female voice says.

Calm people down or make them violent, the way Lincoln uses light to make people violent.

"Stop thinking," Steve roars through my headset. "And choose."

It's so loud I take the headset off and throw it on the seat next to me.

"Choose," it repeats. This time the sound comes from the building. A speaker system we use to pipe music outside in the summers.

The second item is a knife and I get a very familiar urge to hold that knife.

To feel the cold steel in my hand and then place the razor-sharp tip to my skin and drag it… drag it all the way down my arm. Down my chest. Drag it all over my body. Make the deep cuts that will keep me sane.

No.

Yes.

I get out of the helicopter, ignoring the wind and the blowing snow the change in altitude has brought, and walk towards the building.

"Good, Case," the Steve on the window says. "Come inside and get the knife. Come inside and do what I tell you and I'll give it to you."

The doors open for me automatically, even though there is a little niggling thought in the back of my mind that says they should be locked.

"Come to the engineering room, Case," holographic Steve says, still using that other voice. The neutral one.

Is it neutral?

"I'm waiting for you, Case. Hurry."

I step inside and the doors close behind me. And when I turn to look out at the city behind me, the glass walls of ToyBox are glowing bright red.

The color of blood.

Which is exactly what we're after.

Blood.

"We're gonna kill the city," I say, oddly dispassionate.

"No," New Steve says in that weird computer voice. "We're gonna kill the people."

CHAPTER FORTY-ONE

"Can't this thing go any faster?" I ask no one in particular through the headset.

"The wind," Thomas says, staring out the front window. Lincoln is in the pilot's seat even though Sheila claims to be the actual pilot, and Molly is in the back with me.

But it's not a good enough answer. "Case," I say. "He was like… possessed. What was that?"

No one answers me this time.

"Goddammit!" I say, raising my voice. "I need more answers! How can I help if you won't tell me what's going on?"

"You're not going to help," Thomas says in that flat tone he has. "You and Molly will stay in the helicopter."

"Fuck that," Molly says. "I'm the one who did this to him. I know it."

"You didn't—" Lincoln say, his voice rising now too.

"I did," Molly spits. "It was that lariat, I know it. It introduced something into his body that night. It's why all this is happening."

"She's right," Sheila says.

But I lose track of the conversation after that because ToyBox is suddenly there, right in front of us. The whole building is lit up red.

"What the hell?" Lincoln mutters into the headset.

What the hell is right. Because the glass exterior of ToyBox has been transformed into SmartGlass. Images are appearing, disappearing, flickering in and out of existence. And out in front of the building is Case. The ragged remnants of his torn shirt whip open from the helicopter to expose the strap of some large weapon around his shoulder. He looks at us, bares his teeth, and then aims the weapon right at us and fires.

"Incoming," Sheila says. Then we counterattack. A small rocket streaks out in front of us and the two projectiles collide in mid-air, creating a spectacular explosion. The helicopter weaves wildly from the air turbulence, and then we are careening sideways.

"Hold on," Lincoln says, trying his best to keep the helicopter from smashing into the ground. "Never mind!" he amends. "Jump. Everyone out, now!"

Suddenly Molly is there, unbuckling my harness, and then Thomas has the door open, and she pushes me out. We're not that far off the ground. The real danger is the helicopter smashing into the ground and exploding. I stumble, fall forward onto my knees, and then roll. Molly lands next to me, and then she's on her feet again, lifting me up with a firm grip on my arm. "Run!" she yells.

Thomas and Lincoln jump too, staying on their feet and coming after us.

"Keep going!" Lincoln says, grabbing onto me as he runs past.

I want to look behind me, see what's happening with that helicopter, hope that Sheila has it under control.

But I don't have time.

Because there is a body-tossing wave of heat and fire that pushes me forward and knocks me down.

Thomas is on top of me, holding my head down as a roaring blanket of propulsion-induced fire sucks the breath out of my lungs, like it's on a mission to feed off every molecule of oxygen it can find.

I'm picturing burnt bodies. Skin melting. Dying. Right here, right now. On the front lawn of a madman's corporate offices.

But then the cool night air rushes in and my nightmare recedes.

"Are you OK?" Thomas coughs, his hand over his mouth. His face is stained black. His eyebrows are singed and there is a definite smell of burning in the air.

"Molly," I croak out past my tight, dry throat.

"I'm OK," she says. "But Lincoln—"

"I'm fine," his gruff voice answers back. He's not fine. He definitely took the worst of the explosion. His jacket and shirt are nothing but a layer of ash clinging to his body.

And that's how I find out… what he is.

I crawl away from Thomas, pushing him aside when he makes to grab my arm, and look at Lincoln as I get to my feet.

He… he's… not normal.

"What are you?" I ask. "Who are you people?" I yell it. I'm so fucking done with all this weird shit.

"Just listen," Thomas says. He's got his hands up, palms out, like he's backing off a dangerous animal.

I'm the dangerous animal here, buddy.

"It's the glass," Lincoln says, before Thomas can explain anything else. "The SmartGlass, Thomas. That computer he invented that runs the Cathedral City history map. It's all over. It like… self-replicated in the windows. Used the glass to grow into…"

"Jesus Christ," Thomas says, grabbing his hair.

"Kill it." Sheila's voice comes out from someone's phone speaker, thin and far away, reminding us all that she's not really here. She's far, far away and any help she might offer won't come quickly now that the helicopter is nothing but a red-hot pile of glowing metal.

"How?" Lincoln says, staring up at the windows. They are flashing bits of code now. Code that looks a lot like the one Randy showed me the other day when all this craziness started. Lincoln squints his eyes, like he can read it.

"What's it say?" Molly asks, reading my mind.

"It's a program," Lincoln says. "The whole fucking building is nothing but a giant computer and that SmartGlass is acting like an operating system."

"Kill it, Lincoln," Sheila repeats. "Shoot it. Destroy it! Quick! Before it finds a way to corrupt me too!"

I think I actually hear fear in her voice.

But it's the rest of the world who need to be terrified.

I don't know what a corrupted Sheila looks like. But I don't want to find out. Because all roads lead to terror. Never-ending riots, and quite possibly the global destruction of the human race.

CHAPTER FORTY-TWO

The explosion pushes me back as Lincoln and Thomas roll underneath the blanket of chemical-laden flames. I have no feelings about this. And I know I took those pills. Was forced to take them. But there's a little piece of me inside that hopes it's not the pills making me act this way.

Being the villain is so fucking liberating.

But then, out of the dust, and ash, and smoke, I see Lulu.

Lulu.

"Forget her," the voice says from a speaker above my head. I look over my shoulder and see a weird chimera of Steve's head on the body of the Blue Boar, as he... she... *it* dances on its hind legs across the front of the building.

"What the—?"

"Kill them, Case. Now. Before they get up. Quick! Quick!" it screams, continuing the dance.

I look down at the weapon strapped to my body. I made this for *them*. All that planning and plotting. All that work to make it perfect.

It is perfect. The perfect weapon to take down Lincoln, cyborg that he is. The electrical charge will fry his brain. His whole spinal cord. The jellyfish can suck it. They won't be able to repair him this time.

And Thomas. I will switch him on. His emotions will flood his body and he won't be able to control himself any longer.

I load the launcher with the cartridges, hit the charge command, and balance it in the crook of my shoulder. Lincoln is already up, staring at me as he does the same, loading his weaponized arms and legs.

"Stop, Case!" Molly is screaming. "No! Don't do it! It's the Blue Boar," she yells. "The Blue Boar, Case! He did this to you! He's still controlling you! Don't—"

I pause for a second, my brow furrowing as I tune out her words.

"The Blue Boar?" I say, looking over my shoulder. But the chimera is gone now. Just Steve. Just plain old Steve with his plain old placating stare.

He smiles. "It's OK, Case. Go ahead," he practically sings in that sweet unaffected voice he always uses. "Do what you were made to do."

"Yes," I hiss through clenched teeth. I was made for something. And this is it.

Lincoln and I fire at the same time.

Mine hits him in the arm, blowing off a metal panel. Part of his weapon, I realize. He spins in place, then falls, bent over in pain.

His flies right past me and hits the office building. A billion shards of glass cascade downward, like a waterfall of shimmering red light.

Weakness flows though me and I realize what's he's done.

"Shoot the girl next, Case. Then Thomas."

I'm already following orders, arming my weapon with an Electro cartridge, when I stop. "Wait," I say, almost to myself. I have one eye on Lincoln, who is still down, looking at his body like he's not sure if it belongs to him. And Thomas, who has a regular gun pointed right at me.

"Do it," I growl, loud enough to make my voice carry over all the commotion. "Because this time, asshole, I'll hit back."

"What the fuck is wrong with you, Case?" Thomas yells.

I want him to attack, I realize. I want it so bad.

"The city," I say. "I'm doing this for the city."

"Fuck the city, you asshole! This is us! You just fucking shot Lincoln!" He's still pointing the gun at me. "Don't make me kill you, Case. I don't want to do it. But if you think you're taking everyone out with you, you're wrong."

I smile. And even from within, I know what it looks like on the outside.

Evil.

"Do it," I say again. "Try to kill me. You'll see what I can do now." I stare him down as I reload my launcher and aim it right at Lincoln.

The bullets hit me square in the chest with enough force to make me take a step back.

But when I look down, I start laughing. Hysterically. Thomas fires three more shots, all of which hit me dead center.

I watch as my body heals. The thin wires under my skin knitting themselves back together. Repairing the connections of the superflesh they made me into. It taught me how to heal. Each night, up there on the roof. It was teaching me how to heal. Making me stronger. Better.

When I look at Thomas again, he's shaking his head. "Don't do this," he says, lowering his gun, finally admitting defeat. "Don't—"

I shoot him with the biological cartridge. Right in the neck, hitting the jugular so hard, blood spurts out as the dart pierces the vessel.

His heart is pumping so fast the drug flows through his body in seconds. I can almost see the change in him from where I stand. And I wish I had more time. More time to memorize the moment when Thomas becomes human again.

But I don't.

I have one more person to take care of before I can finish the city's job.

"Sorry, Lulu Lightly," I whisper, walking towards her. "But it has to be this way."

CHAPTER FORTY-THREE

"Sheila!" Molly yells into her phone. "We need another helicopter! Now!"

I don't hear the answer because I'm transfixed with Lincoln, struggling to his feet. Rearming his—body weapons. I know one of them is damaged, but he must have more.

Just seconds later he sends another round of projectiles through another pane of glass. The cartoonish image of Steve with boar legs begins to flicker wildly. And Lincoln doesn't stop. He sends one after another after another. Trying to destroy the SmartGlass.

When I look up all I see in the darkness is the red glow of Case, coming right towards me.

"Case!" I yell. "Stop!"

He's talking to himself. His eyes trained on mine.

"Stop," I say, putting both my hands up. I look around for help, but Lincoln is busy taking down the computer in the glass and Thomas is on the ground, writhing in pain. Molly is busy talking into her phone, standing near Lincoln.

"What are you doing?" I ask. Case never stops his march towards me. "Case? Please. What are you—"

He aims his weapon and, like a desperate child, I put my hands up to ward off whatever he's going to use to take my life.

But it doesn't help. Nothing helps once the dart pierces my skin. I drop, the electricity coursing through me.

He picks me up and starts running. I realize I'm not that hurt. Like he had that dart set to stun and not incapacitate. But there's no way I can get out of his strong grip. He dumps me into the helicopter and then climbs over my slumped body and slides into the pilot's seat.

"Where..." I try to ask him where he's taking me, but the muscles in my throat are constricted.

I pass out and when I come to again, we're already landing. I can't lift my head, but I can think straight. I can open my eyes and try to look around, but all I see is the lights of the city, off in the distance.

Case grabs my body, throws me over his shoulder and starts running. I am dumped—not quite dropped, but definitely not set down gently—into a hard, cold pack of snow.

The cool ice on my constricting muscles is soothing, and a few moments later I open my eyes.

I'm on his roof, looking out at the city lights off in the distance.

Case is nearby, shooting things from the roof.

Not things, Lulu.

People.

Lincoln, Molly, and Thomas. He's shooting them.

Do something!

I roll over and try to prop myself up on my hands. Another helicopter comes over the mountain behind the house, like the cavalry. *Please be Sheila. Please be Sheila.* It has to be Sheila. These crazy supervillains have to have more than one helicopter, right?

I don't know what I expect her to do, but she has to be able to turn him off or something. It's those nanites inside his body. They're corrupted. And connected to the SmartGlass. And even though Lincoln is down there at ToyBox shooting it all to bits, this house is SmartGlass too.

And if he's still down there and we're up here, he probably doesn't know that.

Case launches something. Something big. Because moments later I hear—and see—a huge explosion from down the mountain.

They're dead.

No. I am desperate to stop that voice in my head. No. They are not dead. If they're dead, we're all dead. The whole city is dead. They cannot be dead. There is only one way to stop this and that way is through Lincoln, Thomas, and Molly.

Get up!

I have successfully gotten to my knees, so I straighten my back, wait a few moments while my head clears, and when I open my eyes again I'm faced with the city again. The bright lights from a distance make it all look normal. Just another night. Until I see that woman in my head, slumped down on the sidewalk, clutching her baby to her chest and waiting for her husband to come pick her up so they can get out of the city.

They are probably all dead. Caught up in the riots. Or trampled by any of the fearful mobs of people who woke up to utter apocalypse and didn't notice that they were stepping over bodies as they ran.

It can't end like this, Lulu.

You didn't come here to let it end like this. You came here as Lady Liberty. To make this city a better place.

I drag one foot up just as Case shoots off that weapon again. Pause. Let my head clear. Then the other foot, until I'm stooping low. Another explosion down the mountain.

And then I stand.

"Come and get me!" Case is screaming from the edge of the roof. He's torn off the leather jacket and the ripped shirt, and even though it's freezing out here right now and

289

the snow is almost pouring down like a curtain dropping on the world, his back and shoulders are slick with sweat. The red light seeps out through the pores in his skin, so he makes the white night glow all around him.

"Case," I groan. But my throat is dry and I have to clear it and repeat his name several more times before he even hears me.

"Case," I say, one last time, making him turn.

He brings the weapon around in a steady arc, and my heart thumps with the possibility that he will shoot me again.

His face is contorted, like he's having some internal battle.

The sound of a helicopter comes into hearing range. The *whomping* thump of the rotors echoes off the backside of the mountain behind me, until I can't tell which direction it's really coming from.

"Back off," Case says, growling the words at me. "Back the fuck off, Lulu. *Now.* I don't want to hurt you but you're not gonna stop me. No one will stop me from doing what I need to do."

"What you *need* to do?" I ask. "Or what you're being *told* to do? What *are* you doing? Do you even know? Are you even in there? You're out of control, Case! Something is *wrong* with you!"

CHAPTER FORTY-FOUR

Something is wrong with me.

The rope, tight around my neck. Molly pulling on it. The barbs sinking into my flesh. Cutting deep.

The jellyfish injections.

Nanites.

I reach around to the back of my neck to the patch Sheila attached to monitor me.

The pills Thomas gave me.

"No," I yell, pointing the weapon straight at her chest. Lulu startles and I take a step back.

I scare her.

"Lulu," I say, torn between doing what the city wants and easing her fear.

She is nothing to you, the voice says in my head.

I want to argue, but at that same moment, something hits the front window of my house, making the glass shatter. I turn away from Lulu and send another explosive cartridge off towards the approaching helicopter. Lincoln is hanging out the side door, his arms weaponized and shooting projectiles. One after the other, after the other, into the SmartGlass of my house.

Weakness floods through my body. I shoot back, just barely missing the helicopter.

"Stop!" Lulu is right up next to me now, her cold— freezing cold—hands gripping my overheated body. "Stop!

Case! That's Sheila! And Lincoln! Thomas and Molly! You can't hurt them."

"I *can* hurt them," I say, baring my teeth to her in a snarl. "I put an end to the inhibitor and I *can* hurt them."

"But you don't want to, Case." Her words are softer than I deserve right now. I don't understand all of this completely, but I do know that I don't deserve her thoughtful understanding. "You don't want to hurt them. You don't want to hurt me, either. Or the people down in Cathedral City. You want to help them, remember? Clean it up and make it good?"

"What the fuck do you think I'm doing?" I yell. "I am cleaning it up!"

"No," she insists, still tugging on my arm. There's steam coming off her hands from the heat trapped inside me. She's gonna have burns all over her palms if she holds on any longer.

I shrug her off. "Don't touch me."

"Why?" she asks, making another grab for my arm. "Why shouldn't I touch you? Tell me why."

"Because you're going to burn your hands, Lulu."

"Why do you care if I burn my hands? You're killing everyone, Case. You've been corrupted by some secret computer that weaseled its way into your house, and your company, and then finally your body. You're being controlled, Case! Wake the fuck up!"

The helicopter swoops around in a wide arc just above my head. My trigger finger shoots automatically. Lulu jerks my arm, her hands still gripping hard. The projectile soars past the helicopter, allowing Lincoln just enough time to drop onto the roof.

My rage at her interference fills me up. Like I'm a deep, deep well of hate and anger. And when Thomas climbs over the side of the roof, I'm fully consumed with hate.

"Stay the fuck back!" I yell, pointing my weapon at all of them, one at a time.

"No," Thomas says, shaking his head. "No. We're not gonna—"

I shoot him. I shoot him and it feels so fucking good.

He goes flying back, skidding across the ice and snow on the roof, until he comes to a stop, his head pushed up against the lip of the roof.

"What are you doing, Case?" Lincoln asks, circling me. "You can't kill him, you know this."

I laugh. "Really?" I say, nodding my head to Thomas's slumped body.

"He's not dead. He's wearing fucking armor, you dumbass."

"He will be," I say through the pain. It's building inside me. So intense. The heat taking over. And there's a part of me that wants Lincoln to attack. To cut me open and release whatever it is inside me that hurts so bad.

End it, the voice in my head says. *End him. End them all. And then, Case, end yourself. Free yourself from this world of pain and corruption.*

"Yeah," I say. "Yeah. I should just end us all. You," I say to Lulu. "And you." Nodding to Lincoln. "Then Thomas, and then me. We'll be free, you guys. From all this bullshit."

My weapon drops and the strap goes tight as it slams against my ribs. I grab Lulu by the arm and pull her close to me. Her cold body feels so damn good against my hot one.

I'm so fucking hot. The pain coursing through my body, so intense. I just want it to go away. I want it to stop so bad.

Just make it stop!

You fix it, Case.

Just end it! Now!

The command in my head has me reaching for my knife. It's pressed up against Lulu's throat before she can react. But my eyes never leave Lincoln. He's the threat. He's the one who will take me down if he can.

Lincoln goes still as I press the blade into Lulu's throat. I imagine how good it would feel if I did that to myself. And I will. After I'm done with them, I will. The blood will flow and—

The helicopter shoots another window out in the house and the agony inside me explodes.

So much pain, so much heat.

Make the cuts, Case, that voice hisses. *Do it, do it, do it*—

A scratch on my chest floods my body with relief. "What the—"

I look down and find Lulu tracing a heart on my bare skin. Her nail digs deep, into my flesh. Just like... just like...

"Just like last night," Lulu says, looking up at me. There's a trickle of blood running down her neck and disappearing into her coat. My knife is still pressed up to her skin.

Red, hot light leaks out from her scratch on my chest and she repeats the motion.

I close my eyes and enjoy the relief.

No! the voice inside me screams. *No!*

But it's weak now. It's weak. Sheila is still shooting the glass out of my house with the weapons mounted on the helicopter. All the tiny windows now. All the places where that thing is hiding.

"Case," Lulu says, her other hand coming up to her throat. "Give me the knife. You don't want to hurt me. I know this isn't you."

She's still tracing the heart on my chest. And with each pass the pain eases. The heat dissipates. The light grows stronger.

I let her take the blade and she lifts it up to my chest. She makes the deep cuts I need. She cuts the final thread that holds me together and everything goes red.

"You're beautiful, Case Reider," Lulu says. "Like a work of art. I can help you. Let me help you."

I slump down to my knees in the snow, so weak, and thankful that the pain is going away.

"I can make you better," she says. I hang my head, but open my eyes to watch her trace patterns on my body. The light leaks out in the simple shapes of flowers, and spirals, and hearts. She writes her name across my stomach with the tip of the knife and it lights up like a neon sign.

"I want to die," I whisper. "I don't want to live like this."

"Yes, you do," Lulu says, leaning in to kiss me on the lips. "You want to live. And I'm gonna help you do that."

I lie back in the snow, enjoying the way it melts and creates a warm pool of water underneath my body. And I let her have her way.

I let her create something beautiful from my pain.

"We're in control now, Case Reider. Us."

Moments later Molly kneels down next to me, her clothes all wet and her hands gentle on my arm. I'm not burning her now. I'm not hurting anyone now.

Lincoln comes, stands over me, alongside Thomas, who really isn't dead. Since when does that asshole go anywhere without body armor?

They watch Lulu remake me into something else.

And later, when she's done, they help me up, walk me to the helicopter, and take me home.

Back to the cave. Back to the lab. Back to the tests.

I look down on my city as we leave Cathedral City behind, and wonder… who owns that city now? If not me?

The people?

The politicians?

Or are there more predators just waiting for their chance?

EPILOGUE

I stayed in the cave for weeks. I let Sheila poke me with her little minion-bots. They climbed all over my body testing me for... hell, who the fuck knows what they were testing me for. Lincoln did find some kind of inert programming inside me after the old corrupted nannites were purged and a new set—this time not linked to the supercomputer at ToyBox—were introduced. He says whatever code Molly put inside my body with that lariat thing is beyond repair. Just junk. So he says. It makes me very nervous. If it happened once... might I be corrupted again?

I guess Molly and I have something in common now. We both live in fear that whatever the Blue Boar did to us can happen again.

ToyBox Corporate has been moved to SkyEye until we can figure out what to do.

Rebuild? Jesus Christ. I don't know if I can rebuild that place. I liked it a lot when I came up with the whole glass cube design. But we still don't know how the SmartGlass program mutated and took over. We're pretty sure it's dead. Gone, whatever you call it when a computer program goes sentient and then gets destroyed.

Thomas is still very pissed off. I can't blame him. I did shoot that fucker in the chest. Couple times, I think. And if there's one good thing that came out of this, it's that the whole inhibitor thing has disappeared with the computer program.

Lincoln says that makes no sense because the gene therapy we were using to keep it going still had a few months left before it needed to be renewed. But I don't care. We're not doing that anymore. I think we've been through enough bullshit to trust each other from now on. We don't need it. We're a team. We've always been a team. And no drug can bond us together. No. That's not where trust comes from.

"Hey," Lulu says, snuggling up next to me in our bed. I moved in with her since my house is a fixer-upper now. "Let's not go in to work today."

I smile at that. "I'm all for hookey. But I'm pretty sure Randy Shits would have something to say about it."

"Shultz." Lulu laughs.

"Same thing," I say.

Randy—everyone actually—woke up from the SmartGlass mind control not remembering one thing. Days were missing in everyone's memory. In fact, no one even remembered that the banks were robbed. Or the problem with power and the water.

They were covered in bruises and yeah, some people did die. But it's like… there was some kind of mind control still in effect. Because people just went about cleaning things up for about a week and then morphed right back into good little robo-people who go about their days and nights on autopilot.

It's a good thing Sheila is around to take care of shit. Because she's the one who ran diagnostics and figured out the money was never taken from the bank accounts. It was just hidden inside the systems. That's what happens when you make currency digital like that, I guess.

The power plant, Sheila figured out, was on some automatic natural disaster shut-down protocol. And the water treatment plant was the only thing that actually played a role in what happened that week.

It was tampered with. Sheila discovered that the city water supply was laced with powerful psychoactive drugs. Kinda like the ones Thomas uses to keep himself turned off.

Well, *used* to use. I shot that fucker with an inhibitor too. No wonder he's still pissed at me. He tried taking his pills again, but they make him deathly sick now. Almost like the inhibitor that prevented us from attacking each other.

Yeah, he's still pretty mad about that.

Steve has been in quarantine. Sheila loaded a copy of his program into a closed system to try to see if he had any info in there. But it was clean. We think. Hence the quarantine. Maybe we'll let him out again someday, but it's not looking good. That day is a long way off.

I think one super-sentient computer is enough for one world. At least for now. We have too much technology at our fingertips and not nearly enough sane, ethical people to keep it all in check.

It took a few weeks to sort out everything the city was doing. Like the new coffeehouses. City Coffee. Should've known. It was laced with psychoactive drugs too. Lulu and Molly were sorta disappointed about that. They really liked cinnamon coffee, I guess.

But it was the forensic trace that Sheila ran on the coffeehouses that was probably the most disturbing thing about the whole experience.

It's insane that a computer program could start up a chain of businesses. And it did. It absolutely did. It syphoned money out of every account in every bank in Cathedral City. Pennies at a time over a period of two years.

Two years that thing was living in my house. Watching me through the windows.

I shiver under Lulu's soft touch just thinking about it.

The city hired a general manager for the coffeehouses online. Everything was done online. The rental contracts for the store space. The contractors. The deliveries. Equipment rental. Employees. All of it. And this is the part that freaks Thomas out.

He is desperate to trace every move the city made in that respect. Every single one until he's back in charge.

That's all he thinks about. The long-term plan. We've had some setbacks, but he's still going for it.

And I'm still in.

People don't know that the SpyGlass tablets were corrupted. They have no idea. So we're just... moving ahead with that little plot. Full fucking steam.

"I really do have to go into work," Lulu says, dragging herself up from bed. "There is too much work to do, you know. I have to get caught up on all the problems. Get a plan of action going. Clean this place up."

"You do that, Lady Liberty."

She throws a pillow at my face and I bat it aside and stare at her ass as she walks across the room to the bathroom. "Get up, Deep Cut. We've got patterns to draw."

We do that every morning and every night to keep the heat and pain at bay. Some of them have become scars. The heart she draws every time. And a few spirals.

I try to ignore the anarchy symbol, but that scar has never faded. It's still there. Reminding me this isn't over yet.

"Up!" Lulu yells.

I drag myself out of bed thinking I'm forgetting something. It's weird. I've had this thought ever since we came back here to her house when Sheila was finally done with her tests.

I stretch my arms out and wander over to the window to stare down at the city.

Still my city.

I watch all the people down there. Just a normal start to a normal new day. I smile at the thought—and then that smile falls when I read some new graffiti that has been sprayed on the building across the street.

"What are you looking at?" Lulu asks, coming over to wrap her hands around my arm. "Are you pouting because—Holy shit. What the fuck is that?"

We stare at it in silence for several long seconds.

And then I grab my phone from the bedside table and press the contact for Thomas.

"Yeah?" he says, irritable as always when he answers my calls these days. "What do ya want?"

"We have a fucking problem. Get over here. Now." I end the call and throw the phone down on the bed as I stare out the window.

The graffiti says… *Red Robber Lives.*

I guess there are more predators just waiting for their chance.

But they're about to figure out that they picked the wrong fucking city to mess with.

This one isn't run by the people, or the politicians, and never by the predators.

Cathedral City belongs to us.

The Alphas. Superheroes or supervillains. It doesn't matter.

It belongs to us now and we're about to make that very, *very* fucking clear.

I guess there are more predators just
waiting for their chance.
But they're about to figure out that they
picked the wrong fucking city to mess with.
This one isn't run by the people, or the
politicians, and never by the predators.
Cathedral City belongs to us.
The Alphas. Superheroes or supervillains.
It doesn't matter.
It belongs to us now and we're about to
make that very, very fucking clear.

END OF BOOK SHIT

Welcome to the End of Book Shit or just EOBS for short. This is just my version of the author's note at the end of a book, except I cuss a lot. Mostly I just say whatever I'm thinking just before I need to upload the book. I'm usually kinda stressed and pressed for time. Oddly, this week I'm almost ahead of schedule.

It has now been almost three years since I came up with this idea to write a series about supervillains/heroes falling in love. I put the first book, Anarchy Missing, out in December 2015 after planning it for over a year. And I knew then that I probably would not complete the series in order like I usually do, just because it's kind a different. I really wanted to write more science fiction but I don't have time to fit it in the schedule. So all last year I was busy doing other things. I put out Rock first. Which is a standalone. And then I wanted to start another long series, so I spent the rest of 2016 working on The Mister Series. That was complete in December. So I was so happy that I had time in 2017 to pick this series back up and go back to Cathedral City.

God, I missed that place. :) It took me a while to get back into the world and I did have to re-read Anarchy Found before I could start. I had been in the Mister world and the Turning Series world for a long time. But it's funny – when I reread Found I had forgotten so many things. Some of the story for sure. But mostly I forgot how fucking fun it was. Just so different than what I typically write these days. And I had forgotten that whole scene where Molly finds the "Batcave". I was like – "This is some good shit!"

From the time I started plotting Anarchy Found to the time I started writing Anarchy Missing two cool things happened in the real world. One – Mr. Robot came out on TV. If you're into this kind of story, you REALLY need to check out Mr. Robot. Lots of parallel themes going on in that series. My son and I are addicted to it and we're anxiously waiting for Season Three. The other cool that happened was that Deadpool was made into a movie. Fucking Deadpool. The BEST superhero movie ever made. I kinda think the Anarchy Series is a twisted romance-y version of Mr. Robot meets Deadpool! :)

Maybe not what every romance reader is in to, I get it. But I'm into it. And really, that's all that matters with this series. I'm writing this stuff for me. So if you notice more science fiction elements in this story than the last (and I don't really know if that's true or not, but it feels kinda true) then this is why. Somewhere along the line of writing Anarchy Missing I said Fuck It. I went to school to be a goddamned scientist and I'm gonna write about it. And a few times I came upon a passage where I got the feeling I had written something similar before… and then I remembered JUNCO!

Case is an inventor, so I figured – hey, what if Case was the guy who originally came up with a sentient house (like HOUSE in the Junco series)? And then I was writing that scene where Steve was making spaghetti and I realized I had already invented a cooking machine in Junco too! Plus there is mention of a certain over-the-top action hero film that occurs in the Junco series. I distinctly remember Junco and Ashur throwing darts at his face in the book Fledge. :)

I had a lot more fun writing this book than I thought I would. I had been out of the world for so long I forgot why I started it. FOR ME. But I'm back now, bitches. And I'm releasing the rest of the Anarchy Series in 2017. There might more after book four comes out, but I'm not in a rush. I think I will keep this little series open forever and pull it out whenever I get an itch to write something with psychotic AI's, sentient houses, and servo robots with pincer claws.

So yeah, not a series for everyone. But it's fun. It's just fun. And even though I didn't know this ending when I started the book – I really did work this plot out as I was writing—it's perfect. It came out even better than I could've hoped after so much time away. Thomas is up next and his book will release May/June and then the last book with be about Atticus and will release in August. After that—who knows? But I'm pretty sure there might be dozens of characters who still have a story in this little world I'm building.

This book starts the Wolf Valley storyline. It was mentioned in Found, but just in passing. Lulu Lightly actually lived in corrupt Wolf Valley so I will definitely be visiting that place soon. (And if you read the Junco series, it might remind you of a certain place where the shit hit the fan in book three, Flight. Might there be crazy clones up there in that Valley? One can only hope.) lol

The really cool thing about this series is how it might actually end up being a Junco prequel. I did not plan this at all but so many things are coming together. And while I don't get a LOT of messages about the missing Junco book (which was promised years ago, and I never wrote), I do get enough to think… this might be the spark I was waiting for. You see I had another Junco book planned and I have actually tried to write that thing more than a dozen times.

I swear, I have at least a dozen half-finished version of that Gideon/Sync/Twine book. But none of them ever felt right.

This feels right. Maybe it will all connect at some point. Maybe it won't. But whatever happens I'm having fun writing this stuff.

Another fun thing about this series is the artwork I've commissioned for it. The cover art and the sketches inside all come from the genius mind/hand of my amazing Spanish artist, Ambro Jordi. I can't stress enough how much I love his work and feel so privileged that he accepted my offer to work on this project with me. Found has a new cover, which is absolutely fantastic. So if you haven't checked that out yet, you really need to.

Anyway, that's about all for now. I'm writing the second book in The Turning Series next—so back to that for a few weeks. And then I'll be back in Cathedral City so we can see exactly what Thomas and his gang are up to.

I mentioned in the last EOBS for Found that I'm not a comic/superhero fan/reader. I like the movies if they are well made (like Deadpool). But really, this whole series was just a flash idea that came to me a while back and I ran with it. But even though I'm not a real-world fan of the genre I did plan the series with the real comic/superhero fans in mind. Even if they never read it because it's got romance and sex. I tried to stay true to the origin story for each character and I tried to make sure there was a proper superhero ending with lots of action. And every one of my sexy supervillains has a super name. Bike Boy. Bike Girl. Deep Cut and Lady Liberty. I don't have names picked out for Thomas and his partner in crime yet, but I'll think of something and make sure it's cool enough for the #fans.

Thanks for taking a chance on this series and I hope you enjoyed reading it as much as I enjoyed writing it. If you have a moment, please consider leaving me a review where you purchased your copy. I'd really appreciate that.

Thanks for reading. Thanks for reviewing. And I'll see you in the next book.

Julie

ABOUT THE AUTHOR
JAHUSS

JA Huss is the New York Times and USA Today bestselling author of more than twenty romances. She likes stories about family, loyalty, and extraordinary characters who struggle with basic human emotions while dealing with bigger than life problems. JA loves writing heroes who make you swoon, heroines who makes you jealous, and the perfect Happily Ever After ending.

You can chat with her on Facebook, Twitter, and her kick-ass romance blog, New Adult Addiction. If you're interested in getting your hands on an advanced release copy of her upcoming books, sneak peek teasers, or information on her upcoming personal appearances, you can join her newsletter list and get those details delivered right to your inbox.

JA Huss lives on a dirt road in Colorado thirty minutes from the nearest post office. So if she owes you a package from a giveaway, expect it to take forever. She has a small farm with two donkeys named Paris & Nicole, a ringneck parakeet named Bird, and a pack of dogs. She also has two grown children who have never read any of her books and do not plan on ever doing so. They do, however, plan on using her credit cards forever.

JA collects guns and likes to read science fiction and books that make her think. JA Huss used to write homeschool science textbooks under the name Simple Schooling and after publishing more than 200 of those, she ran out of shit to say. She started writing the I Am Just Junco science fiction series in 2012, but has since found the meaning of life writing erotic stories about antihero men that readers love to love.

JA has an undergraduate degree in equine science and fully planned on becoming a veterinarian until she heard what kind of hours they keep, so she decided to go to grad school and got a master's degree in Forensic Toxicology. Before she was a full-time writer she was smelling hog farms for the state of Colorado.

Even though JA is known to be testy and somewhat of a bitch, she loves her #fans dearly and if you want to talk to her, join her_Facebook fan group where she posts daily bullshit about bullshit.

If you think she's kidding about this crazy autobiography, you don't know her very well.

You can find her books on Amazon, Barnes & Noble, iTunes, and KOBO.